Fortuné Du Boisgobey

Cash on Delivery

Rubis sur l'Ongle

Fortuné Du Boisgobey

Cash on Delivery
Rubis sur l'Ongle

ISBN/EAN: 9783337226282

Printed in Europe, USA, Canada, Australia, Japan

Cover: Foto ©Andreas Hilbeck / pixelio.de

More available books at **www.hansebooks.com**

CASH ON DELIVERY

(RUBIS SUR L'ONGLE)

A Novel of Love and the Passion for Gaming

BY

FORTUNÉ DU BOISGOBEY

AUTHOR OF "THE CONDEMNED DOOR," "DEATH OR DIS-
HONOUR," "THE RED BAND," "THE CRY OF BLOOD,"
"THE BLUE VEIL," ETC., ETC.

SOLE AND AUTHORISED COPYRIGHT TRANSLATION

LONDON
JOHN AND ROBERT MAXWELL
MILTON HOUSE, ST. BRIDE STREET, LUDGATE CIRCUS
AND
SHOE LANE, FLEET STREET, E.C.

CASH ON DELIVERY.

CHAPTER I.

It was a cold, stormy winter's night. The wind was blowing a gale and the rain and sleet cut and stung the faces of the unfortunate pedestrians who were laboriously making their way up the broad Boulevard Montmartre, like a thousand tiny whip-cords. As a natural consequence they endeavored to shield their faces with their umbrellas, and this being the case, collisions were of frequent occurrence.

"Take care, you nearly knocked me down!" exclaimed one victim.

"Confound you! you've ruined a hat for me, and a brand-new one at that."

After this interchange of amenities, the two men lifted their umbrellas high above their heads, and looked at each other.

"What! is it you?" they both exclaimed, in the same breath.

They were both young, but they did not resemble each other in the least.

One was tall, slender, dark-complexioned and remarkably handsome. The other had broad shoulders, a slight tendency to embonpoint, chestnut hair, a full beard of the same color, and a face, not ugly, but insignificant, which is a thousand times worse.

Though he was the elder of the two men he certainly could not have been more than twenty-five years of age.

"What a piece of good luck!" exclaimed the dark-complexioned youth. "Do you know, my dear Gustave, that we have not met since we were comrades in the 24th Dragoons at Dinan?"

"That was in '79, my friend, more than six years ago, and I am delighted to see you again. What are you doing now, and how does life serve you?"

"Tolerably well, my dear fellow. I am acting as Labitte's private secretary, now."

"Labitte, the banker on the Rue d'Enghien? A good house that."

"Excellent, and I am very nicely fixed there. My father was an intimate-friend of my employer, who treats me like a spoiled child."

"You get about three hundred francs a month, probably?"

"Five hundred; and I hope to soon have an interest in the business. And you, Gustave, how are you getting on?"

"Oh, I've no particular cause to complain; I've been speculating a little of late, and with very fair success."

"You have some capital, then?"

"Yes. You wonder at it, of course; as I was not rolling in wealth by any means when we were both members of the same regiment. The truth is, I was not born a millionaire. My mother had to strain every nerve to raise the necessary amount to save me from the three years of obligatory military service; and the poor woman died, leaving me nothing but debts to pay. She was a widow, so my prospects were by no means brilliant, but I've managed to get along all the same."

"I congratulate you. I should certainly have had a hard time of it if I had been in your place. How did you manage it?"

"Oh, I have a natural talent for speculation, I think. Besides, in Paris, a little shrewdness is all one needs to start one on the road to fortune, and though I am not rich yet, I shall be sooner or later, and in the meantime, I am living very comfortably. I have been very lucky, it is true, inasmuch as a large capitalist has taken a fancy to me, and given me an interest in his operations, and as I am generally fortunate, I have made a good deal of money already. If you have any capital to invest you had better apply to me. I will see that it is put where it will yield you handsome returns."

"I have none, unfortunately."

"I thought your parents were very rich."

"They had four or five hundred thousand francs worth of real estate in the department of Ille et Vilaine, and that was all my father left at his death. My mother, who resides in Rennes, has half the income, and I get along very nicely on the other half and my salary."

"A total of above twelve thousand francs per annum, as the English say. That is not an enormous sum, but one can live very comfortably on it; besides, you are just the fellow to make a wealthy marriage. You are contemplating one now, I am sure."

"You are very much mistaken. I am only an insignificant clerk. No heiress would look at me."

"You are too modest. You have a name, to say nothing of your personal attractions. Robert de Becherel— that sounds well—and I know plenty of rich young girls who would be proud to bear it. Under the Republic rank is an even more desirable possession than in times past. You are a prize in the matrimonial market, while I, Gustave Piton, shall not be considered an eligible *parti* until I become the possessor of a couple of millions at least."

"I hope that happy day will soon dawn, my friend. I, myself, am less ambitious. I shall be perfectly satisfied to marry some well-bred and pretty girl, with a fortune about equal to my own."

"In that case, I know the very person you are looking

for. She has five hundred thousand francs in cash, and expectations; twenty-four years old, and an orphan; very handsome, very intelligent and very well-bred. Has a childless uncle who is wealthy, apoplectic, and a sexagenarian. She has been from childhood under the care of a highly respectable lady—a countess, by the way, who is very anxious to marry her ward to a nobleman. I'll introduce you to her whenever you like."

" Oh, I'm in no hurry about it."

" But you do not absolutely refuse, and I feel sure that you will thank me for introducing you into one of the pleasantest and most popular houses in Paris. I am on my way there now, and I'll take you with me."

" This evening? What can you be thinking of? I am not in evening dress; besides, I'm covered with mud."

" So am I, for that matter, but we can have our boots blacked a few steps from here, and then take a carriage. It is not one of my lady's grand reception days, so you will be graciously received, even in a frock coat."

" But under what pretext will you take me there, simpleton?"

" I am a friend of the family, and have full permission to bring any old comrade I please. I can insure you a hearty welcome and a very pleasant time, and you needn't feel under the slightest obligation to pay court to Mademoiselle Herminia des Andrieux, the heiress in question, unless you choose."

" Her name is Herminia, then?" exclaimed Robert, bursting into a hearty laugh.

" Alas! yes. It is her only fault, however. But I repeat that you will be perfectly free to do as you please. Once introduced to the countess, you can either listen to some very excellent music, take a seat at the card-table, or have a chat with some very agreeable ladies—just as the mood seizes you."

" So they play there?"

"Oh, yes; whist, écarté and other innocent games. Don't fancy I'm trying to inveigle you into a gambling-den, though, if I remember rightly, you were not afraid of a little baccarat in days gone by. At Madame de Malvoisine's they play only for amusement, however, and the evening usually ends with a dance, followed by a nice little supper."

"Yet you say this is not her regular reception night. What do they do there on gala occasions?"

"Nothing more. To tell you the truth, there is always a good time going on at the house of this kind-hearted countess, and when you've once had a taste of it, I predict that you'll cry for more. The programme for to-night is rather attractive, you must admit."

"Yes, if it were not for that introduction with a view to matrimony."

"Oh, set your mind at rest upon that score. The fair Herminia doesn't want for suitors, and will not see a possible one in you. You'll have a chance to see her, and the sight will cost you nothing. Come, let us step into the bootblack's."

Robert still retained a very pleasant recollection of his former acquaintance with this good-natured friend, and was by no means loath to renew it. Besides, Robert dearly loved surprises, and the idea of spending the evening at the house of this countess whom he had never seen, seemed both original and amusing to him. He said to himself that it might be necessary for him to be a little on his guard, in this unknown world into which his friend was about to take him, but he felt sure of not compromising himself, though he had a weakness for card-playing. This weakness his father had transmitted to him with his blood, for this father had lost at least half of his fortune at the card-table; but Robert, protected by the very smallness of his income, had succeeded in curing himself of this hereditary fault; at least he thought so. He therefore decided, though not without some hesitation, to accept the invitation of this agreeable friend, and when the operation of restoring the polish their boots had lost on the muddy boulevard was concluded, they both entered a carriage they were fortunate enough to find on the corner of the Rue Vivienne.

But had Robert known what was in store for him, he certainly would never have set foot in that vehicle.

"Where does your friend the countess live?" he inquired.

"At the upper end of the Rue du Rocher. It is quite a distance, but it is only nine o'clock, so we shall get there in very good season. You will have an opportunity to hear Mademoiselle Violette, who sings divinely."

"And who is Mademoiselle Violette?"

"Mademoiselle Herminia's music teacher, and a very pretty girl she is, upon my word! But she hasn't a penny unfortunately, so I advise you not to turn your eyes in that direction. But what nonsense! You have a sweetheart, of course. I am almost sure you were going to see her when I met you."

"You are very much mistaken, my dear fellow. I have no sweetheart, and when we ran into each other a few minutes ago, I was just returning from the Rue de l'Arcade, where my employer had sent me to deliver ten thousand francs to a client I did not find at home, unfortunately."

"So you still have the ten thousand francs in your possession?" inquired Gustave.

"Certainly," replied Robert, "and as the banking-house on the Rue d'Enghien is now closed, I shall not be able to return the money to the cashier until morning. But why do you ask the question?"

"Why, because they play cards at the house of the countess, as I said before," replied Gustave, "and if you should allow yourself to yield to temptation—"

"What do you take me for? This is not the first time I have carried large sums of money that did not belong to me, and I assure you that I have never felt the slightest inclination to touch them."

"Oh, I don't doubt your honesty in the least, only ' the man who has drunk, will drink,' the proverb says. You used to be very fond of cards; you must still be fond of them, and you always will be fond of them, so perhaps the opportunity only is lacking. I wanted to warn you of the danger, that is all. Still, even if you should lose the ten thousand francs, you would be able to refund the money. Real estate was made to be mortgaged, you know. Yours is still free from incumbrance, I suppose?"

"Yes, and I hope it always will be."

The conversation ceased here, and about fifteen minutes afterward the carriage drew up in front of an iron gateway on the Rue du Rocher.

"Here we are," remarked Gustave, opening the carriage door. "It is still raining. I have a great mind to keep the carriage."

"As you please."

"Then I will do so, provided you allow me to pay the coachman when he takes us home. You are my guest, and it is only fair that I should defray the expenses of the evening's entertainment."

And leaping from the carriage, Gustave gave an order to the coachman before ringing the bell.

Robert alighted in his turn, and saw that the house was eminently respectable in appearance, though not large. Every window from basement to garret was brilliantly lighted; three handsome private coupés were standing before the door, and in the court-yard stood a servant in livery, armed with an umbrella, which he held over each newcomer.

The friends divested themselves of their overcoats in a hall that strongly resembled a conservatory, so lavishly was it adorned with rare exotics, and were then ushered into a drawing-room where they found about twenty persons assembled.

The majority of the guests were men, but there were several ladies, at least three of whom were young. The others were of an uncertain age, but still had some pretensions to good looks. In the center of the largest feminine group the Countess de Malvoisine sat enthroned—an imposing matron, with a very low-necked dress, and blazing with diamonds.

When Robert de Becherel, escorted by his friend, advanced to pay his respects to her, a low murmur of admiration rose from the ladies, who unanimously declared him charming.

Gustave presented him to the countess, who received him very graciously, and when Robert apologized for not being in evening dress, she said suavely:

" With a name like yours, one doesn't need to be in full dress to be welcome anywhere. I am delighted to see you, and very grateful to our friend Gustave for bringing you here."

Robert bowed his thanks for the compliment, but had considerable difficulty in repressing a strong desire to laugh.

The countess seemed a rather grotesque person to him; and he already began to feel strong doubts of the authenticity of the title she bore.

" From this moment my house is open to you," she continued graciously, " and I hope to see you here often. Now make yourself perfectly at home. Gustave will pilot you through my salon, where you will find that every one does exactly as he pleases."

" We will begin by paying our respects to Mademoiselle Herminia," exclaimed Gustave, pushing Robert toward the piano, by which three young ladies were standing, talking, only a few steps from a table where two gentlemen were playing écarté, surrounded by several other guests.

The center of this little group, which any lover of the classics would undoubtedly have compared to the Three

Graces, the handsome Herminia instantly attracted attention by reason of her almost masculine stature.

One could see her from afar off, and there could be no doubt that she was the heiress Gustave had described. There was something in her very bearing that proclaimed the richly dowered maiden who looks down superciliously upon other young people from the height of her grandeur. She seemed to say, "Adore me. I shall be worth a million some day."

She was really very handsome, and would have been a great belle under the Directory unquestionably. The happy possessor of rather coarse but regular features, large black eyes, superb shoulders, and a majestic figure, she would have been adorable dressed as Mme. Tallien dressed in Barras's time; but the costume of the present day that suits *sveltes* forms so well was less becoming to her, as it revealed her rather massive proportions too plainly. In short, Herminia lacked both grace and distinction; but to compensate for this she possessed a complexion of wonderful freshness, and dazzling white teeth that she displayed freely on all occasions.

Robert was neither charmed nor intimidated when presented to her by his friend. He confined himself to bowing politely, leaving to the obliging Gustave the task of sounding the praises of his friend M. de Becherel, a gentleman of ancient lineage.

The aristocracy were evidently held in high esteem in Mme. de Malvoisine's drawing-room, and seemed to be the subject of frequent discussion there, for Mlle. Herminia remarked graciously:

"The name of Becherel is one of the oldest in Burgundy."

"I do not know whether there are any Becherels in Burgundy or not," replied Robert, smiling, "but I am sure that my family does not belong in that province."

"You are from Brittany, are you not, sir?" asked one

of the other young ladies—a dark-eyed blonde, with a very sweet voice.

"Yes, mademoiselle. Can it be that you are a compatriot of mine?"

"No, monsieur; but when I was a child I spent several years at the Convent of the Visitation in Rennes, and I remember the name very well. It was borne by a lady who was justly considered one of the kindest and most generous friends of the sisterhood."

"It must have been my mother, mademoiselle. She and I are the last of the Becherels."

"These reminiscences are very interesting," said Herminia, dryly; "but I am sure that these gentlemen would like to hear you play, my dear Violette, so do me the favor to seat yourself at the piano."

Violette's eyes drooped, and she obeyed without a word. The poor girl was not there for her own pleasure. The countess paid her to play, so play she must; but she certainly had a right to think that her ungrateful pupil was punishing her too severely for having ventured to take part in the conversation for an instant.

Robert, incensed by this display of arrogance on the part of the heiress, was strongly tempted to make a stinging retort. He was also seized with a profound compassion for the unfortunate musician who was subjected to the humiliation of being treated as a servant by the necessity of earning her own livelihood.

Gustave gave him a warning glance; and just as he did so Mme. de Malvoisine called her young charge, who bowed coldly to the gentlemen and walked away, evidently much displeased, to rejoin the countess.

The third young lady—an insignificant blonde—followed Herminia, and the two friends were left standing alone near the piano.

"Well, what do you think of the majestic Herminia?" asked Gustave. "Confess that she is magnificent."

" One couldn't find a finer Goddess of Liberty. She reminds me of the statue of Marseilles on the Place de la Concorde."

" You are certainly hard to please. I admit that she hasn't a wasp-like waist; but I, for my part, greatly prefer her to that puny-looking governess who seems to have taken your fancy."

" Each one to his taste, my dear fellow."

" That is true; and as I did not come here to flirt with the young ladies, I am going to try my luck at écarté awhile. There is plenty of money to be won here; and I shouldn't be sorry if my evening yielded me a hundred louis or so."

" I wish you good luck, I am sure."

" That is to say you intend to take yourself off after the English fashion, without saying anything to anybody. Just as you please. I brought you here because I thought you would enjoy yourself; but you are not obliged to remain if you are beginning to find it tiresome. I advise you to wait awhile, however. In the first place, you will have an opportunity to hear your favorite, Mademoiselle Violette, who has remarkable musical talent; and in the second place, the rooms are just beginning to fill up. There is a crowd of new-comers now and several ladies, you see. Possibly you will find some one more to your taste. But in any case, I hope we shall see each other again. Where do you live?"

" No. 29 Faubourg Poissonnière. And you?"

" No. 24 Rue Drouot. I am not often at home; but you need only drop me a line to find me at any time. We will dine together any day you name."

Having said this, Gustave walked to the card-table, and Robert approached Mlle. Violette, who was looking over the music portfolios in search of the piece she was to play.

No one was paying any attention to her; and Robert, seeing that her eyes were full of tears, endeavored to console her.

" Will you permit me to play your accompaniment,

mademoiselle?" he said, gently. " I am not a very brilliant
performer; but if the music is not too difficult I think I
can manage it."

" Thank you, monsieur; but I am in the habit of playing my own accompaniments," murmured the young girl,
who was evidently greatly embarrassed.

" Very well. I will turn the pages for you then. Please
do not send me away. I have met you this evening for the
first time, and yet it seems to me that I have known you
for years."

" I must admit that I can not rid myself of a similar
impression," said the young girl, forcing back her tears,
" though I am very sure that we never met before."

" I am equally sure of it, for if I had ever seen you I
should not have forgotten it. But there is already a bond
between us—my mother's name—that you heard in days
gone by, and that you have remembered. We were evidently predestined to meet some day; and I feel very grateful to my friend Gustave for bringing me this evening to a
house where I never set foot before."

" And which you will never visit again, I presume?"

" I certainly had no intention of doing so a few moments
ago, but I have changed my mind. It would be too much
of a deprivation never to see you again."

Mlle. Violette blushed to the very tips of her little ears;
but instead of making any reply to this complimentary
speech she struck a few chords, apparently at random, upon
the piano. Robert perceived that she had beautiful hands
—the hands of a duchess, white and slender, with pink,
almond-shaped nails—and lowering his voice, he added:

" I shall come again, but solely on your account, as I
can see you only at the house of this countess, who doesn't
impress me very favorably, I must admit."

This time Violette turned pale; and drawing up her slender form haughtily she replied, without pausing in her pre-
lude:

"Why do you speak to me in this way? I do not deserve that you should treat me as if I were one of those silly women who are flattered by any commonplace compliment. You evinced sympathy for me just now, and I feel grateful to you for your interest in a poor and friendless girl; but that is no reason why you should amuse yourself at my expense."

Then seeing that Robert was about to protest, she added, firmly:

"Do not deny it. To hear you one would suppose you had fallen in love with me at first sight; but I am neither a simpleton nor a coquette, and I know exactly what such protestations are worth. Do not attempt to thus mar my peace of mind. I have trouble enough now. What would my existence be if I should listen to you?"

The deep feeling that was so apparent beneath the sound good sense of this appeal surprised and charmed Robert de Becherel, who was utterly unprepared for it.

"I swear to you that I will never be guilty of a similar offense again, mademoiselle," he said, earnestly; "and now I have given you this assurance, will you allow me to remain near you while you sing?"

"Very willingly," exclaimed the young girl, who seemed to have regained all her wonted cheerfulness. "As you accept my conditions, I shall be delighted to talk with you; and there is nothing to prevent it, for I am not going to sing. What would be the use? They would not listen to me."

"These gentlemen and ladies do not evince much desire to hear you, strange as it may appear. They are all chattering like magpies; and I really can not understand why Mademoiselle Herminia asked you to go to the piano."

"The same thing happens almost every evening. The *habitués* of the house like to talk to the sound of instrumental music provided it is not too loud. It drowns the asides, you see. If I should sing they would perhaps feel obliged to applaud occasionally, and their approval is a matter of no consequence to me, so I play Mozart to them in a subdued way so as not to disturb them.''

" You are a lover of Mozart's music, are you not, mademoiselle?'' inquired Robert, who adored the great composer.

" Yes; from my earliest childhood, when I began to take lessons upon the piano I happened to hear my teacher play an air from the ' Magic Flute ' one day. It made such an impression upon me that before light the next morning I slipped into the music-room and began to play with one finger the air that had so charmed me. The Mother Superior heard me, and after a severe reprimand ordered me from the room. I rebelled—Mozart must have intoxicated me—I think—Heaven forgive me!—that I even struck the venerable mother. There was a terrible fuss made about it, and I came very near being expelled. "

" I can hardly believe that you ever struck any one, mademoiselle. ''

" Then it is probably because I have had no cause to do so since that memorable day, for if you think that Heaven has endowed me with an angelic disposition you are very much mistaken, monsieur. I am very quick-tempered, and I fly into furious passions sometimes. ''

" Against the majestic Herminia or against the countess?'' inquired Robert, laughing.

" No. They give me no cause. They pay me liberally for my lessons and my music, and I do my duty faithfully, so we are even. An occasional snub or slight is to be expected, and I endure them uncomplainingly. But we are talking too much. I see that people are beginning to look at us. What piece of Mozart's would you like to hear?''

" Any selection from ' Don Juan ' that you please. Of all his operas that is my favorite.''

Violette instantly began to play the serenade, and to play it as it should be played—softly and with exquisite feeling.

Robert forgot everything—Mme. de Malvoisine, her ponderous ward, and her noisy guests—in the charm of this delicious music that transported him to the land of dreams.

Then came the trio of the maskers, Zerlina's gay aria, and then the gloomy duet between Don Juan and the Statue of the Commander, "Pentiti! No! No!" played for Robert alone, for no one else pretended to listen.

"Do you know that you would be wonderfully successful on the stage?" exclaimed Becherel, enthusiastically.

"I have thought of that sometimes," replied the young girl, "but I prefer quiet happiness to brilliant triumphs."

"Happiness! How can you be happy in a house where you are treated with so little consideration? How can you bear the idea of always enduring the fate to which some undeserved misfortune has condemned you?"

Instead of replying to this invitation to relate the history of her life, Violette only smiled sadly, and began one of Beethoven's sonatas.

"I must beg you not to remain with me any longer," she said softly. "Herminia will never forgive me if I engross too much of your attention. Besides, we can see each other again before the end of the evening, for I shall not be able to leave the piano. I shall have to begin playing for them to dance presently."

"And I shall not even have the consolation of waltzing with you?"

"No, for I shall be tied fast to the piano; but while they are at supper we shall perhaps have an opportunity for a little chat. Now I ask you in all seriousness to leave me."

There was nothing for Robert to do but obey; but before he rose he exchanged a last glance with the fair girl beside him, and he fancied he read in her eyes that she was not in the least offended by his evident interest in her. The main thing now was to find some way of whiling away the time that must elapse before he could rejoin her; and he was at a loss how to dispose of it, for he did not care to join the circle that had formed around the countess.

He felt strangely incensed against Herminia, and he distrusted Mme. de Malvoisine. Gustave had told him enough for him to understand that this majestic dame was trying to marry off her ward, and that he, Robert de Becherel, would be gladly welcomed as a suitor for the young lady's hand.

He had not the slightest intention of encouraging either lady in any such hope, but as he had determined to stay for the sake of securing another brief conversation with Mlle. Violette, he could hardly hope to escape the rather fulsome flattery of his hostess; but being anxious to postpone the evil hour as long as possible, he approached the card-table, where he found Gustave losing heavily, for just as Robert reached the table, he saw a gentleman who had just played the king pull a very good-sized pile of gold and bank-notes toward him.

"I have just lost my last sou," Gustave whispered. "Loan me fifty louis."

"I would gladly do so, if I had it about me," replied Becherel, considerably surprised by this unexpected call upon his purse.

"You have that amount, and a good deal more."

"But it belongs to my employer, and I must return it to-morrow morning."

"Don't be alarmed. You shall have the money back. We can go round by my lodgings when we leave here, and as I have fifteen thousand francs in my secretary, and an account at the Credit Lyonnais, I can pay you."

"I don't doubt it; still—"

"Oh, I see! You distrust me. Ah, well, let us say no more about it. I know what your friendship is worth now, and shall feel under no obligation to speak a good word for you to the golden-haired *pianiste* you seem to have taken such a fancy to."

Not much troubled by this threat, but greatly annoyed at being obliged to refuse an old friend a favor, Robert said to himself that he had one hundred louis laid by, and that if worst came to worst, and Gustave should fail to repay the loan, he would only have to take a thousand francs from his private purse.

"Here is a one thousand-franc note," he said, taking one from the package in his pocket-book. "I do not doubt your word, and shall certainly expect you to return the money to-morrow morning."

"Good! I have found my friend Becherel of the 24th Dragoons again; and, to show you that I bear you no ill-will on account of your hesitation, I will take you into partnership with me. You shall have half my winnings, and, as I feel it in my bones that I am going to have a wonderful run of luck, you will find yourself the possessor of a handsome sum before the evening is over."

"Very well; I accept your offer so far as—"

Robert did not have a chance to finish the sentence. Some one had just tapped him on the shoulder, and he turned hastily to see who had accosted him so familiarly.

Gustave took advantage of his opportunity, and rushed toward the card-table, flourishing the thousand franc note, and crying:

"It is my turn now. I claim my revenge!"

Robert found himself face to face with a gentleman about fifty years of age, tall, slim, and straight as a poplar, and wearing the rosette of an officer of the Legion of Honor in his button-hole.

"You here, colonel!" murmured Becherel, hanging his head like a school-boy detected in some grave misdemeanor.

"Yes, my boy," replied the new-comer, pulling his gray mustache; "so you are surprised to see me here? Ah, well! that proves you have never set foot here before, for I come here very often, and never think of concealing the fact. I am not married; I have an income of forty thousand francs, and, since I left the army, I am as free as air; so I take my pleasure wherever I can find it. But what brings you here?"

"Nothing in particular. A friend I happened to meet this evening brought me."

"That big fellow who just borrowed that thousand franc note of you? He is one of the *habitués* of the house. How the deuce did you make his acquaintance?"

"We were in the same regiment."

"Yes; during your years of compulsory service, I suppose. If your father had listened to me, you would have enlisted again, and been an officer by this time."

"I would have asked nothing better than to remain in the army; but while I was serving out my term of enlistment, my mother became a widow, you know—"

"And she wanted you home again. I don't see that she is much better off now, however, as you are in Paris and she in Rennes. But you have a very good situation, at least I heard so when I was down in Brittany last summer. You have some property left, too, I hear. Your father didn't succeed in spending it all. Why have you never called on me since you have been living in Paris?"

"I really beg your pardon, colonel; I didn't know your address."

"A poor excuse, my boy. You could have discovered it at the War Department if you had taken the trouble to inquire. Besides, I am as well known as a white wolf. You had only to write to Monsieur Louis de Mornac, Retired Lieutenant-colonel, and your letter would have gone straight to No. 64 Rue de la Boëtie."

"I will atone for my neglect by calling very soon, if you allow me."

"I will not only permit it, but urge you to do so. I was very fond of your father, and you must need a word of advice from an old codger occasionally. Oh, don't be afraid! I've no intention of preaching to you, but I'll serve as your pilot through the dangerous shoals and rapids of Parisian life if you wish. It is filled with wrecks—this stormy sea—I know all the rocks, and I will point them out to you. To begin with, would you like me to enlighten you about these people here?''

" I was just on the point of asking you to do so.''

" Oh, well! it is a very easy matter. We will begin with the mistress of the house. I don't know where she obtained her title of countess, but I do know that she has never been married.''

" I suspected as much. She is an adventuress, I suppose, who has succeeded in making a fortune.''

" No; she was formerly a dress-maker, and made a fortune in the business. She has had several partners in the course of her long career—and has a silent partner even now—''

" He is here, probably. Point him out to me, colonel.''

" No, he is not here. He is never here. He takes good care to keep away, but he and Madame de Malvoisine are as firmly united as the fingers of one's hand, for their interests are identical. There is a dead man between them.''

" A dead man?''

" Yes; they must have committed some crime that served as the foundation of their fortune. No one ever told me so, but I would wager my right hand that they did. Besides, there is the child—''

" What child?''

" Why, Herminia, of course. Your friend Gustave probably told you that she was Madame de Malvoisine's ward, but if you had used your eyes, you would have seen that she was her daughter. They look as much alike as two drops of water.''

" That is true; though I didn't notice the fact before. The father, I suppose—''

" Is Madame de Malvoisine's silent partner. They have never acknowledged her, so they can leave her their whole fortune without violating the provision of the code that limits the portion of illegitimate children to one half of their parents' income. Besides, the father is legally married, perhaps. No one has ever seen his wife, but there is strong reason to suppose that she exists, nevertheless."

"A nice set, these people are! Would you believe it? Gustave had the assurance to pretend that I could secure the hand of this heiress if I chose—"

"He is right. The so-called countess and her partner would deem themselves only too fortunate if they could secure a son-in-law like yourself. It matters very little to them if this son-in-law is poor, provided he bears an honorable name. But I suppose you are not particularly anxious to enter this charming family?"

"I would rather marry a respectable washer-woman."

"You are a good, sensible fellow, and I hope that you will not hesitate to call upon me if I can ever be of the slightest service to you."

"Thank you, colonel," said Robert, quickly; "and I assure you that you will never have reason to blush for me. But I am surprised that Gustave should have advised me to enter the lists as a suitor."

"He is paid for it, probably. The father employs him in his speculations at the Bourse, and thus enables him to make a good deal of money. The father passes as the majestic Herminia's uncle, and it is more than likely that your friend Gustave doesn't know the real facts of the case. Like many other people, he is trying to make a fortune, and doesn't think it advisable to inquire too closely into the antecedents of the powerful financier who employs him. I have heard nothing to his discredit, but I would nevertheless advise you not to become too intimate with him."

"Oh, I will be prudent, never fear!"

"Your father was not, if you are; and his want of caution in such respects cost him dear. Profit by his experience, and don't frequent the society of people like these."

"I don't intend to; but it seems to me that you yourself, colonel, would do well—"

"Oh, it's very different with me! I'm an old stager, and I can enjoy myself when I please without much danger."

"And you enjoy yourself here?" asked Becherel, smiling. "Mademoiselle Herminia can hardly be the attraction, I think, nor her imposing mother."

"You don't understand the situation. This house is always filled with people who certainly would not be admitted into your mother's house, but who are not all hardened wretches, by any means. Indeed, among the number there are two or three ladies who are really very agreeable and worthy of interest. As for the men, the majority of them are persons one can associate with without compromising one's self. I see here, at this very moment, two gentlemen of my acquaintance, and members of the same club to which I belong. You will say, perhaps, that they gamble here. That is true, but the countess is too well off to feel any desire to make money out of her guests; and I am almost certain that there is no cheating. I know some highly respectable clubs of which one could not say as much."

"I don't want to bore you, colonel," said Robert, anxious to question him about a person in whom he already felt a deep interest; "but as you have so kindly enlightened me in regard to the mistress of the house, will you have the goodness to tell me what you think of the young lady at the piano?"

"Little Violette? She is a pearl, my dear young friend. Pretty as a pink, full of grace and talent, a musician of the first order, and as pure as a lily."

"I am satisfied of that. But what is her origin? Has she any relatives?"

"Not one. She was a foundling, I believe, or something of the kind. "I heard her story once, but I have almost forgotten it. There is some mystery under it all, I believe. Ask the girl to tell you, and be as polite to her as you please; only recollect that as you don't think of marrying her, you would be doing very wrong if you amused yourself by turning her head. But now, my dear boy, I must leave you. I see a great friend of mine, the widow of a sea-captain, sitting over there in the corner, and I am going to take advantage of this opportunity to join her. I shall probably leave before you do. Come and take breakfast with me whenever you like—the sooner the better."

Having said this, M. de Mornac turned away, and in another minute or two Robert saw him cautiously making his way toward the fair widow.

Several new groups had formed, and Herminia was surrounded by a number of admiring young men, while the countess was chatting with a party of older gentlemen.

Violette, who seemed to be more alone than ever, continued her playing, though no one made any pretense of listening. She had forbidden Robert to rejoin her, and not daring to disobey the order, he could think of nothing better to do than mingle with the men who were crowding around the card-table.

His stakes were upon the table, as he had had the weakness to consent to the partnership proposed by Gustave, and he was not sorry to see how the game was progressing.

He believed himself capable of watching it, too, without any undue emotion, for he flattered himself that he was cured of the hereditary weakness of the Becherels.

He little thought that the demon of play was lying in wait for him there.

The mere sight of the gold spread out upon the table made him forget poor Violette, who was sadly performing the dreary task of a paid musician not far from the card-table.

Gustave already had his cards in his hand, and Robert reached the table just in time to hear him say, in a loud voice:

"I'll play against the crowd, gentlemen."

For one to engage in such a contest with any chance of success, a large amount of money is an absolute necessity; and Becherel asked himself if his friend had not lost his senses to thus enter the lists armed with only a one thousand franc note against gentlemen who were beginning with bets of five and even ten louis.

Already there were at least thirty-five louis on the table.

"He certainly must be mad," thought Robert. "However, I am involved only to the extent of the one thousand franc note, and if he should come to grief, I have the means of replacing the amount I was weak enough to loan him out of my employer's money, and if this hard-headed Gustave wants to play any more it will be at his own risk."

Robert had quite forgotten that he had not had time to add a restrictive clause to his acceptance of the proposed copartnership, when the colonel startled him by tapping him on the shoulder.

Just then Gustave glanced up, and, perceiving him, cried:

"Look here, my dear fellow, you have no right to watch these gentlemen's play, as you are in partnership with me. Come over on my side."

Becherel was strongly inclined to reply that the company was limited, as they say in England, when the liabilities of stockholders do not exceed a certain figure; but all eyes were fixed upon him, so he said nothing, but consoled himself with the thought that it would be time enough to withdraw when the money he had advanced was lost, and docilely placed himself behind his friend who had just covered the stakes of the other gentlemen with the banknote borrowed from Robert.

"Recollect that you are to give me no advice," said Gustave, carelessly. "I know how to play écarté, and I don't need your counsel."

Robert also prided himself upon being an excellent

player, but he was not at all anxious to take part in the contest, and for fear of becoming interested in it in spite of himself, he began to watch Violette instead of the cards.

That young lady had not left the piano, but she was no longer alone there. A man with a red beard had just planted himself behind the piano-stool, and was endeavoring to talk with her in a very confidential manner. She did her best to escape the fop's compliments and assiduous attentions, but failing, she finally struck up the liveliest quadrille the *habitués* of the Bal de l'Opera ever danced, and the noise drowned the voice of her admirer, who was obliged to cease his compliments and beat a retreat, though not without one last impertinent remark which Robert fortunately did not hear, for he would have promptly espoused the cause of the persecuted girl.

" The king!" announced Gustave, as he turned the eleventh card. " One point for me."

His opponent played first, and lost.

" Two more points!" exclaimed Gustave. " That makes three for me."

This was quite enough to make Becherel forget, at least momentarily, the scene he had just witnessed. The passion for play had seized him again, and he concentrated his whole attention upon the game so promisingly begun.

It ended still better, for Gustave took every trick on the deal that followed, and won.

This brilliant success did not elate Robert much, however. It was not the money that he cared for, it was the excitement of play; and he had not had a chance to experience much of that, owing to the fact that he and his friend had had it all their own way.

" Put up your money, gentlemen," said Gustave.

They did so, and the stakes amounted to quite a large sum, for nearly all who had been defeated doubled the amount of their bets.

This time the game was closely contested, and his adversaries gained four points before Gustave scored a single one; but he worked his way up, point by point, and the fortunate turning of a king of hearts on the fifth deal won him the game.

"Will you try another game?" he asked, drawing his winnings toward him.

There was some grumbling among the losers, who did not seem inclined to contend with a run of luck that threatened to become really formidable.

"What are the stakes?" cried the gentleman Violette had just snubbed so unmercifully.

"Whatever you please," replied Gustave, loftily.

"What! is it you, Piton?" responded the other, with a rather scornful air. "You are playing against the crowd! Can it be you have become a millionaire?"

"Not yet, my prince of brokers, but I have the wherewithal to pay you—if you win."

"Five hundred louis to begin with then."

"The devil!"

"I warn you that if you refuse, I shall play against the crowd in your place. That is the rule, you know."

During this conversation Robert examined the newcomer closely, and was not at all prepossessed in his favor. This young man who talked of beginning with a bet of ten thousand francs was extremely loud, both in manner and coloring. Everything about him indicated the *parvenu*, from his insolent air to the enormous gold watch chain that dangled upon his black vest. Becherel hated him already for having forced his unwelcome attentions upon Violette, and would willingly have given a year's salary for the privilege of boxing his ears, but he hoped that Gustave would firmly decline this unreasonable proposal.

But Gustave, after hesitating an instant, replied:

"Here goes for five hundred louis then!"

"Very well. I'll play on those conditions. Bring out

your money, my dear fellow. I play only on a cash basis, and you haven't ten thousand francs there before you."

As he spoke he deposited upon the table a pocket-book stuffed with bank-notes.

"My partner will complete the amount," said Gustave. "Robert, my good fellow, pass me the reserve."

Becherel opened his lips to say that he would risk no more money, when he saw that the young *parvenu* was survey- ing him with a supercilious, even sneering air, and the pride and anger aroused by this impertinence deprived him of his usual prudence and good sense to such an extent that he drew from his pocket the nine one thousand franc notes that remained there, and handed them to his imprudent companion without a word.

At that moment he would have risked his entire patri- mony rather than flinch before this purse-proud and vulgar youth, who now turned to Gustave with the sneering remark:

"This gentleman is your banker, it seems. I should never have suspected it."

"And why, sir?" demanded Becherel, in a more and more aggressive tone.

"Simply because you don't look like a capitalist. One can't have everything in this world, you know."

"I at least have a habit of correcting ill-bred persons, and I—"

"Gentlemen! gentlemen!" cried the other players.

"I will take you at your word, and we will settle this affair after this game is ended."

"Whenever you please."

"Let me see, whose deal is it? Yours, Piton, I believe. Try not to turn the king of hearts too often — of all hearts"—he added, with a side glance at Becherel, who, though inwardly boiling with rage, took no notice of this allusion to his personal charms.

Gustave not only failed to turn the king, but gave it to his opponent, who scored a point with it.

The game began badly for Gustave and his friend, and the next deal proved equally unfavorable.

"Two and one make three, in my arithmetic," said the enemy coarsely, as he slapped his last card down upon the table.

Gustave began to look anxious, but Robert, who had forgotten everything in his anger against Violette's persecutor, was only waiting for the end of the game in order to challenge this odious creature.

Gustave dealt a second time; his opponent asked for the cards, and Gustave, being in doubt, concluded to consult his friend.

"Advise me," he said.

"No," replied Robert, unwilling to assume the responsibility of giving advice under such circumstances.

"No?" repeated Gustave, questioningly.

"Very well, then, I will play," replied his opponent quickly, spreading out three cards upon the table, "and you have lost, for I have the ace and the queen of trumps. I planned to make two points by refusal, and unless you have the king—"

"But I did not refuse—"

"Pardon me, your partner said no."

"That was only in reply to the question I put to him. Besides, I alone have the right to reply, as I am the person who holds the cards."

"Granted, but you, too, replied with a distinctly uttered no. I leave it to these gentlemen."

The by-standers unanimously declared Gustave in the wrong, and he was now obliged to yield.

"You have had enough, I fancy," remarked the victor, as he pocketed the spoil.

"On the contrary, I'll play another game for the same stakes," said Gustave, angrily.

"For cash, or on time?"

"If I lose you shall be paid before noon to-morrow."

"That is contrary to my principles. Still, I'll do it this once to oblige you."

"Let us draw for deal, then."

Robert said to himself: "I have nothing to do with it this time, for Gustave did not ask me if I wanted my revenge or not."

The game began, and Gustave lost it on the third deal.

"It is all your own fault, my dear fellow," his opponent remarked to him. "You ought to know that the strongest side always wins the victory. Don't trouble yourself about the payment of the money. If you give it to me to-morrow after the Bourse closes that will be time enough. Now, gentlemen," he added, turning to the other players, "I'll take Piton's place, and give you all a chance at me."

"Don't forget that you and I have another matter to settle," said Robert de Becherel, whose wrath had only been increased by Gustave's defeat.

"I am aware of that," replied the victor, dryly. "Send your seconds to me whenever you please. Your friend Piton will give you my address."

"Put up your money, gentlemen."

Gustave, who had risen from the table in very bad humor, dragged Becherel into one corner of the room, and said to him angrily:

"What has put this absurd idea of fighting with Galimas into your head?"

"Galimas is your late opponent, I suppose?"

"Yes, and he is one of the richest brokers in Paris."

"I don't care if he is."

"But I do. He has put me in the way of making a good deal of money at the Bourse, and I .on't want to get in a quarrel with him, I assure you. You are angry with him because he ventured to pay the fair Violette a few compliments. That is no reason for challenging him.

Besides, before carrying this absurd altercation any further, we must pay him what we owe him.''

"Very true. I was foolish enough to go shares with you in the game for one thousand francs, so I am a loser to the amount of five hundred francs.''

"You don't seem to understand the situation, my dear fellow. The ten thousand francs you gave me represent your share of the loss. I will pay Galimas the other ten thousand, and we shall then be square.''

"I do not see the matter in this light," said Robert, hastily. "Our copartnership was not unlimited. You chose to risk twenty thousand francs on two games of écarté. You might have risked and lost one hundred thousand just as well, for you did it without consulting me.''

"Then you ought to have announced your determination to withdraw, but you not only failed to say anything of the kind, but placed yourself directly behind me as if to publicly declare yourself my partner. Besides, everybody saw you hand me the bank-notes. If you choose to deny your obligations now, well and good. I thought you a man of honor. I was mistaken, and I must take the consequences.''

Becherel turned pale with anger, but he managed to control himself.

"Listen, Gustave,'' he said. "No one else could say what you have just said to me with impunity, but I don't want to quarrel with an old comrade, and as you really seem to consider me your partner in this loss, I will consent to pay half the amount. But I haven't the money, as you know very well, so I must ask you to loan it to me for a few days—just long enough to write to my mother and receive her reply. She will send me the money, I am sure, even if she has to mortgage some of our real estate to obtain it.''

"I can settle with Galimas to-morrow, on a pinch, as I

have fifteen thousand francs at home, but I haven't twenty thousand, and you must return to your employer's safe to-morrow morning the ten thousand francs that just found their way into that lucky dog's pocket."

"Then there is nothing left for me to do but blow my brains out," said Becherel, gloomily.

"How absurdly you talk! When one has four hundred thousand francs worth of real estate a man needn't worry himself about a paltry ten thousand francs. If he needs that amount he has only to borrow it."

"Of whom? You haven't the money, and I must have it to-morrow morning."

"Of Cash on Delivery."

"What do you mean?"

"Of Marcaudier, then."

"And who is Marcaudier, pray?"

"A usurer who has accommodated me in a similar way at least a dozen times."

"But he doesn't know me."

"He knows me, and he will be ready and willing to loan you ten thousand francs, and even a much larger amount on my recommendation. He is not so very exorbitant in his charges either. He won't ask you more than thirty per cent. interest, and that will include everything."

"How very reasonable he must be in his demands," said Becherel, with an ironical grimace. "I am in no situation to haggle about terms, however. And you think the matter can be arranged in the morning?"

"I'll answer for that."

"And you will go with me when I call on him?"

"No. If I did, he would perhaps regard it merely as an act of complaisance on my part, prompted by a desire to oblige an old friend. It would be better for me to see him alone, I think. I will call on him to-morrow morning at eight o'clock, and explain your situation and your resources. He has great confidence in me, and if you will drop in at nine o'clock I feel sure that you can have your money ten minutes afterward."

" I hope you will not tell him that the money so foolishly lost did not belong to me."

" Certainly not. I shall not even tell him that you are in Labitte's employ. I shall represent you in the light of a young spendthrift."

" That makes no difference to me. I will call on this man at nine o'clock precisely. Where does he live?"

" In a dingy little street known as the Rue Rodier, between the Rue Choron and the Avenue Trudaine."

" I shall have no difficulty in finding it, I think."

" Well, Marcaudier lives on the third floor of No. 24. The porter will tell you which staircase to take; and when you reach his door ring three times in quick succession. Marcaudier doesn't open his doors to everybody. He is afraid of thieves and of gossips, but he will admit you, for I will warn him of your intended visit. When you are once in his office tell him what you want plainly, and don't be afraid to assert yourself. Usurers of his stamp are like women—to obtain what you want of them you must bully them a little."

" I'll follow your advice as far as possible; and as you are going to intercede in my behalf, I shall count upon taking the ten thousand francs away with me. I shall have no difficulty in obtaining the money through my attorney at Rennes before the note I have to give this old Shylock matures. Now to change the subject, will you act as my second?"

" What! are you really in earnest about fighting with Galimas?"

" I shall fight with him unless the man is a coward."

" Oh, he's not a coward. He fights just like everybody else when he has to, and isn't a bad shot I've heard, though I don't know much about it. I wouldn't think of fighting with him though if I were in your place. He has the worst

tongue of any man I know; and if you insist upon fighting
with him he will tell everybody that it is on account of your
pretty *pianiste,* and he will not hesitate to ruin the poor
girl's reputation if he can. The countess will be sure to
dismiss her; and Mademoiselle Violette will be left without
a home and without resources."

"I should be very sorry indeed to injure her, but I can
not allow the matter to end here. Galimas just told me
that he should expect a visit from my seconds."

"Ah, well, come and breakfast with me at Champeaux
to-morrow morning at eleven o'clock, and we'll talk the
matter over. You can tell me, too, about your visit to
Marcaudier, and afterward we will go together to the
Bourse, and I'll manage to bring about an interview with
Galimas, who will apologize, I promise you, if you will
leave the matter to me."

"If he is willing to do that I shall accept his apology,
of course. So it is decided, to-morrow morning, after
restitution's made, I shall ask my employer for a day's
leave, and he will not refuse my request, I am sure."

"I am not a bad fellow at heart, you see, my friend,"
remarked Gustave. "It was a great pity that I brought
you here, as we have both lost quite a large sum in consequence of our visit; but I·have devised a means of
getting you out of the scrape; and as for the loss we
have sustained, it won't prove the death of us. It has
made me terribly hungry though. Come, let's go and
get something to eat."

"No, thank you. I am going home. I've had
enough of your countesses and rich young brokers.
You can remain longer if you choose, but I am going
to take my departure."

"Very well; just as you please. You won't go without
taking leave of your new divinity, I suppose. It seems
to me that she is gazing rather anxiously in this direction. Don't keep her pining. I'm going into the dining-
room to make the acquaintance of a *pâté de foie-gras.*

until to-morrow. Take the carriage that brought us here. I can easily find another if I want it."

The card-playing was still in progress; but the room had undergone a decided change in aspect. All the ladies, including Mme. de Malvoisine and Mlle. Herminia, had gone out to supper; Colonel Mornac was nowhere to be seen; Violette was still playing waltzes and quadrilles.

Robert joined her, and was greatly surprised to find her in tears.

" What is the matter, mademoiselle?" he asked, almost affectionately.

" I have heard all that has passed," faltered the young girl. " You have had a quarrel—you are going to fight—"

" Do not worry about that, mademoiselle. The affair is likely to be amicably adjusted; and if you have no other cause for anxiety—"

" Madame de Malvoisine has just given me my dismissal. My engagement with her ceases to-morrow."

" This is infamous! What is her pretext? Of what does she accuse you? Of having answered when I spoke to you? It would seem that I am the cause of this misfortune."

" That fact need not grieve you, sir. I have long been weary of the humiliations I am forced to endure here. I shall live as I have always lived—by my music—and I shall at least be my own mistress."

" And am I never to see you again?" exclaimed Robert.

" Why not? I feel sure that I can trust you. Tell me where I can write to you; and if you will promise me to offer me only your friendship, I—"

Robert drew a card from his pocket-book and slipped it into the hand of Violette, who as she took it, whispered:

" Leave me now, I entreat you. Those gentlemen are watching us with evident curiosity."

Robert bowed and hastened from the room, carrying with him a hope that in a measure consoled him for his pecuniary losses.

CHAPTER II.

THOUGH he was twenty-four years old, Robert de Becherel
still cherished many of the illusions and much of the enthusiasm of youth.

This was due in a very great measure to the training he
had received as well as to his temperament.

The son of a pleasure-loving father, and a mother pious
almost to austerity, tender almost to weakness, and ignorant
of the world and its wickedness, Robert had inherited many
of the virtues and faults of both parents. .

From his father he had inherited a heedlessness or perhaps rather an unconsciousness of the duties and responsi-
bilities of life—from his mother, wonderful kindness of
heart and delicacy of feeling, as well as a dangerous credu-
lousness and naïveté.

Three years spent in the ancient capital of Brittany after
his term of military service had expired had been a disadvantage rather than an advantage to him.

In Rennes, where his name opened every door to him, he
soon became a great favorite.   His handsome face, his dis-
tinguished manners and appearance, and his genial disposition made him the admiration of every heiress in the town
in spite of the smallness of his fortune, which had been
seriously impaired by the author of his being.   They forgave him everything—his fondness for play, as well as his
conquests outside of the aristocratic circles, whose spoiled
darling he was.

Consequently there had been nothing to prevent him
from making a brilliant marriage in his native province.
His mother desired it very much; and he adored his mother; but he soon became surfeited with these provincial triumphs, and one fine day he took it into his head to try
Parisian life for awhile.

One of his father's old friends, M. Labitte, was the head of a large banking-house, and had offered him a position as private secretary. Mme. de Becherel had finally become reconciled to the separation from her son, for she felt that the change might be an advantage to him, and thus far she had no cause to regret her decision, for Robert had shown a decided taste for his new duties and had fulfilled them with exemplary zeal.

He had been cured, too, in a great measure, of his conceit; his natural refinement had preserved him from vice; and in the maelstrom of Parisian life, where all ranks are confounded, he had conducted himself in an eminently respectable and praiseworthy manner.

All this, however, had been due to chance rather than to any remarkable strength of character, as the ease with which he had been enticed into the salon where he had just seen and heard so many startling things and lost ten thousand francs that did not belong to him conclusively proved.

He reached home about two o'clock in the morning, and slept but little the rest of the night, so deeply was his mind engrossed with the folly of which he had been guilty.

And yet his losses at the card-table did not trouble him very much, for he felt comparatively sure of being able to borrow the money the next morning, and cared very little about the heavy rate of interest he would be compelled to pay for it.

The culpable act of which he had been guilty in making this disposition of M. Labitte's money did not strike him very forcibly; and he would have been greatly surprised if any one had told him that he had been guilty of a breach of confidence. The all-important thing, in his eyes, was to restore the money; and if he had found it impossible to make restitution he would not have hesitated to confess the truth to his employer.

The moral side of the act escaped his notice entirely;

but, strange to say, he bitterly reproached himself for thus grieving his mother, who would be sure to learn sooner or later that her son had been obliged to mortgage his property to meet the demands of an usurer.

Such was this young man, endowed by nature with many admirable traits of character, but subsequently spoiled by the example of a dissipated father and the excessive indulgence of an angelic mother. His heart was all that could be desired: he lacked only firmness and strength of character.

During the hours that elapsed between his departure from the salon on the Rue du Rocher and his compulsory visit to M. Marcaudier, the lovely Violette was ever in his thoughts; for the mystery that surrounded her only enhanced her charms in the eyes of a person endowed with such a vivid imagination.

Whence came this beautiful young girl; this beautiful *artiste?* and what strange series of events had transformed the child reared in the convent at Rennes into the paid musician of a spurious countess? Colonel Mornac, whose judgment could certainly be relied on in such matters, did not hesitate to vouch for her virtue, and even the skeptical Gustave had naught but good to say of her.

Robert, who was more than willing to believe them, anxiously asked himself what would become of her now that Mme. de Malvoisine had dismissed her? Had she been living in the house on the Rue du Rocher? He had neglected to ask; and as he never intended to set foot there again he was by no means sure that he would ever see her. She had accepted his card, it is true, but would she write to him? And even if she did, how could he be of any assistance to her in the trying position in which she was placed?

These questions and many of a similar nature disturbed his slumbers much more than the recollection of the game of écarté and his quarrel with Galimas; and finally after thinking over the situation long and carefully he resolved to embrace the first opportunity to call upon the colonel, who certainly would not refuse to give him all the information in his power and perhaps some good advice as well.

A little consoled by the hope of soon solving this mystery Robert rose about half past seven o'clock and rang for his groom—for this secretary with a salary of five hundred francs a month had a groom and a very charming suite of bachelor apartments, exactly as if he had lived in those days when the heroes of Paul de Kock's romances kept their cabriolets and lived sumptuously upon a yearly income of six thousand francs.

The groom was the son of one of his tenants who resided near Prevalaye, and who was devotedly attached to his young master.

The rooms had been furnished by Mme. de Becherel, who had come up to Paris for the express purpose of seeing her son comfortably established there, and she had done things very handsomely. Robert had a parlor, a bedroom and a smoking-room, all furnished in exquisite taste. Nothing was wanting, not even objects of art: and Robert enjoyed these pleasant surroundings so much that he breakfasted there almost every day, Jean, his groom, having sufficient knowledge of cookery to prepare the traditional cutlet and eggs very creditably.

His duties as private secretary occupied Robert only two hours in the morning and two hours in the afternoon, so he had plenty of leisure time; and he generally employed it in a pretty sensible fashion.

That day he began by writing to M. Labitte, asking to be excused from coming to the office that morning, but making no allusion to the ten thousand francs; for he felt sure that his employer would not think of inquiring if the money had been delivered, and he wanted to have time to secure the loan that would enable him to reimburse the amount.

Having finished this note and intrusted it to Jean for delivery, Robert made a hasty toilet and started out to pay his visit to Marcaudier.

The Rue Rodier, where the usurer lived, was not far from the Boulevard Poissonnière, so as it was only half past eight Robert had plenty of time to reach the place before the appointed hour without taking a carriage.   Gustave had warned him that Marcaudier did not reside in a palace; but the house bearing the number mentioned by his friend was so unprepossessing in its aspect that Robert was loath to enter it.

" It looks like a den of infamy," he muttered, " and as it shelters a usurer, I suspect that it is.   It is hard to believe that any capitalist would live in such a dingy hole; but what of that? provided he gives me the ten thousand francs I want, here and now, that is all I ask."

He finally concluded to cross the threshold, and, while groping his way through a dark hall, he stumbled over the first step of a rickety staircase.   Keeping a tight hold on the baluster, he had cautiously mounted about a dozen steps, when he saw a lurid light, and heard a husky voice cry:

" What do you want?"

The sound proceeded from a sort of niche in the wall, and Robert had considerable difficulty in discerning the person who thus addressed him.   He was only partially successful in his efforts, in fact; but the strong smell of cooking that greeted his nostrils satisfied him that the dim light that was flickering before his eyes came from a fire on which some of the dishes particularly affected by porters and portresses were in course of preparation.

" Did you come for the locks?"

This time Becherel perceived that the voice was that of a woman, and he attempted to enter her den, but the shrill mew of a cat made him start back.

" Take care! you came near stepping on Mistigris!" cried the same voice that had first addressed him.

Mistigris was a cat whose green eyes shone weirdly

through the darkness, as if to complete the diabolical aspect of this porter's lodge, which is one's very ideal of a witch's den.

"I want to see Monsieur Marcaudier," said Robert.

Instead of replying, the woman stooped over the fire, and, rising with a lighted candle in her hand, advanced to the door.

A more hideous old hag never startled the eyes of man. The most prominent feature of her repulsive face was her hooked nose, which instantly reminded one of the beak of a bird of prey. Her clothing was nothing more or less than a mass of rags of every texture and color; and though she peered at Robert closely with her round owl-like eyes, she seemed in no haste to reply.

"Have you lost your tongue?" cried Becherel, stamping his foot impatiently.

The woman recoiled, and the frightened cat darted out upon the staircase where she crouched, growling sullenly.

"What do you want of Monsieur Marcaudier?" inquired the portress at last.

"That is none of your business, and as you don't seem inclined to answer me, I am going up. I know that his rooms are on the third floor, and I shall certainly be able to find the door."

The old hag retreated into her den, mumbling some insult, and after ascending a few steps higher, Becherel was able to see his way a little more clearly, for the dingy frames of a window which must have opened upon some inner court-yard or well admitted sufficient light for him to be able to distinguish two doors upon the landing. They were both closed, however, and were probably no longer in use, for there was neither knob or lock upon them.

"A strange house, this!" Robert said to himself. "This usurer can't derive much of an income from this old rookery, for he don't seem to have many tenants. Indeed, if the next story is like this he hasn't any."

On reaching the landing on the floor above, he again found himself confronted by two doors which bore no name or inscription, but he perceived that one of them was slightly ajar, so he pushed it open, and found that it led into a dimly lighted passage the further end of which he could not see.

"This house is a perfect labyrinth," he muttered. "Gustave, before sending me here, ought to have given me a plan of it to aid me in finding my way. Mr. Cash on Delivery is perhaps to be found at the end of this corridor, so I'll try it."

He was obliged to walk some distance before he reached the end of the passage.

"I had no idea that this narrow old rookery was half so deep," he thought. "It 'seems to extend way back to the Rue des Martyrs. It's as dark as a pocket here, and if I go on much further, I shall dash my brains out against the wall or fall into some hole. Can it be that Gustave was playing a joke on me?"

He was about to retrace his steps when he heard a low moaning sound that seemed to come from further down the corridor.

"Can it be they are murdering somebody in this den?" he muttered. "Or, is it the usurer's victims who are groaning as if he were putting them to the torture? I mean to find out what is going on here."

And without any further hesitation, he again started down the corridor. The further he went the more distinct the sound became, and soon there was no longer any room for doubt. It was the voice of some one moaning and weeping, and the voice seemed to be that of a woman.

After groping a few steps further through the darkness, Becherel encountered an obstacle that prevented any further progress, and on feeling it with his hands he found that this obstacle was an iron door, secured by ponderous locks and bars like those of a prison.

To satisfy himself that he was not mistaken, he applied his ear to the door, and now fancied he heard incoherent words as well as sobs.

He could distinguish only one word, however, but that was repeated again and again, and sounded like " Mignonne."

The ending was certainly " onne."

This word too seemed to be rather an appeal than a complaint. To whom could it be addressed? Robert had no idea, but he said to himself that when one cried out in this way it was because one needed aid, so he rapped loudly on the door, and cried at the top of his voice:

" I say, who are you in there? What do you want? What can I do for you?"

There was not only no reply, but the sound suddenly ceased.

Becherel pounded on the door again, with all his might this time, but with no better success than before.

The person who had been weeping and moaning so wildly a few minutes before was silent now, as a dog confined in his kennel ceases to howl when he hears the crack of his master's whip.

" The deuce take the woman!" muttered Becherel. " I'm a fool to trouble myself about the whimpering of a girl who can't answer when she is spoken to, and as I've evidently made a mistake in the door, I'll make one more attempt to find Marcaudier. He has strange goings-on in his house, and I intend to tell him so if I succeed in finding him. To tell the truth, I'm terribly afraid of falling through some trap-door in this infernal corridor."

He succeeded in making his way out of it without any accident, however, and finally found himself in front of the other door, which was locked and provided with a bell. He perceived, too, for the first time, that the lock of the door he had pushed open was missing, and understood now why the portress had inquired if he was the locksmith.

In compliance with the instructions he had received from Gustave, Robert rang three times in quick succession.

Several minutes elapsed before any notice was taken of the summons, and Robert was on the point of ringing again, when a face, illumined by a pair of tawny eyes, suddenly appeared behind a small opening in the wall.

"I would like to see Monsieur Marcaudier," said Robert.

"I am he," replied a deep bass voice. "Who are you?"

"I was sent here by my friend, Gustave Piton."

A bolt was drawn; the door opened, and the voice replied in gentler tones:

"I was expecting you. Come in, my dear sir."

"This man is certainly very familiar," thought Becherel. "He never saw me before, and yet he calls me dear sir. This extreme politeness is likely to cost me dear."

To his very great surprise, Robert found himself in a large and elegantly furnished room. There was a Louis Seize desk of richly carved mahogany, several luxurious arm-chairs, a profusion of costly ornaments, and even a book-case filled with richly bound volumes.

Though it was now nine o'clock in the morning, the room was lighted by two large lamps, and this fact was a surprise, though one would not have suspected that it was daylight without, for the windows—if there were any—were entirely concealed by hangings of antique tapestry.

"Will you take a chair, my dear sir?" continued Marcaudier, seating himself at his desk. "I have just received a visit from our mutual friend, Piton, and know to what I am indebted for the honor of this call."

"Then it is unnecessary for me to explain—"

"Entirely unnecessary. Gustave has told me all. You accompanied him to the house of the Countess de Malvoisine last evening, and while there you both took part in a game of écarté, in which you lost ten thousand francs, which must be paid this morning, as you owe the money to Galimas, who will not trust you for twenty-four hours; so you have come to ask me to loan you the money."

"Yes. Gustave assured me that you would be willing to do so."

"And he was perfectly right, my dear sir. I like to accommodate young gentlemen when the state of my finances permits me to do so without personal inconvenience; so I am going to let you have the ten thousand francs you need. I am anxious, first, to say a word or two about myself, however. You thought, probably, that your friend had sent you to a common usurer; you must see now that I do not look like one.''

This was certainly the truth. Marcaudier had a pleasant face; he was dressed like a gentleman, and did not appear to be over forty-five years of age.

Robert was so amazed at this preamble that he could only bow his assent.

"You are not to understand from this that I oblige those who apply to me without some compensation," continued Marcaudier. "In return for the ten thousand francs I am going to loan you, you must give me your note for eleven thousand francs, payable three months from date; so I loan you the money at a rate of interest which fools call usurious, but I have my own ideas on this subject. I hold that money is a commodity whose value varies as much as that of a house which is rented more or less dearly according to the difficulty its owner meets with in securing tenants. The fact that the Bank of France raises or lowers its rate of discount, according to the scarcity or abundance of the commodity, is certainly sufficient proof of the justice of my reasoinng.''

"He evidently intends to put me through a course of political economy," thought Becherel.

" And, to conclude with another case in point, you would not have applied to me if you had not found yourself in pressing need of money. The security you can offer would enable you to secure a loan of a much larger amount through any notary, and at a rate of interest certainly not exceeding five per cent."

" It was Gustave who told you this."

" I have not relied upon him alone for my information. I have known you for some time, or rather, I have been acquainted with your financial condition. Your fortune is not large, but it is substantial, as it consists of unencumbered real estate. You wonder how I happen to be so well informed. I am acquainted with Monsieur Labitte, and he has spoken of you."

" I hope you will not mention this matter to him," exclaimed Robert.

" For what do you take me? I am discreet by profession, like a physician; besides, I can very readily understand your unwillingness to be regarded as a gambler by your employer. The negotiation we have just concluded will be known only to you and me. I forgot to mention Piton, but, though he is rather thoughtless, he is too intimate with you to say anything that would be likely to injure you."

" He is not such an intimate friend as you perhaps suppose. I used to know him quite well, but we had not seen each other for years, when I happened to meet him last evening."

" Yes; he told me all about it, and, believe me, he has some very excellent traits in spite of his foibles. He does very wrong to squander money as he does; but he makes a good deal. He is a shrewd fellow—a man of brains, unquestionably. He will certainly succeed in making a large fortune some day, and he might, perhaps, assist you in making yours."

" That is a subject on which I am not bestowing much thought just now," said Becherel, with an impatient movement.

Marcaudier saw the gesture, and it was in an entirely different tone that he said:

"Pardon me, sir. When I find myself in congenial company, I am too prone to talk, and to neglect business matters as in the present instance. The negotiation is virtually concluded, however, and there is nothing more to be done but for you to give me your note in exchange for the ten thousand francs. Here they are. I always pay cash on delivery."

As he spoke, he placed upon the desk a package of bank-notes he had just taken from one of the drawers.

"You smile," he remarked, glancing at Becherel. "I see that Gustave has told you the name I go by—Cash on Delivery. It is an expression I frequently use in my business, so the gay young men who make it the business of their lives to enjoy themselves, and poke fun at more serious-minded people, have fallen into the habit of calling me by that name. I believe they even style me Father Cash on Delivery—I, who have never had either wife or children, and who am an incorrigible old bachelor. But pardon me, my dear sir, for again wandering from the subject. Will you have the goodness to sign this, and add your address to your name? Oh, yes, and write above your name, 'Good for eleven thousand francs.' I will fill out the rest of the note myself. The time is to be three months, is it not?"

"Three months," repeated Robert.

"That is all. Please take the trouble to count the notes."

"They are all right," replied Becherel, rising and slipping the money into his pocket. "There is nothing left for me to do now, sir, but compliment you on the courtesy with which you transact business matters, and bid you good-morning."

"One word more, my dear sir, before you go. This is the first time you ever did me the honor to call on me, and you are doubtless astonished to find me in such a miserable old barrack."

"I must admit that the external appearance of your house rather surprised me," replied Robert.

"Why do you not frankly admit that it frightened you?" returned Marcaudier, laughing. "You must excuse me for having received you here. Gustave ought simply to have taken you with him to the Bourse to-day. I go there every day, and he knows where to find me. It is true, however, that I seldom get there before one o'clock, and that you were in a hurry for the money. Gustave knows my habits. I attend to matters of this kind here between the hours of eight and ten in the morning, but I do not reside in this old rookery, I assure you. On the contrary, I have a very cozy little house on the Rue Mozart, in Passy. The old rattle-trap in which you find me was a part of the inheritance I received from an uncle, so I have furnished a room here, and left the rest of the house in charge of a woman as old and hideous as the building she guards. It is a convenient place to meet people who desire my services and whom I do not care to receive in my own home. As for the old woman you must have seen in the porter's lodge she was in the employ of my deceased uncle, and is devoted to me."

"She took me for a locksmith."

"Impossible!"

"But she did. She nearly snapped my head off when I inquired if you were at home, and then she asked me if I had come for the locks."

"She could not have seen you very plainly. It's as dark as Egypt on the stairs."

"So dark that I had a good deal of difficulty in finding my way up, especially as I met no one."

"Naturally. I have made no effort to rent the other apartments, which are only fit for kennels. I have even had the doors nailed up."

"You are not alone in the house, however."

"Pardon me. I am entirely alone—unless you count Mother Rembriche, my portress."

"But I have reason to know that the room at the end of the other passage on this floor is occupied."

"You are mistaken. The door next to mine opens into a dark passage that has no other outlet."

"I found the door standing ajar; the lock had been removed, and I entered the passage."

Here Marcaudier gave a nervous start that did not escape Becherel's attentive eye.

"Yes, I entered it," he continued, "and walked down to the end of the passage."

"If you did, you must have broken your nose," sneered Marcaudier, who had already regained his self-possession. "I have never explored the passage you speak of, but I know that there is a solid wall at the further end of it."

"There is a wall, I admit, but there is a door in it."

"Indeed?"

"Yes, a door heavily barred with iron. There is nothing to prevent you from convincing yourself of the fact if you wish to do so."

"What good would it do. This house adjoins another, in regard to whose owner and inmates I know positively nothing. Possibly both houses once belonged to the same person, but they were sold separately, and my uncle must have closed up all communication between them. You found the door securely locked, I suppose?"

"Very securely. I pounded upon it, and even kicked it, but it showed no signs of yielding."

"But why were you so determined to gain an entrance, my dear sir?" asked Marcaudier, laughing.

"Because I heard some one—a woman I think—moaning and crying on the other side of the door, but as soon as I began to rap the sound ceased. I should not have mentioned the fact, however, if you had not told me that there was no one in the house but yourself.''

"I am greatly indebted to you for the information, I assure you, and I shall send for a mason and have the door leading into this passage, as well as into the adjoining house, walled up immediately, so if you ever honor me with another visit, as I sincerely hope you will, you will not be subjected to a similar annoyance."

Becherel bowed without replying, for he was resolved to have no further dealings with M. Marcaudier, and he was already maneuvering to reach the door when the usurer remarked, with real or pretended carelessness:

"May I venture to ask if you spent a pleasant evening at Madame de Malvoisine's?''

"Not sufficiently agreeable to console me for the loss of ten thousand francs," replied Robert, dryly.

"True! But aside from that slight misfortune—which has already been repaired—you must have enjoyed yourself, and must certainly have noticed Mademoiselle Herminia des Andrieux."

"Gustave introduced me to her."

"She is a charming young lady, is she not? And she will be very rich some day, a fact that certainly does not detract from her good looks. I know her uncle well. He is worth several millions, and will leave all his property to her. If you are looking for a wife, you certainly could not find a more desirable one than the young lady in question."

"I have no intention of marrying at present," Robert answered brusquely.

"Then you are making a great mistake. Of course I understand that at your age a young man likes to enjoy himself, but one need not prevent the other, and you really ought to think of the future."

"I am greatly obliged to you, sir, for your advice, but it is time for me to be at the office, and—"

" Excuse me, excuse me, my dear sir. What I said was entirely on your own account, but I have no right to dictate to you, and I bitterly reproach myself for having detained you so long when Monsieur Labitte is waiting for you," added Marcaudier, stepping aside to let Becherel pass.

The latter heaved a sigh of relief on finding himself again in the street, with the money safe in his pocket, for though he could not but be grateful to Gustave Piton for sending him to this usurer, he could not help wondering if he had not fallen into bad hands.

Mr. Cash on Delivery seemed to him a very suspicious character, and he fancied there must be some sort of a bond between him and Mme. de Malvoisine; besides, he said to himself, that in ordinary life a loan like that he had just negotiated was not treated so lightly. He suspected, too, that the moans he had heard in the corridor were not those of a sick woman, and that they did not come from an adjoining house, as Marcaudier had declared.

" Still, why should I worry myself into a fever about these matters?" he exclaimed, trying to drive these unpleasant suspicions from his mind. " I have the money, and three months to pay it in. They can't compel me to marry the huge Herminia, so what do I care for all their plotting and planning."

He was anxious to return the ten thousand francs to his employer's safe as soon as possible now. He might postpone doing so until the following day, as he had just written to M. Labitte that he would not be at the office that day, but he thought it would be better to get the money out of his hands without delay.

He was not to breakfast with Gustave until eleven o'clock, so he had plenty of time to go to the Rue d'Enghien before the hour appointed for meeting his friend at the restaurant on the Place de la Bourse.

He accordingly wended his way there, but instead of going straight into the banker's office as usual, he paused in the office of the cashier—a kind-hearted old man with whom he was on the best of terms.

"My dear Maringard," he remarked, "Monsieur Labitte requested me to deliver ten thousand francs last evening to one of the clients of the house, a Monsieur de Brangue, who resides on the Rue de l'Arcade. I did not find the gentleman at home, so I have brought the money back."

"You had better give it to Monsieur Labitte," replied the cashier. "He probably took it from his own private purse, and I am not authorized to receive it."

"Put it in the safe. It won't make any difference, and I don't want to see Monsieur Labitte, for I wrote to him just now requesting leave of absence for to-day."

"He can not have received your note then, for he is expecting you. I received a message from him just now, requesting me to send you into his private office as soon as you came in."

"The deuce! I'm afraid he'll keep me, and I had planned to spend my day very differently. There seems to be no help for it, though, so I shall have to make the best of it. I hope he won't keep me long."

M. Labitte's office adjoined that of the cashier, and Robert had only to open the door to enter it.

He found the banker engaged in writing a letter.

"I have brought back the ten thousand francs you intrusted to me, sir," Robert began. "Monsieur de Brangue was not at home, and—"

"Sit down," interrupted M. Labitte, without pausing in his writing. "I want to speak to you."

The banker was a tall, spare, and rather austere-looking man about sixty years of age. His smoothly shaven face and suit of black broadcloth made him look very much like a magistrate, and all his clerks stood in great awe of him.

Robert, who had always been treated with exceptional kindness, was greatly surprised at this reception, but he took a seat and waited, still holding the bank-notes in his hand.

M. Labitte finished his letter, placed it in an envelope, wrote the address, and after laying it on top of a pile on the desk, said, turning to his secretary:

" So you have the money?"

" Here it is, sir."

" Where did you obtain it?"

" What do you mean?" stammered Robert.

" You certainly did not have it two hours ago, when you wrote to me asking permission to absent yourself to-day. Of whom did you borrow it?"

Robert turned very pale, and was about to protest when M. Labitte checked him by saying, coldly:

" Spare yourself the humiliation of telling a falsehood. I know that you lost the money I intrusted to you last night at the card-table. I even know where, and to whom you lost it."

" Who told you?" demanded Becherel quickly.

" That is not of the slightest consequence. I know it, and you can not deny it."

" Pardon me, sir. I did lose that amount, it is true, and the bank-notes that I lost were yours, but I had ten thousand francs of my own, and more, so I only risked my own money, as I was in a position to make the loss good this morning. And here is the money," he added, laying the notes on the desk.

" I can hardly believe that you only had to take the money out of one of your drawers," said the banker coldly. " I am perfectly well aware that you would have been able to repay the money sooner or later, but your only worldly possessions consist of real estate, in which your mother holds a life interest, for I do not believe that you have saved ten thousand francs out of the salary I give you.

Besides, if you really had the money on hand, as you pretend, you would not have written to me this morning, asking me to grant you leave of absence until to-morrow. You wanted to give yourself time to procure the money. You succeeded in doing this sooner than you expected, so here you are."

As he spoke the banker looked searchingly at Becherel, as if anxious to discern some sign of contrition, or, at least, of the embarrassment that precedes a confession in his countenance, but Robert, instead of blushing, met his gaze calmly, even haughtily. His pride stifled the voice of conscience, and he replied, carelessly:

"I have no reason to reproach myself. You intrusted ten thousand francs to me yesterday. I return the money to you this morning. What more can you ask?"

"Then you think that restitution will suffice to destroy the recollection of a breach of confidence?"

"Sir!" cried Robert, springing up in a furious passion.

"Yes, a breach of confidence," repeated M. Labitte. "I repeat the words, because I know no other name for the offense you have committed; and you must have very mistaken ideas in regard to honor if you think it enough to return the property of another person after you have appropriated it to your own use for a day, or even for an hour. Even if you spoke the truth when you said that you were in possession of a sum of money equal to that you had lost you would be none the less to blame for having betrayed a trust that should have been sacred to you. I would rather never have seen the money again than hear that you had used it at the card-table. So much the worse for you, young man, if you do not realize the gravity of such an offense. Remember there are not two codes of morals; there is but one. Was it your father who taught you the one you seem to believe?"

"I forbid you to speak of my father in this manner."

"Your father was my friend; and it is because he was

my friend that I have a right to remind you that he, too, would never look at these matters seriously, and that this unfortunate habit cost him dear. He died—partially ruined in purse, and—almost disgraced. I forgave him his faults, though they had cost me dear; but I tell you frankly that his death was most fortunate, for if he had lived much longer Heaven only knows how he would have ended. His example was one which you would do well to shun."

" Enough, sir."

" Will you be kind enough to hear me out? I have a word to say to you in relation to your mother. She is a saint; and she has suffered much. Have you thought of the fresh grief you are about to cause her? The letter I was finishing when you came in was to her. When she hears to-morrow that I have been obliged to dismiss you it will be the severest blow she has received since your father's death. Only a week ago I wrote her that I was very much pleased with you; now I am obliged to announce a misfortune for which I was as utterly unprepared as she can possibly be."

This allusion to his mother touched Robert deeply, and his eyes filled with tears; but his wounded pride soon regained its ascendancy, and conquering his emotion he said, dryly:

" You dismiss me, then? You have no further use for me?" he added, gazing at M. Labitte with a defiant air.

" You leave me no alternative; besides, I feel convinced that what I am doing is for your own good. I do not underestimate your good qualities. I have had plenty of time to recognize and appreciate them during the past year, and I do ample justice to your intelligence and activity. But you turn from the path of rectitude at the very first opportunity that presents itself. Other opportunities will be offered, and you will again yield to temptation; so I think it will be best for you to give up a position in which you will constantly be exposed to new temptations. Choose a profession in which you will never have any financial responsibility. It will be your only salvation. I wish you success, and I will assist you if I can."

"Thanks!" said Robert, ironically. "Our acquaintance, however, had better cease here and now; but I should like to know what you wrote to my mother."

"I wrote her that you had been gambling, and that I could not keep you in my employ any longer. I refrained from adding that you had lost money that did not belong to you. I should not have told her that even if you had not returned the money. My decision is irrevocable, however."

"I shall not make any attempt to change it, I assure you. The only thing left for me now is to ask you once more to whom I am indebted for a dismissal for which I shall have very little trouble in consoling myself, however?"

"I am under no obligation to give you the name of my informant; and I am surprised that you should try to wound one who has certainly proved himself a friend, by such bitter words. All I have to say is that if you were more familiar with Paris and Parisian life you would know that the house where you met with this mishap is one of those where thoughtless gossip is quite the order of the day. It is frequented by all sorts of people who do not consider themselves under the slightest obligation to keep what happens there a secret. The merest chance brought to my office this morning a person who met you there last night, and who told me nothing but the truth, as you yourself have been obliged to admit. We had better let the subject drop now, I think. You can rely upon my keeping the affair a secret. Your mother alone will know what has occurred. There will be nothing to prevent you from giving your friends to understand that you left me of your own accord."

A cold bow from the banker terminated the interview.

Robert scarcely deigned to return it, and left the office without another word.

But once out of his former employer's sight, all his pretended indifference vanished; and he left the building crushed and stunned, like a man who had just received a severe blow on the head. He staggered as he descended the steps, and when he reached the street he walked aimlessly on without even knowing where he was going. The shock was the more severe from the fact that he received it just as he was rejoicing over his miraculous escape from the embarrassing position into which his imprudence had plunged him.

To his credit be it said, however, that he was less troubled about the loss of his situation than the grief his mother would experience on receiving M. Labitte's letter.

"I, too, will write to my mother," he murmured, "and tell her that this man is a cold and unfeeling creature who is pleased to consider a mere peccadillo a heinous crime. I will tell her that the whole difficulty can be adjusted by raising, by means of a mortgage, a sum of money that will make no appreciable difference in our fortune, and that I can easily find another situation in place of the one I have lost. Colonel Mornac, who knows almost everybody in Paris, will cheerfully find me one, I am sure. My mother, who knows him, will feel reassured when she hears that I have met him and that he still takes an interest in me. Nevertheless, I would give all the ready money I have left to know the name of the scoundrel who denounced me. I haven't the slightest idea who it could have been. The *habitués* of Madame de Malvoisine's house are not business men, and would not be likely to have any dealings with Labitte. But now I think of it, Galimas is a stock-broker, and stock-brokers often visit banking-houses to solicit orders. Galimas must have learned through Gustave that I was Labitte's private secretary, so he hurried to the bank this morning to regale my employer with the history of my escapade. I have an old score to settle with him, and he shall settle with me for this at the same time. I will insult him in the presence of the whole Stock Exchange. Gustave offered to take me there after breakfast, and I intend to accept the invitation. After I have given Galimas a lesson I will go down to Rennes and spend a month with my mother to console her.''

When he reached the corner of the Rue du Faubourg Poissonnière, where he lived, he recollected that the hour of his appointment with Gustave was eleven o'clock, and as it lacked only a few minutes of that time he turned his steps in the direction of the Bourse instead of returning home to write to his mother as he had previously intended.

'' It will answer every purpose if my letter is mailed by five o'clock,'' he thought; '' and it is of the utmost importance for me to see Gustave this morning, not only to tell him what has happened, but to remind him that he promised to serve as my second against the scoundrel who has not only insulted me but acted the part of a cowardly informer.''

The clock was just striking eleven when he reached the door of the restaurant where he was to meet his friend. There was quite a crowd in the square already, and he had considerable difficulty in crossing the street on account of the numerous carriages that were flying about in every direction.

There was almost as much bustle and confusion in the restaurant as in the square. Every table was occupied; and he was obliged to exercise considerable skill and patience to reach that at which Gustave was just finishing a dozen oysters.

'' I began without you,'' he remarked; '' but I have ordered cutlets and eggs fried with truffles for two, and here are your oysters. Sit down and begin your breakfast. We've no time to lose.''

'' Why are you in such a hurry?''

" To-morrow is liquidation day; and the day is likely to be an exciting one, especially as there are all sorts of rumors afloat. But that is neither here nor there. Did you have a satisfactory interview with Cash on Delivery?"

" Yes; he seemed to be expecting me; and the interview was not a long one. After a conversation of about a quarter of an hour he gave me the ten thousand francs."

" I prophesied as much, you recollect. He's a very pleasant sort of a fellow to deal with, don't you think so?"

" Oh, yes; very pleasant," replied Becherei. " So pleasant, in fact, that I don't altogether trust him."

" And why?" inquired Gustave.

" Because no one ever saw a usurer before who was ready and willing to loan so large a sum of money to a person he knew nothing about."

" You forget I had told him all about you before you went there. He knew that you belonged to a highly respectable family, and that you were the possessor of quite a snug little fortune, which your mother shares with you now, but which will be all your own some day. And then your name had its effect with him, as with everybody else."

" My name! One would suppose I was a direct descendant of the dukes of Brittany to hear you talk. We belong to a respectable old country family, that is all."

" But that is quite enough for people who would be loath to mention their grandfather's calling. It is very evident that you know nothing about these *parvenues*. Marcaudier's father was a waiter in a restaurant; and that accounts for his weakness for persons with a title or even a *de* before their names."

" Are Madame de Malvoisine and Mademoiselle des Andrieux *parvenues* too?" inquired Robert, ironically.

" I shouldn't wonder," replied Gustave laughing. " I certainly should not be willing to guarantee that their ancestors figured among the Crusaders."

" Nor that the fair Herminia is not the daughter of the countess who passes her off as her ward, eh?"

" What! you know that?"

" An old friend of my father's, who was there last evening, told me so."

" Then it is useless to try to conceal it from you. Herminia is an illegitimate child; but she will have a dowry large enough to make up for that; but I repeat that you could hardly do better than to marry her."

" Marcaudier made the same remark to me. There seems to be a sort of conspiracy in all this. But I warn you that it will prove a failure. Such a marriage would not suit me at all."

" Oh, well, don't get angry. No one has any intention of compelling you to marry the girl against your will."

" I presume not: so suppose we change the subject. Do you know what has befallen me?"

" No, upon my word, I do not."

" Labitte has just dismissed me as he would dismiss a servant, and even more summarily, for he didn't even give me a week's notice."

" And why?"

" Because the scoundrel who won all your money last night at écarté went to him this morning and told him that I lost ten thousand francs at cards last night."

" Galimas? the rascal!"

" Yes, my friend, the scoundrel denounced me. I am almost sure of it. I hope you will not take his part now as you did after our quarrel at the card-table last evening; and I warn you that on leaving here I intend to go straight to the Bourse for the express purpose of boxing his ears."

" That will be pretty rough treatment; but he certainly deserves it—that is, unless he was actuated by no malicious motive in disclosing what he did. He could have had no suspicion that the money you handed me at the beginning of the game belonged to your employer, and on dropping into Labitte's office for orders, as he is in the habit of doing every morning, he must have thoughtlessly let the cat out of the bag."

"There you are trying to excuse him again! You had better be trying to excuse yourself for not having told me that the fellow knew Labitte."

"I did very wrong, I admit."

The conversation ceased for awhile. Robert was thinking of the vengeance he was determined to wreak upon Galimas; and Gustave too seemed to be deeply absorbed in thought—a very unusual thing for him.

"Listen," resumed Gustave after quite a long silence, "Galimas has acted infamously. I am going to pay him the ten thousand francs I owe him, and then I intend to tell him exactly what I think of his conduct. He will find that he has two duels on hand instead of one. But now let us talk over your plans. What are you going to do now you have lost your situation?"

"I haven't the slightest idea. If nothing better offers I shall return to Rennes."

"I should call that a last resort. How would you like to remain in Paris, and go into a business that would yield you from one to two thousand francs a month to begin with?"

"Don't try to make fun of me. I am in no jesting mood, I assure you."

"I am not jesting. If you will go into partnership with me, I'll guarantee you at least that much."

"Become a speculator? Never! In the first place, I know nothing in the world about stocks."

"What did you do at Labitte's?"

"I had charge of his correspondence. He never sent me to the Bourse. He promised my mother he would not—"

"Ah! so you are afraid of displeasing your mother?"

"I am my own master, but I repeat that I have no taste
3

and no talent for the business you propose to me. Besides,
I know nothing at all about it."

"I will teach you, and in five or six lessons you will
know more than I do."

"Thanks, but I am sure it is not my vocation," replied
Robert, brusquely, "so we had better say no more about
it. Tell me instead, what occurred at Madame de Malvoisine's after my departure. Did that young lady—Mademoiselle Violette—remain in the drawing-room until the
close of the evening?"

"So you are still thinking about that young lady, are
you?" cried Gustave. "Ah, well, she left the drawing-
room shortly after you did, and later in the evening the
countess told me that she had dismissed her. Mademoiselle Violette consequently finds herself without a situation; and you two certainly ought to sympathize with each
other. But you need feel no uneasiness about her. She
will have no trouble about finding another, for she has
great musical talent. She might do much better for herself pecuniarily if she chose, for Galimas would be only
too glad to lavish his money upon her."

"That man again! Can it be that you have sworn to
exasperate me beyond endurance?" cried Robert, striking
the table with his clinched fist.

"Don't fly into a passion, my dear fellow. Mademoiselle Violette is quite capable of taking care of herself.
Galimas will have his labor for his pains. Besides, you
can protect her if necessary. Though if you have any intention of doing that you had better try to make a little
money. Money is power, you know, and I am going to put
you in the way to make some to-day."

"Much obliged, but I don't want to run any risk of
losing, and with my experience of last night still fresh in
my mind—"

"Oh! I'm not going to associate you with me in my
speculations unless I have a sure thing of it. Do you see

that tall man who is coming toward us? Ah, well! let me have about three minutes conversation with him, and I shall then know exactly what to depend upon."

Gustave rose, shook hands with the new-comer, took him off behind a large flowering shrub planted in a box a few yards from the table, and began a confidential conversation with him.

This new-comer was a light-complexioned, tolerably good-looking man, whose costume was one of studied elegance. At the first glance one might have taken him for a man of rank and culture, but on looking at him more attentively Robert perceived that he had a treacherous eye and a crafty face. After a few minutes he walked away, and Gustave rushed back to the table.

"Make haste and drink your coffee. You can finish your cigar under the colonnade. Time is money this morning."

"Why?"

"You will see presently. Waiter, bring the bill."

As his friend made his way toward the door, Robert, who was following him closely, saw several men with hooked noses and a Hebrew cast of countenance endeavor to speak to him, but Gustave, without even pausing, waved them aside with a gesture that said more plainly than any words: "I have nothing to tell you."

"Do they take you for an oracle?" asked Becherel.

"For a sub-oracle, and they are not far from right. I have just heard a valuable piece of news, and I intend to keep it to myself. By the time they hear it my game will be won."

"So you intend to speculate to-day?"

"What a question! Do you suppose I am going to enter that building merely to contemplate the frescoes that adorn the ceiling?"

Becherel said no more, but allowed himself to be dragged toward the Grecian temple where the devotees of Mammon worship with such frenzied devotion. A long line of carriages bordered the sidewalk, and others were constantly driving up with speculators and brokers, who hardly waited for the horse to stop before leaping to the ground, for the hour for opening the Bourse had come, and the sound of excited voices could already be heard. The belated ones were mounting the steps, three at a time, and the peristyle and colonnades were already thronged.

Everybody was running wildly about, shouting and gesticulating frantically.

"I never visited a lunatic asylum," thought Becherel, "but I fancy that the inmates of one do not appear as demented and boisterous as these gentlemen."

Gustave did not allow him much time for reflection, however.

"Come with me," he cried, darting up the steps, "and whatever I say or do, maintain a prudent silence. I ask only one favor of you, and that is to keep your mouth shut."

On reaching the colonnade he turned to the left, and led Becherel to the place where the north gallery intersects the grand staircase.

"Remain here and you will see an exciting spectacle," he remarked.

"But I came here to box Galimas's ears, not to watch the brokers."

"You can do that by and by, and I will help you—after I've finished the little business transaction we have on hand."

"*You* have on hand, you mean. I don't want to have anything to do with it."

Gustave did not wait to hear the end of the protest, but darted into the crowd, where he was immediately surrounded by a dozen excited men, from whom he finally succeeded in making his escape, though not without a desperate struggle.

Several young men rushed by Robert, note-book in hand, to give the prices of the various stocks to their clients under the colonnade, soon returning to again plunge into the fiery furnace, which must be in full blast, judging from the noise it made. Soon this handsome and rather distinguished-looking young gentleman attracted their attention, and they paused for a second as they passed, to enlighten him, too, in regard to prices, by thrusting their note-books under his nose, a courtesy which Robert felt obliged to acknowledge by a " Thanks, monsieur," that seemed to surprise them very much, not being accustomed to such politeness.

" They take me for a speculator, that is evident," thought Beecherel. " I've a great mind to get out of here. But no, I can't go until I have seen Gustave again, that is, unless Galimas should happen to pass."

So he resolved to wait as patiently as he could, and accordingly made an attempt to divert his mind by listening to the conversation that was going on around him, though much of it was more unintelligible than Greek to him.

" How are they selling now?" he heard one man ask.

" They are falling rapidly. 82¼ were the last figures."

" And they opened at 83. That is a sharp decline."

" What is the cause of it?"

" Bad news from Tonquin."

" Is the news official?"

" It hasn't been published yet, but big Gustave is always well posted. He has a friend of the minister of war at his elbow. He has just sold three hundred thousand francs' worth."

" He must be sure of the fact then. He is too shrewd to be caught. But he must have somebody to back him; he hasn't credit enough for transactions of that magnitude."

Things went on in this way for at least twenty minutes, and Robert, in his bewilderment, began to wonder if his friend had gone mad. He finally concluded that it would be advisable to make some further inquiries, and seeing a rather pleasant-faced young broker standing alone a few steps from him, he stepped up to him, and touching his hat politely, inquired:

" Can you tell me what all this means, sir?"

" Certainly, sir. Government securities are going down because Monsieur de Bismarck is selling."

" What, sir?"

" You see that big man over there with a red nose and mutton-chop whiskers. Well, he is Prince Bismarck's private secretary, and he has been sent here by his master for the express purpose of unloading his stock."

Robert perceived now that the young man was making open fun of him. He turned pale with anger, and was about to answer him in kind, when another broker rushed up, and seizing his facetious friend by the collar, exclaimed:

" What are you doing here? Canler is looking for you everywhere. The news from Tonquin was only a *canard*. Rentes are going up again like mad. In less than five minutes they will be above the opening price. They are selling at 82½ already."

They both rushed off, and were out of sight and hearing before Becherel could find the stinging retort with which he proposed to annihilate the impertinent young man to whom he had applied for information.

" I must look like a greenhorn," he muttered, savagely. " If I ever see that fellow again I'll pay him for his impertinence. What a rude, unmannerly set these brokers are. I'm not used to associating with such people, and I certainly am not going to begin now."

And he was about taking his departure when he saw Gustave rushing toward him, puffing and panting.

" So you've come at last!" exclaimed Becherel. " I was just going. What were you thinking of to leave me here?

Will you do me the favor to tell me why you insisted upon bringing me here?"

"To make some money for you, you great simpleton," replied Gustave, dragging his friend out of the crowd. "Our little scheme proved a success."

"What little scheme?"

"On reaching the Bourse we sold three hundred thousand francs worth of rentes at the rate of eighty-two francs seventy-five centimes, and we just repurchased them at the rate of eighty-two francs twenty-five centimes."

"I don't understand you."

"What! you don't understand that we make a profit of fifty centimes a share by the operation—an aggregate of one hundred and fifty thousand francs—less commission!"

"You must be jesting. In the first place, I did not authorize you to embark in any speculation on my account; besides, if I had lost such an amount I should not have been able to pay it; so it is impossible for me to accept any share of the profits. It would not be honest in me, and I absolutely refuse to do so."

"You refuse!" exclaimed Gustave. "What an absurd and unreasonable creature you are. I bring you a snug little fortune almost, and you turn up your nose at it. It is ridiculous in you. I'll set your mind at rest, my dear fellow, for you must understand that if it had not been for you I shouldn't have been able to manipulate three hundred thousand francs worth of securities. I made use of your name and your credit in the transaction."

"My credit? You must be crazy."

"No, listen, and I'll explain how I managed it. I have a friend who is in a position to get hold of trustworthy information—or what passes for such—the tall, light-complexioned fellow you saw in the restaurant, and it is enough for him to be seen talking with me for people to suppose that he has just confided a government secret to me. As I wanted to speculate a little on my own account to-day, and didn't have credit enough, I took your name, and Monsieur de Becherel, a wealthy real estate owner in Brittany has figured quite extensively here to-day, through my agency of course. A broker who has great confidence in me bought and sold the stocks for me without asking me any questions, and we repurchased just one minute before the official dispatch denying the news of the disaster in Tonquin was affixed to the bulletin board, and now you have only to accompany me to the office of our broker on the fourth day of next month to receive the one hundred and fifty thousand francs we have cleared by the operation. I shall have to give one half of the amount to the person who gave me the information, and we will divide the rest, so there'll be about thirty-five thousand francs apiece for us. What do you say to that? Wasn't I right when I told you that the business was a good one?"

"I don't know what you think about it, but I consider the circulation of false reports for the purpose of influencing the market nothing more or less than a swindle, and as I said before, I absolutely refuse to profit by it."

"You can do as you please about that, of course, but I hope you won't refuse to go and draw the money. I can't get it if you don't, for the transaction was conducted in your name. You needn't take any of the money of course, unless you choose to do so, but you will have to sign the receipt. You surely won't make me lose the money I've made."

"Very well, I will draw it for you, but I shall tell the broker how I happened to be mixed up in the affair."

"That would be even worse, for you would ruin my credit completely. If it should become known that I had operated in your name, without your knowledge or consent, I should never find another firm that would be willing to fill an order for me. There would be nothing left for me but to jump into the Seine, and you would be the cause of my death. A nice way of thanking me for putting thirty-five thousand francs in your pocket."

"I won't take the money, I tell you."

"Of course you will do exactly as you please about that. I only venture to remind you that it is three times the amount you lost last night at Madame de Malvoisine's, and that it will come in very conveniently, now you have lost your situation. So far as your scruples are concerned. I must say that they are utterly absurd. Do you suppose that even the virtuous Labitte would refuse to profit by any information that came in his way? I'll warrant that if he had known what my friend just told me, he would have sold securities by the armful and made his millions—instead of thousands—for he operates on a colossal scale. Don't be a child. Look at life as it really is, a perpetual struggle in which all that is not forbidden is permissible. This morning before breakfast you were groaning about your debts, and talking of going back to Rennes to bury yourself there, and deploring your inability to render the charming Violette some assistance. The wheel of fortune has turned for you now. You are the possessor of a snug little sum; there is nothing to compel you to leave Paris or to prevent you from coming to the aid of your new divinity. Money is the sinews of war, in love as in everything else."

"Enough. If I decide to take the money it will only be to repay Marcaudier. As for Galimas—"

"I had no idea that you were such a man to bear malice. I, when I have such a run of good luck, feel like forgiving all my enemies. I just saw Galimas. He scarcely had time to take the ten thousand francs I owed him. He wasn't as well posted as I was, and was caught. He's been losing money like fury, and.—"

"I hope he'll be ruined."

"What a hard-hearted creature you are! I don't think there's any danger of his being ruined, but you can rest assured that he'll lose a good round sum, and in that case he'll have something else to do than run after Mademoiselle

Violette. But I can't waste any more time talking to you. I must go back and see what they're doing in there. If you'll take my advice you'll let Galimas alone. He's forgotten all about you and the seconds you were to send him, and if he did tell Labitte, which I am strongly inclined to doubt, he did you a service, though unwittingly, as you are now on the road to fortune. You'll receive a statement from our broker to-morrow, and I hope that I've succeeded in converting you to more sensible notions and that you will cease to spurn the favors Fate has bestowed upon you. *Au revoir.*"

Robert, once more left alone, asked himself if he had not been dreaming. He could not accustom himself to the idea that his situation had just been entirely changed by the stroke of a fairy's wand, and that he owed this miracle to the burly fellow whom chance had thrown in his path only the evening before.

He could not yet congratulate himself upon having met Gustave, but he was less firmly resolved to refuse his share of the ill-acquired gains. He said to himself that with this money he should be able to pay the debt that weighed so heavily upon him, and without being obliged to grieve his mother by mortgaging their property.

In the meantime he must write to his mother, and if he wished his letter to reach her at the same time as that of M. Labitte he had no time to lose, so he hastened to his lodgings.

On arriving there, he found a letter that had been left during his absence. The handwriting was unknown to him, but on carelessly breaking the seal, he was not a little surprised to see these lines:

"I must have a few minutes conversation with you. If you feel any interest in my welfare, meet me at two o'clock to-morrow on the terrace near the orangery.

"VIOLETTE."

CHAPTER III.

THE month of February was drawing to a close, and the near approach of spring was apparent. The sun was shining brightly from a cloudless sky, and departing winter seemed to be trying to atone for her past severity by granting the Parisians a warm and serene day.

More delightful weather for a promenade could hardly be imagined, and the privileged persons who were not chained to the desk or work-shop by stern necessity, were crowding the streets, and the Champs Elysées was thronged with equipages on their way to the Bois.

At a quarter of two o'clock, Robert de Becherel entered the garden of the Tuileries, and walked rapidly toward the Orangery.

After writing to his mother he had spent the rest of the evening before in reviewing the events of that day and of the preceding night.

He was still undecided as to the course he would pursue. The wisest thing for him to do probably, was to return to Rennes, and allow Gustave to get out of the scrape as best he could; but the other course had its attractions. To remain in Paris, and acquire a competence there through the acquaintance and advice of this Gustave who knew how to make seventy thousand francs in twenty minutes, was certainly a very tempting prospect to a secretary who was out of employment, especially as he said to himself that he might be able to make money honestly and without resorting to such trickery as his friend had used that morning.

At all events, he could not leave the city without seeing the fair young girl who had made such a favorable impression upon him, and who now asked his aid and advice with such flattering frankness. He accordingly resolved to defer his final decision until after this interview, and also until after he had stated his case to Colonel Mornac.

Upon the long terrace that overlooks the Place de la Concorde, there were only a few nurses and children, and two or three old men who had come there to sun themselves, for the spot is but little frequented except in summer, though it commands a magnificent view of the Seine and of the Trocadero and the hills of Meudon in the distance.

Robert hastened on, without pausing to admire it, however, for he had but one thought, to discover the young girl of whom he as yet saw no sign, and he feared he had arrived too late.

He caught sight of her at last, as he passed the corner of the Orangery. She was coming straight toward him, and he thought her even more charming than the evening before. In the drawing-room on the Rue du Rocher he could judge only of her face, and one really judges of a woman's charms only after one has seen her walking in broad daylight. Many women who are beautiful, seated, and seen by gas-light, lose greatly when subjected to this test, but Mlle. Violette was a gainer by it. Her figure was perfect, her gait at once easy and graceful, and there was a perfect harmony, not only of proportions, but of movements.

She was not very tall, nor was she the fraction of an inch too short; and she was dressed very simply though tastefully, for the neatly fitting black dress she wore enhanced the fairness of her skin, the brilliancy of her large dark eyes, and the rich gold of her tresses.

She did not seem at all embarrassed as she extended a little daintily gloved hand to Robert, and said:

"I thank you for coming. I felt sure that you would, I admit, and I am glad to see that I judged you correctly."

"And I, mademoiselle," replied Robert, smiling, "am proud to have inspired sufficient confidence for you not to feel afraid to apply to me in this hour of trouble."

"What could I possibly have to fear? We have exchanged only a few words, it is true, but I flatter myself that we understand each other. Besides, at the very beginning of our acquaintance, I made known the conditions upon which a continuation of it depended, and you accepted them."

"It cost me quite a sacrifice to do it, but I can not deny that I promised not to make love to you."

"That is all I ask."

"But I did not promise not to love you."

"Ah, well, love me with a frank and cordial affection. then. You will perhaps declare that such a feeling can exist only between persons of the same sex, but I hope to convince you to the contrary."

"I will try to oblige you, but I can not vouch for my success."

"I will undertake your conversion at my own risk, but I warn you that at the very first violation of the compact I shall instantly terminate our friendly relations, highly as I value them."

"You value them no more highly than I do, since I am glad to accept even the meager and unsatisfactory ones you offer me."

"Is the assurance of mutual esteem and sincere sympathy in all the trials of life nothing? You may reply that our situations are not identical, and that all the advantages are on my side, as you are rich and—"

"Less rich than you suppose, mademoiselle," interrupted Becherel. "My financial condition is not all that could be desired, by any means, and I have just lost the situation upon which I am partially dependent for support.

"Is this really true?" exclaimed the young girl. "And I have sent for you to tell you about my own troubles. Pray do not waste your time and thought upon me. I shall be able to get out of the difficulty somehow. Think of yourself, sir, and forget that I am in trouble."

This was said with such earnestness, and in a tone of such sincerity that it dispelled the suspicion that had arisen in Robert's mind. She had said: "You are rich," and he had fancied that this was the preamble to an appeal to his purse, but he now regretted the injustice he had done her, and replied, cheerfully:

"Oh, my troubles are as nothing in comparison with yours. My mother has some property, and I—"

"Your mother! oh, sir, if you are in trouble, go to her without delay. If I was so fortunate as to have a mother it is with her that I would take refuge in a time like this."

"Yes, I know that you are an orphan."

"Who told you so?"

"An old friend of my father, whom I met at Madame de Malvoisines night before last."

"You mean Colonel Mornac, do you not?"

"Do you know him?"

"I have frequently met him in Madame de Malvoisine's salon, and he has always been particularly kind to me."

"He spoke of you in the highest terms, and gave me to understand that there was some mystery connected with your past life. If I dared I would ask you—"

"To tell you my story? If I did you would be the only person to whom I have confided all—"

"I should certainly be deeply touched by such a proof of confidence on your part."

The girl hesitated.

"So be it," she said, after a long silence. "When you know my history I shall feel less unwillingness to ask the favor I desire of you, for my past will explain my present situation. I warn you that my story will be a long one, and if you wish to hear it we had better take a seat on that bench yonder."

"Very well: I am listening, mademoiselle," remarked Robert, who needed no urging to induce him to seat himself beside the young girl.

"Then I will begin, but I warn you that I shall be obliged to go very far back, even to the days of my infancy."

"Those days can hardly date back to the Dark Ages," interrupted Robert, gayly. "You are barely nineteen years of age I am sure."

"Possibly twenty—possibly eighteen. I do not know my exact age, nor do I know the place of my birth, the name of my parents, or even my Christian name."

"Then that of Violette—"

"Is only a surname that was given me for reasons I will explain presently, but pray do not interrupt me again. The first in my series of recollections is that of a very insignificant fact. I must have been about three years old when a woman, my nurse, probably, carried me out upon a sort of terrace surrounded with water."

"A terrace surrounded with water! It must have been a pier or jetty."

"So people have told me since, and I think they are right. There was a crowd on this pier, and I was looking around me when suddenly an enormous dark object passed by me—a huge black mass that looked like a moving house."

"It was a ship coming into port probably."

"Yes, but into what port? That is something I never knew, and never shall know probably."

"Why not? I feel sure that I could find this town, and that you would recognize it if I took you there."

"Perhaps so, but that day I was terribly frightened, and uttered such shrieks that my nurse was obliged to take me away. An incident like that makes an indelible impression upon a child's mind, while other much more important events leave no trace upon it. I should perhaps recognize the place where I wept, but I should not know the town. I have no recollection of it whatever."

"But you must remember your parents—at least your mother."

"Very vaguely. I sometimes see, in fancy, the face of a lady who embraced me tenderly, and whose voice was as sweet as the sweetest music. I remember, too, that this lady—who must have been my mother—often repeated a word which I have never been able to recall, but which I think must have been my name."

"Have you ever looked over a list of names to see if you could find it there?"

"Yes, but without success."

"Do you recollect nothing about the house in which you lived?"

"It seems to me that this house was large, and that there was a garden with flowers and gravel walks connected with it, but that is all I can remember."

"If you were only three years old at the time this is not to be wondered at. But afterward, when your mind developed and you became able to talk and listen and reason, you must have had a much clearer idea of your situation, and so retained a more distinct recollection of the persons and things that surrounded you."

"One would suppose so, but for some time after the event I speak of my life seems to have been a perfect blank. Sometimes I am almost inclined to believe that I slept for two or three days, for I can recollect nothing more until I found myself in the orphan asylum at Rennes, your native town."

"That is strange. You were born in a seaport, and Rennes is an inland town. Some one must have taken you there."

"Yes; but how or why I am unable to say. I was picked up one summer morning at the end of the Promenade du Thabor, where I had spent the night asleep on a bench. I could not speak distinctly, though I seemed to be at least four years old, and people at first supposed I was an idiot. There was no scrap of paper or clew to my identity about me, but I was well dressed, and I wore very fine linen, from which the mark had been removed, however. From this fact it was generally supposed that my parents were wealthy, and that they had purposely abandoned me."

"Was no attempt made to find these inhuman parents?" exclaimed Robert.

"Yes; but these efforts proving futile, I was placed in an orphan asylum, where I was taught first to talk, and afterward to read, write, sew and embroider. I was learning the dress-maker's trade, at which I was fast becoming an adept, when the directress of the institution discovered that I had a decided talent for music, and a very good voice, so I was made to sing in the church where we attended service. It soon became rumored that one of the children of the Home was a musical prodigy, so the Mother Superior of the Convent of the Visitation came to hear me sing. She expressed herself much pleased, and offered to take charge of my education. I eagerly availed myself of the opportunity thus afforded, and the happiest days of my life were spent with the sisterhood."

" Why did you leave the convent?"

" I had no intention of leaving it, for I was leading a tranquil, pleasant life there, untroubled by any anxiety in regard to the future, when one day, about three years ago, the mother superior asked me if I intended to take the veil when I became old enough. I had a profound respect and love for religion, but I did not feel that the life of a nun was really my vocation, and I frankly told her so. She praised my sincerity, but said that the sisters could not keep me any longer unless I intended to enter upon a religious life, and that I must choose a way of earning a livelihood. There was nothing I could do but become a governess, or give lessons in music and singing, and as a very respectable lady who kept a boarding-school at Saint Mande had just written to the superior asking if there was among her pupils any one she could recommend to fill the position of assist-

ant music teacher in the school, the situation was offered
to me, and there was nothing for me to do but accept it,
for I was obliged to leave the convent, and what would become of me, alone in the world, without relatives, influential friends, or money? So I went to Saint Maude, where
I was very graciously received by Madame Valbert. She
took a great fancy to me, and I was very much pleased
with her, so I immediately entered upon my duties. I remained in the institution a year.''

"And left it to enter Madame de Malvoisine's employ."

"Yes, very unfortunately, and I will tell you how it happened. I had become accustomed to my new life, which was
much more gay than at the convent. Madame Valbert was
very kind, and my pupils seemed to be exceedingly fond of
me, and I must do them the justice to say that they never
tried to humiliate me by alluding to my unfortunate past.''

"Perhaps they were ignorant of it."

"That is true. They were ignorant of it, though Madame Valbert was not. She kept my secret, and I ought
to feel grateful to her for it, though if Madame de Malvoisine had known the truth I should still be at Saint
Maude. On certain days—her birthday for example—Madame Valbert was in the habit of giving entertainments
and *musicales*, to which not only the parents of the
scholars, but former pupils, were invited. Herminia des
Andrieux had left the school two years before I entered it,
but she always attended these reunions, chaperoned by
Madame de Malvoisine, and they never heard me sing without quite overpowering me with compliments. I did not
fancy the countess very much, but I rather liked Herminia.
She is really not bad at heart, her worst fault being her
vanity; besides, I did not know her then as well as I have
since learned to know her."

"So you unfortunately consented to enter the house on
the Rue du Rocher?''

"Certainly, though had I known more of the company

that frequented it, and foreseen my brutal dismissal, I should not have accepted Madame de Malvoisine's offer, liberal as it was, for she offered me my board and a salary of four hundred francs a month. I was to take my meals at her house, and lodge in a room rented and furnished at her expense. She also gave Madame Valbert to understand that I stood a very good chance of finding a husband among the gentlemen who frequented her salon, and that lady strongly advised me not to refuse a situation that seemed in every way desirable. We both made a great mistake, however, in not ascertaining exactly what would be required of me. Madame de Malvoisine gave us to understand that her daughter needed a companion to assist her in completing her musical education. I was fully competent to do this, as I had had excellent masters at Rennes, and had worked very hard. I did not suspect for an instant that the lady had engaged me with the expectation that I would make myself generally useful in her household."

" What! that woman dared to make a servant of you!"

" Oh, no; at least, not apparently. I was treated to all appearance as an equal, but if you only knew what was expected of me! I had not a moment that I could call my own. I was obliged to be at the house by nine o'clock, and wait until it suited Herminia to come and take a singing lesson. After breakfast, at which Madame de Malvoisine seldom made her appearance, I was expected to remain at the disposal of the ladies, and if they had no shopping or errands to be done they made me read to them —and such reading! All this was nothing, of course, and a poor girl like myself ought not to complain of the tasks imposed upon her. I was paid for performing them, but the evenings—"

" How intolerable they must have been to you!"

" Yes; I suffered more than you can possibly imagine. At first I was hardly competent to judge of the characters of the persons who frequented Madame de Malvoisine's drawing-room, for all I knew about life was from the little I had seen of it in a convent, and in a young ladies' boarding-school; but it seemed to me that there must be circles in which one met better-bred men and less vapid women. One evening, a few words uttered by Monsieur de Mornac, who seemed to take a friendly interest in me, opened my eyes, and I perceived that I had made a great mistake. About the same time it happened, too, that some of the gentlemen began to pay me too much attention to please Madame de Malvoisine. I certainly did not encourage them, but I could not be forgiven for unintentionally attracting their notice. The reason of all this was apparent. Herminia was anxious to marry, and any gentlemen who do not pay court to her are not welcome in the countess's drawing-room."

"I must be in dire disgrace then," remarked Becherel, smiling.

"Less so than you suppose. Herminia is now and will be, very wealthy, so she is not looking for money, but for a name—and yours suits her. You please her too, in other respects, so you may expect to receive a pressing invitation to honor Madame de Malvoisine's house with your presence on any and all occasions."

"She can invite me if she likes, but I shall never accept the invitation."

"You are at liberty to do as you please about that, of course, but let me finish my sad story. It was not until about a year ago that my position became absolutely intolerable. Madame Valbert inquired about me from time to time, and the countess, who could find no just cause of complaint against me, dared not dismiss me without a cause, so she decided upon another way of getting rid of me. She tried to marry me to a gentleman of her acquaintance who was willing to take me without a dowry; but the gentleman had excited my intense aversion from the very first, and I declined the honor he thought he conferred upon me. From that day I was the victim of Madame de Malvoisine's continual displeasure, and Herminia never attempted to take my part. I was now reduced to the humiliating position of a hireling. I continued to appear in the drawing-room, it is true; but I was forbidden to take any part in the conversation, and was expected to play almost constantly, sometimes until as late as three o'clock in the morning.''

'' I wonder that you endured this life as long as you did.''

'' I had resolved to make a change, and was only waiting for an opportunity. That has presented itself, and I leave Madame de Malvoisine without the slightest regret. There is but one thing that troubles me. That is a fear lest she should slander me to Madame Valbert, and I prize the good opinion of my former employer too highly to be willing to lose it.''

'' And you are sure that Madame de Malvoisine did not know your story?''

'' Perfectly sure. You doubt it, probably, because you wonder that the countess would take any young girl without a family name into her household. But I had one that was manufactured for me in Rennes. I forgot to tell you that I was baptized at the orphan asylum. The directress was my godmother, and I was named Marie Thabor, from the walk on which I was found. Afterward I was called Violette, from my intense love for the flower of that name, and the surname clung to me. Madame de Malvoisine fancied it, and never called me by any other name. She never made any inquiries about my parents; she thinks they are dead, and it is more than probable that she is right. But the time has now come for me to tell you the favor I desire of you; but first I want to enlighten you in regard to the state of my finances. If I were in pecuniary distress I should not have applied to you. I am too proud to ask alms of any one. But I am not in need of money. My stay with Madame de Malvoisine was an advantage inasmuch as it enabled me to save the greater part of my earnings. I have not spent more than one fourth of my salary during the past two years; besides, my room rent is paid for six months to come. She was certainly very generous to me in these matters, and the injustice she has done me will never make me forget her benefits. I have enough to live on for at least eighteen months, and in that time I certainly ought to be able to better my condition—I certainly intend to try."

" You will succeed, I am sure; but in Paris it is a very difficult matter for a young girl to earn an honest livelihood, and—"

" You will perhaps think me very presumptuous, but I have been told so often that I possess remarkable talents, both as a pianist and singer, that I have really come to believe it, and I would like to put this talent to some practical use."

" In giving concerts? Your success would be certain, but I doubt if you would derive much pecuniary benefit from this success."

" I, too, doubt it, so I am thinking of something else."

" Of the stage, perhaps?"

" Yes, of the stage," replied Violette, promptly.

Robert's face clouded.

" I can see that you do not approve of the plan, and I foresee the objections you are going to make. You think that I shall be rushing to my ruin. I am aware that it is a dangerous career, but I realize the danger, and am not afraid to confront it if I can find a friend to sustain me, a friend who will encourage me and aid me with his advice. I am not wanting in energy, but I lack experience, and I must have that of a friend to rely upon. You have offered to be this friend—"

"And I will keep that promise; but, alas! I do not know much more about the career upon which you wish to enter than you do. I see the dangers, as every one sees them, and as you yourself see them, but I do not know how I can help you to avoid them."

"You fail to understand my meaning. I thought that through you I might be brought into communication with some theatrical manager. Colonel Mornac knows them all. He told me so, and I might have applied directly to him, but I did not dare. Do you blame me for thinking that you would perhaps consent to act as an intermediary between him and me?"

"No, mademoiselle," replied Robert, rather coldly. "I will do what you ask; I even hope that the colonel will consent to comply with your request, and I admit that you are almost sure to succeed in the career you have chosen. But what then! What will your life be? Do you know how actresses live? Do you think they are content with their salaries—when they get any?"

"I shall be content with mine. You must recollect that I was able to live upon a fourth of what Madame de Malvoisine paid me."

"You forget that you were at no expense while you were with her; but if you go upon the stage the toilets that will be required of you will absorb all the money you earn and more. You will say, perhaps, that you will marry. Would you be willing to marry an actor?"

"No."

"Can you hope that any man of the world, no matter how ardently he might admire your talent, would ask your hand in marriage?"

"Still less," replied Violette, sadly.

Her eyes filled with tears, and this touched Robert, who already began to regret his sternness.

"Forgive me, mademoiselle," he said, kindly, "for thus destroying your illusions, but I think them exceedingly dangerous, and I am too truly your friend to encourage you in them.''

Violette wiped her eyes, and lifting her head and looking Robert full in the face, responded firmly:

"I do not blame you in the least, but my mind is fully made up, and I have sufficient confidence in myself to feel sure that I shall be able to avoid the perils you point out to me. It is enough for me that you do not entirely desert me; that is, that you will not refuse me your counsel when I apply to you. I am alone in the world, and I have no one to depend upon but you. I ask you to see my work before you judge me. If you do not consider my conduct irreproachable, if you find me unworthy of your friendship and interest, I will not ask you to trouble yourself any further about me, but until that time comes do not refuse me your friendship and assistance.''

"Both are already yours, mademoiselle,'' replied Robert, quickly, "and as you desire it, I will see Colonel Mornac and ask him to do all in his power to facilitate your entrance upon the career you have chosen, and I do not doubt that he will comply with your request. Where can I inform you of his decision?''

"At No. 47 Rue de Constantinople. You can either write or call on me there to-morrow afternoon, at three o'clock, as best suits your convenience.''

"I will call if you have no objections, mademoiselle,'' he replied, promptly, "and I will perhaps bring the colonel with me.''

Then a new idea suddenly occurring to him, he asked, suddenly:

"Has the idea of trying to find your parents never occurred to you?''

"Never! I knew too well that I should not succeed.''

"Are you willing that I should try?''

"You, my friend!'' exclaimed the young girl. Then suddenly recollecting herself: "Pardon me, sir,'' she said,

" I do not know that you will permit me to call you by that title."

" Do you still doubt it?" asked Robert, smiling. " Well, to convince you that you have the right, must I call you Violette?"

" I should be very glad if you would."

" That is, until I can call you by your own name—the name that your mother gave you and that you have forgotten."

" Mother! what a sweet word!" murmured the orphan. " And I shall never see her to whom I should be so glad to apply it!"

" Who knows? She is still living probably—you are so young."

" I would rather believe she was dead than think that she abandoned me."

" There is nothing to prove that she did. You may have been stolen from her, and she may still be deploring your loss."

" If I could only believe that—"

" What would you do?"

" I would search for her everywhere. But that is impossible. The mother superior of the convent at Rennes on describing when and where I was found, told me that my story was published in all the newspapers, and that a description of me was sent to all the principal towns of France. If my mother had been living she would have come to claim me, that is unless she lost me intentionally."

" But your father—have you no recollection of him?"

" Only a very vague one. It seems to me that at the time I was being carried about in my nurse's arms that a man often scolded me in a loud voice that frightened me."

" You would recognize the voice, perhaps, if you heard it again."

" I doubt it very much. I can not recall the man's face at all."

"But you would perhaps recognize the house in which you lived if it were shown to you."

"I am afraid not."

"I am inclined to think that you must have lived in Havre. You have spoken of a pier extending out into the sea, and of a large ship coming into port. There is one answering to that description at Havre, where the residents of that city go to see the foreign steamers come into port."

"So I have been told; but I never visited that city. The only towns I know anything about are Rennes and Paris; and my acquaintance with these places is very limited. At the convent we went out but once a week, and then only for a short walk. At Saint Maude we never went further than the Bois de Vincennes. While I was at Madame de Malvoisine's I did occasionally venture as far as the Park Monceau, and once or twice as far as the garden of the Tuileries."

"But you must have attended the theater with the countess."

"No, I never set foot in a theater in my life."

"And yet you wish to go upon the stage?"

"It is very audacious in me I know; but the untried has its charms. And I am sure that I shall not be troubled with stage fright—for the same reason that a conscript who is ignorant of the danger goes so bravely into battle."

Robert was surprised to hear Violette speak in this way; but it was no time to discourage her.

"Will you go to the Opera or to the Opera Comique with me?" he asked.

"With the greatest pleasure," replied the young girl, gratefully. "To hear 'Don Juan,' the 'Huguenots,' 'Carmen,' all the *chefs d'œuvres* I know by heart, that is one of the dreams of my life!"

"A dream that can be easily realized. But as you seem to trust me, why will you not allow me to escort you to

Havre! I should like to see if you would recognize the jetty, and we could try to find the house with the garden."

"I am not at all confident that I should recognize it; but I will do as you think best, for I do trust you, and feel sure that you would never compel me to remind you of our compact. Now I must leave you, for I want to see Madame Valbert to-day. If I do not explain the situation to her without delay Madame de Malvoisine may succeed in prejudicing her against me, so I am going out to Saint Maude in the omnibus, and shall return in the same way. Good-bye until to-morrow," concluded Violette, rising and offering Robert a hand that he pressed warmly.

"What a strange girl!" Becherel said to himself as he stood watching her until she disappeared from sight. "Heaven only knows how all this will end; but I can not make up my mind to desert her. Her plan of going on the stage is arrant folly, and I shall try to induce her to abandon it. But why shouldn't I try to find her relatives? It would be a worthy and charitable act which I am sure my mother would heartily approve if I consulted her; and I shall consult her as soon as I am able to see my way a little more clearly, for I must first get out of the scrape Gustave has got me into."

While thus soliloquizing, Robert turned mechanically to leave the garden by the same path he had entered, and he was walking slowly along with his head bowed upon his breast when he was suddenly aroused from his reverie by a voice that cried:

"Well, what are you doing here?"

Robert glanced up and perceived Colonel Mornac.

"You came here to meet some fair lady, of course," continued the old soldier. "Oh, I don't blame you. It's only natural in one of your years. Even I—though I'm rather more than twenty-five—came here on a similar errand. My divinity just left me, however."

"So did mine," replied Robert, smiling.

" Then I guessed correctly. Well, I'm not sorry to meet you. Come, let's have a talk."

" Willingly, colonel, for I have a host of things to say to you. In fact I was intending to come and breakfast with you to-morrow morning."

" Good! I shall count upon seeing you punctually at twelve to-morrow. In the meantime come and take a turn in the Champs Elysées with me. How have you been spending your time since night before last?"

" Very badly, colonel."

" What have you been doing? Oh, I know. While I was chatting with the fair widow the other evening I saw you at the card-table. You played and lost, I suppose?"

" If that were all—"

" You certainly can't mean—"

" Monsieur Labitte has found out that I've been gambling and has dismissed me."

" The deuce! this is a nice piece of news for your mother!"

" I've written to her."

" And a fine situation you are in—without employment and without money—for I doubt if you had enough to pay your indebtedness, for they play heavily at the house of our dear countess."

" I borrowed the money."

" Another act of folly. Of whom did you borrow it?"

" Of a usurer that was recommended to me."

" Worse and worse! Why didn't you come to me, you young idiot?"

" I didn't dare. It was a matter of ten thousand francs."

" Zounds! you have certainly begun well! Of course you'll be obliged to mortgage your property to meet the note when it becomes due. You are following in your father's footsteps, my boy; and you'll probably do worse than he did, for he was fortunate enough to die in time. You'll reduce your mother to want, unquestionably."

" I'll blow my brains out first."

" You'll do that too without a doubt if you keep on. You'd better enlist at once. You had better be a soldier than a loafer."

" I don't intend to remain idle. There is nothing to prevent me from making a good deal of money if I choose."

" In what way, pray?"

" At the Bourse."

" That is to say by speculating. Was it your friend Gustave that put this idea into your head?"

" I don't see why I should conceal the fact that he associated me with him yesterday—without my knowledge—in a little speculation that he considered a sure thing, and that turned out very well, as my share of the profits amounts to about thirty-five thousand francs."

" There's a generous speculator for you! Have you drawn your share of the profits yet?"

" Not yet. In fact I felt some hesitation about doing so, as he speculated for me without my knowledge or consent; and if he had lost I should not have been able to pay my share of the loss, at least not immediately."

" In that case I don't see how you can hesitate. You must leave the money in the broker's hands and tell Mr. Gustave not to make use of your name in any of his swindling operations hereafter."

" Is that really your advice?"

" It certainly is."

" Very well; I shall follow it then; at least I shall draw the money and hand every penny of it over to Gustave."

" Who will immediately try the same game over again. If you do that you are lost, and I shall not trouble myself any more about you. I can take an interest in a young man who rashly squanders his patrimony, but not in a weak and unprincipled man who trifles with his honor.

Listen, my boy. I was your father's friend, and I will be yours upon certain conditions, the first of which is that you will have nothing more to do with this unscrupulous speculator. Let him get out of the scrape as best he can; and if he makes any fuss send him to me. I'll see that he gives you no further trouble."

"I have no desire to see him again," said Becherel.

"So much the better. Now what are your plans for the future?"

"I have made none yet."

"Then you had better return to Rennes and become a provincial swell again. You'll probably capture some heiress eventually. That is the best thing that could happen to you, unquestionably; and as you stand a better chance of success in your native town than in Paris, I would advise you to return there without delay."

"I would like to, but it is impossible."

"And why?"

"Circumstances forbid."

"Explain, if you please."

"Mademoiselle Violette has been dismissed on my account, and is now living alone in the lodgings she has been occupying for some time past at No. 47 Rue de Constantinople."

"And she asks your protection? She certainly has chosen a singular mentor."

"Whether she has acted wisely or not, would you advise me to refuse her my aid?"

"That depends. What does she want of you?"

"She is anxious to go on the stage, and she asks me to aid her by interesting you in her behalf, as you can be of much greater service to her in this matter than I can."

"I always thought she would come to that sooner or later; and I am satisfied that she will be a success, for she has a superb voice and musical talent of the highest order."

" Then you will not refuse to do what you can for her?"

" Why should I? With beauty like hers she is sure to turn out badly, so it had better be as an actress. The profession gives a certain *prestige* to the fall. I am acquainted with the manager of a new theater who is seeking new attractions. I will introduce your protégée to him, and when he has heard her I feel sure that he will engage her on very liberal terms. The consequences of all this are no business of mine."

" She told me her story just now; and since I have heard it I am inclined to think that she will succeed."

" I know her story too, at least in part, but I have kept it to myself. The mistress of the boarding-school at Saint Maude told it to me; but Madame de Malvoisine doesn't know a word of it. This Violette, who is certainly rightly named, by the way, was found on a public promenade in Rennes; but she can not be the offspring of a laborer or mechanic, for she shows blood to her very finger-tips. I have always fancied that her parents were people of wealth who lost her on purpose."

" I haven't the slightest doubt of it."

" Then why don't you try to find these barbarous and probably wealthy parents, as you seem to take such an interest in the girl? It would certainly be an eminently meritorious work, and one that would suit a person of your romantic tastes. Then, too, if you should succeed in restoring her to the bosom of her family, she would not be obliged to go on the stage. Her relatives probably would not receive her with open arms, but there might be a handsome inheritance awaiting her now or in the future."

" I am glad to hear you say this, for I had decided to enter upon this very work immediately."

" Is the girl able to give you any information that would assist you in your researches?"

" She says she has a vague recollection of some seaport town—Havre, perhaps—and also of the face and voice of a lady, who must have been her mother, and also of a large house with a garden."

"Have you seen her since the evening you spent on the Rue du Rocher?"

"She wrote to me asking me to meet her here to-day at two o'clock. We had a long talk, and she left me only a few moments ago to pay her former employer at Saint Maude a visit, for she fears that Madame de Malvoisine will make an effort to rob her of that lady's esteem and friendship."

"She is right; the countess will do everything in her power to injure her; there's no question about that. But I will see Madame Valbert myself, and tell her what I know about the affair. Now let us sum up our conclusions, for I must be off. In the first place, it is agreed that you are going to renounce Satan and all his works—that is to say, the young man named Gustave and his operations at the Bourse."

"Willingly."

"In the second place, I will attend to paying the usurer from whom you borrowed the money; and I shall do it at once, so you would greatly oblige me by informing him that you intend to take up the note two days from now. Thirdly and lastly, I will immediately interest myself in your fair protégée's behalf, and endeavor to secure her an engagement at the Fantasies Lyriques. I will also assist you in your efforts to discover her missing relatives. I will even accompany you on your voyage of discovery to Havre and elsewhere, if you desire it. I must go now, so good-bye. Don't forget that you are to breakfast with me at twelve to-morrow."

CHAPTER IV

AFTER his conversation with Colonel Mornac, Robert de Becherel returned home, greatly encouraged.

The philosophical colonel was the very mentor he needed, an indulgent but resolute mentor, who excused his faults, even while he set his face firmly against any deviation from the path of honor.

Considerably reassured, and well-nigh consoled for his recent misfortune, Robert finished the day quite cheerfully by dining at an excellent restaurant, after which he went to hear a popular singer who seemed to him greatly inferior to Violette both in talent and beauty.

His enjoyment was slightly marred by a chance meeting. Galimas was enthroned in an orchestra-chair only a short distance from him, and Robert was not a little surprised to receive an almost obsequious bow, of which he took not the slightest notice, however. He tried to divine the cause of this extraordinary politeness, and finally concluded that Galimas saluted in him the fortunate speculator who had just gained a large sum of money. He even asked himself if Galimas had not had a hand in the matter, and this suspicion only strengthened him in his resolve to have nothing more to do with Gustave, either in a social or business way. The evening ended without any other incident of importance. Galimas left the hall before the close of the performance, and Robert, who remained until the conclusion of it, went quietly home and to bed, where he slept much better than on the preceding night, and woke greatly refreshed, shortly after sunrise the next morning.

The business of the day had been marked out for him in advance; at nine o'clock he was to pay a visit to Marcaudier; at twelve o'clock, he was to breakfast with Colonel

Mornac, and at three o'clock he was to have an interview with Violette on the Rue de Constantinople.

The visit to Marcaudier gave him very little uneasiness, for what money-lender ever objected to receiving the amount of a note before it became due?

"One thousand francs for the use of ten thousand for three days is not bad, even for a scoundrel who loans money at the rate of forty per cent. a year," Robert said to himself, as he walked up the Rue Rodier, more and more astonished that a wealthy capitalist would be willing to stay there, even temporarily, for the neighborhood seemed even more intolerable than on his first visit.

The house of which Cash on Delivery was an inmate was even more dingy and dilapidated in appearance than those around it, and when Becherel reached the door, he again shrunk from entering the dark passage leading to the staircase guarded by the repulsive-looking *concierge* known as Mother Rembriche.

Glancing up at the house, he perceived that all the windows were protected by heavy wooden shutters that seemed to be rarely opened, and that needed only iron bars to give the house the appearance of a prison.

Becherel also noticed that this strange dwelling, though it adjoined another house on one side, was separated from the nearest dwelling on the other by a dark and narrow alley that seemed to have no outlet at the further end.

But Becherel had not come here to study the topography of this strange locality, so after a minute's hesitation he boldly entered the house. The portress was not in her lodge, but on reaching the landing above she suddenly confronted him, broom in hand.

"Monsieur Marcaudier is not at home," the old hag exclaimed, in a voice husky with anger; "so clear out, and be quick about it."

"Monsieur Marcaudier is expecting me."

"That's a lie! and I tell you that you sha'n't go up and

play the spy, and listen at doors, as you did the other day. You got the best of me then; but you won't again. No rascally detective will succeed in forcing his way into this house while I'm here.''

"You deserve a sound thrashing, but I respect myself too much to administer it. I want to speak to Monsieur Marcaudier. Stand aside!"

"So you can go prowling about the house, listening at doors, as you did before. I'm not such a fool! I've no intention of losing my place through you. My master went out a few minutes ago; but even if he was at home, I wouldn't let you go up, for he has forbidden it.''

Robert hesitated. He was strongly tempted to push the old hag aside, and ring at the usurer's door; but she was quite capable of clinging to his clothing and uttering shrieks and yells that would be sure to call in the neighbors. Indeed, there was nothing to prevent her from rushing down into the street to summon assistance, and as he did not care to get into a difficulty with the police or brave the scandal a quarrel in the open air would be sure to create, he concluded that it would be better for him to restrain his anger and beat a retreat.

"Enough, you old fool! I am going,'' he exclaimed; "but you will hear from me again. I shall write to Monsieur Marcaudier, and tell him how you treat people who call to see him on business in his absence, and we'll see what he says about the scandalous way in which you perform your duties as portress."

"Portress, indeed!" yelled the Rembriche, who wished to have the more honorable appellation of *concierge* applied to her. "So you want to insult me now, you miserable fop! I'll run you out of the house, I will!"

And she brandished her broom with such a threatening air that Robert, concluding that discretion was the better part of valor, rushed down-stairs four steps at a time.

This ridiculous scene not only irritated Becherel, but confused him; but he had scarcely reached the street when he came to the conclusion that this woman would not have assumed the responsibiilty of thus insulting a visitor who had been previously admitted by Marcaudier himself, and that in refusing him admission she had only obeyed her master's orders.

If this was indeed the case, why had Cash on Delivery resolved to close his doors in the face of the debtor he had received so graciously only two days before? Could it be because he was determined to remain Robert de Becherel's creditor, and because he guessed that Robert had come for the express purpose of notifying him that the note would be paid on the morrow? This conjecture seemed highly improbable, however; that is, unless he had been informed of the large amount of money his young client had cleared by a fortunate speculation at the Bourse. And even if he had been apprised of the fact, what possible interest could he have in preventing the payment of the money?

Robert could not imagine, but in mentally reviewing the particulars of his quarrel with Mother Rembriche, he recollected that she had accused him of being a detective, and this opprobrious epithet seemed to have been bestowed upon him in consequence of his exploration of the dark passage leading to an iron door on the third floor, and if this act had given such grave offense, it must certainly be because the usurer had some special reason for desiring that no visitor should be aware of the existence of the door in question.

Hence, this door must conceal a mystery that Marcaudier did not desire solved, and the explanation he had given of the cries and moans heard there, was only a series of falsehoods. There was no dentist's office, or sick woman on the other side of that door, but some wretched prisoner detained there by force.

Having come to this rather rash conclusion, Becherel's imagination began to indulge in the most extravagant lights, and to see in Marcaudier one of those villains of mediæval times, who kept some dethroned queen a prisoner in a lonely tower.

From this to the resolve to deliver her was but a step to a person of Robert's temperament, and this step was soon taken.

Indeed, the idea took such possession of his mind that he forgot for the moment his intention of searching for Violette's parents. He had plenty of time before him in which to make his voyage of discovery to Havre, while, on the contrary, the best opportunity to solve the mystery of the Rue Rodier seemed to be the present moment.

To accomplish this, he must find a way to gain an entrance into the fortress in which the victim he hoped to succor was pining, and he now knew, by experience, that he would not succeed in entering it from the Rue Rodier. The Rembriche was there to effectually prevent that.

Before opening the siege, he must know something more about the surroundings of the place, in order to decide upon the best point of attack, so he could hardly spend the rest of the morning to better advantage than in exploring these surroundings; so he softly retraced his steps, and after satisfying himself that the old portress was nowhere in sight, he slipped cautiously into the alley on the north side of the house.

He soon discovered that this alley was obstructed at the further end by a wall, and bordered on the right by the side of a house in which there were no windows or openings of any kind. On the left side, and running parallel with this house which fronted upon the Rue Rodier, was a long building that seemed to be an extension of Marcaudier's house.

Both these tall buildings were as gloomy in aspect as the exterior of a prison. Of whom could he ask information? He saw no one; besides, he did not feel inclined to question the first person he met. He resolved to explore this alley thoroughly, however, and his labor was not lost; for near the wall that obstructed it, he saw a strange building, almost as high as a tower, and surmounted with a sort of glass cage that had probably served as a photographer's studio; but the artist must have long since abandoned it, for many of the panes of glass were broken, and the roof that covered this aerial conservatory was already in ruins.

Robert, on approaching it, saw that the work of demolishing it had begun. The window-shutters and the door had already been removed. A huge pile of plaster filled the hall, and *débris* of all kinds strewed the alley in front of the house; but for some cause or other the workmen had paused in their work of demolition, thus leaving the dilapidated structure open to any one who wished to enter it.

The staircase was still intact—a winding staircase that led up to the glass top of this donjon—a very fortunate thing for Becherel, who was in search of an observatory that would command a view of the neighboring houses.

The ascent was not particularly easy, for the stairs trembled beneath his tread, and the dust that flew from the walls almost blinded him, but when he reached the top he was amply repaid for his labor, for the tower upon whose summit he was standing was not only considerably taller than the surrounding dwellings, but overlooked a garden, or rather a walled inclosure, for it was entirely destitute of both turf and flowers—which extended back quite a distance to a street that ran parallel with the Rue Rodier.

On his left, and in the immediate vicinity of the tower, this inclosure was separated by a tall and substantial iron fence from another garden—a genuine garden, this—a miniature park adorned with shrubbery and evergreens, through which one could discern a small house that must front upon the same street, a street whose name Robert did not know, however, as he had never explored this part of the city before.

The house did not seem to be occupied, however; for no

smoke emerged from the brick chimneys, but the well-kept turf and walks indicated that the dwelling, even though unoccupied, was not permanently abandoned.

Robert de Becherel, not being in a position to solve the problem, concentrated his attention upon Marcaudier's house, from which he was separated only by the alley.

This house, though so narrow that there was room for only a single front window in each story, was so deep that it encroached considerably upon the smaller garden out of which its roof rose like a sort of promontory. This roof was covered with tiles, and in it were two sliding windows, which were standing open.

Were there any windows in the side of the roof that overlooked the garden? Robert could not see from the place where he was standing. but he was able to satisfy himself upon one point, viz., that the extension of the usurer's house adjoined no other house on the side next to this garden.

It was not impossible, however, that this building and its long extension was divided into two separate dwellings by a party-wall, and that part of it belonged to the owner of the house and garden? but in that case, the owner, who must be a person of means, would not have rented to a dentist or midwife rooms that could be reached only by passing through his own house and garden, so Marcaudier must have told a falsehood, when he declared that the woman who was moaning and weeping on the other side of the iron door was not an inmate of his house and that he knew nothing about her.

But how was his victim to be wrested from him? By denouncing him to the authorities? That would certainly be the easiest way, but would it be the most efficacious? The authorities always act with great prudence, or in other words very slowly, and they would not be likely to issue a search warrant upon the complaint of a young man who was a comparative stranger in Paris, and who could furnish no proofs to substantiate his accusations against a respectable citizen.   Any magistrate or commissioner of police would begin by summoning Marcaudier, and demanding an explanation; and Marcaudier being thus warned, would have time to remove his prisoner to some other place of confinement.

Robert could succeed only by taking the matter into his own hands, and this was what he had resolved to do, though it would be no easy matter for him to gain access to the usurer's captive.

To go to the door of the house he saw at the other end of the garden and ask the permission of its occupants—if it had any — to examine this suspicious building more closely was almost as impracticable as to risk a leap over a space fifteen feet in width and nearly thirty in depth.

It was more than likely that these people would take him for a fool, and laugh in his face, to say nothing of the fact that even if he should be allowed to enter the garden, he would probably be no wiser than he was now, for it was very doubtful if there was any way of gaining an entrance into the Marcaudier house on that side.

Robert was beginning to despair, when he suddenly discerned upon a wall beyond and above the roof of Marcaudier's house the inscription: " Hotel de la Providence " in huge black letters.   This sign must be that of a hotel on the Rue Rodier, below Marcaudier's house, and this hotel had side windows which were only five or six feet above the windows in the roof of the extension.

It would only be necessary for Robert to hire one of these desirably located rooms, install himself there, and when evening came, lower himself by a rope to reach this roof, to which there was no way of gaining access from the street.   Once upon this roof, he would have no difficulty in reaching one of the windows and letting down a lantern that would enable him to see what was going on in this mysterious garret.

This plan seemed so admirable that he resolved to carry it into execution at the earliest possible moment.

He asked himself once more, and for the last time, however, if he could possibly be mistaken in his conjectures; if this house did indeed serve as a prison for some unfortunate fellow-creature, or if he was about to risk his life for nothing?

The idea of attempting to discover whether this back building was really occupied or not occurred to him, and gathering up a handful of plaster he threw it into the window nearest him.

Twice he failed, and the bits of plaster rolled down the roof into the gutter, but the third attempt proving more successful, Robert hoped that the prisoner, if there was one, would throw the plaster back again, to indicate his presence. He waited with this expectation, but in vain; and finally becoming discouraged, he concluded to leave this tower where there was very little chance of making any further discoveries.

He had scarcely set foot in the alley, however, when something struck him on the shoulder, and bounding off rolled across the alley to the foot of the opposite wall. Of course when Becherel was hit by this object that seemed to have fallen from the skies, his first impulse was to glance upward, and seeing no one at the windows of the tower he had just quitted, he speedily concluded that the projectile must have come from the casement into which he had thrown the plaster a few moments before, for the other house had no windows on the side next the alley.

The desired response had come at last in the form of some round object, about the size of a billiard ball, but not as large and heavy, and wrapped in a scrap of coarse paper. Robert sprung forward to pick it up, and was surprised to find it an apple of inferior size and quality. At first the discovery disconcerted him not a little, but after some reflection, he came to the conclusion that the prisoner, in her

anxiety to give some signs of life to those without, had
seized the first thing she could lay her hands upon; but
with it she must have sent some word of explanation.

Robert hastily unfolded the scrap of coarse paper in
which the apple was enveloped—a scrap of paper which
seemed to have been torn from some grocer's day-book,
and upon which Robert could at first discern only columns
of figures.   But on examining it more closely, he perceived
some red letters that seemed to have been traced with the
point of a pin or a nail.

The next thing to be done was to decipher them, and
this proved no easy matter.

Becherel finally succeeded in deciphering the word,
"Help!" and several indistinct letters that seemed to
compose the last syllable of another word.   This syllable
was either "one, or onne," but the first syllable had become so blurred that it was impossible to make it out.

The discovery was one of great importance, nevertheless, for the word, "Help" must have been written by the
person who had just thrown this strange projectile, so she
must be forcibly detained, and very unkindly treated, as
she was reduced to writing with her own blood, and to
using a pin or a nail as a substitute for a pen.

Moreover, the ending of the illegible word suddenly reminded Robert of the sounds he had heard through the iron
door two days before—those plaintive appeals terminating
in "onne," and repeated again and again.

Putting the scrap of writing carefully in his pocket,
Becherel left the alley, and started up the Rue Rodier without even glancing behind him.   He had gone but a few
yards, however, when he saw Gustave approaching, and it
was impossible to avoid a meeting, for his former comrade
had seen him, and was coming straight toward him.

"So much the better!" thought Robert.   "This is just
as good an opportunity to settle the matter as I shall ever
have, probably."

" You have been to see Cash on Delivery, I suppose,'' cried Gustave.

" Yes, but I did not find him at home.''

" That is because you came too late. Marcaudier is here only from nine to ten, and it is after eleven now.''

" His charming portress told me he had gone out, but he may be at home to you.''

" I have no intention of calling on him. I am on my way to a client who resides on the Rue Trudaine, and whom I must see before I go to breakfast. What did you want with our financier?''

" I wanted to notify him that I would be ready to pay the note I gave him to-morrow.''

" But the note is not due.''

" That makes no difference. I don't want my note to remain in this usurer's hands.''

" The deuce! you've become very proud, it seems to me, since our little speculation turned out so well.''

" I shall not touch a cent of that money.''

" Don't talk nonsense. Yesterday I took the trouble to explain that you could hardly do otherwise, and you promised me you would draw the money.''

" I have changed my mind.''

" All this is really too absurd. Besides, I really think you might be more considerate than to place me in such an embarrassing position. I want my share, and so does my partner—the gentleman who gave me the information that enabled me to make the money.''

" Then you must devise some way of getting it without my help. You certainly shall not touch a cent of mine, however. ''

Gustave turned pale with anger, but he managed to control himself, though he said, with a sneer:

" You seem to have been seized with another attack of morbid conscientiousness, but you'll get over it.''

" I think not,'' replied Becherel, coldly.

" So you have decided to play me false! You ought to have warned me that you intended to let me get out of the scrape the best way I could."

" On the contrary, it was your duty to have told me that you wanted the use of my name in carrying out your scheme. I should have refused it. But I said all this to you yesterday, and it is useless for me to repeat it. You may rest assured of one thing, however. I shall not touch one cent of the money."

" Very well. Then you have no objections to our acquaintance ending here, I suppose."

" If you desire it."

" Look here, Robert, you certainly would not sever your relations with a friend without some cause. Confess that some one has been prejudicing you against me. It can not be Galimas, for you haven't seen him since the evening you met him at Madame de Malvoisine's."

" I am only obeying the dictates of my own conscience."

" Oh, I know. It was Violette. She never liked me, though I can't imagine why, for I have always treated her with the greatest deference."

" You would greatly oblige me by not dragging Mademoiselle Violette's name into the conversation."

" So you have constituted yourself her champion. I congratulate you; she is certainly a very pretty girl. She's a shrewd one, too, and I would advise you to be on your guard."

" I do not recognize your right to meddle with my affairs, and I forbid you to mention that young lady's name again."

" So that is the way you treat my advice! Ah, well, you had better go your way, and I'll go mine. You have got me into a fine scrape, but I shall get out of it, all the same. Still, you needn't be surprised if I pay you back for this shabby treatment some day."

"Do your worst!" cried Robert, angrily.

And he passed on without any attempt on the part of Gustave to detain him. The rupture was complete, and Becherel was not sorry, for he had seen enough of this rather disreputable acquaintance, and he wished to return to the companionship of honorable men.

Colonel Mornac must be expecting him at that very moment, and as he was anxious to consult him before continuing the investigation so fortunately begun, he resolved to repair to that gentleman's lodgings immediately.

He was admitted by the colonel's valet, who was neatly dressed in black, and he instantly perceived that his own cozy quarters in the Faubourg Poissonnière looked poor and mean in comparison with these luxurious apartments.

The colonel was not only a good deal richer than his protégé, but he had remarkably correct ideas of elegance and comfort, so his rooms were perfection. There was not only plenty of light and space, but each room was admirably suited to the use for which it was intended, nor was there a single blunder in the furnishing, nor a color that did not harmonize in this interior planned by an intelligent man of the world. There were ornaments enough, but not one too many. A few books and pictures, but all admirably chosen—more curiosities picked up on his travels than costly knickknacks bought at auctions at the risk of the purchaser—and M. de Mornac enjoyed and appreciated these spacious and luxurious quarters the more from the fact that he had spent at least twenty-five years of his life in a garrison or in camp.

Robert found him reclining on a sofa in a large dressing-room, which was a model of its kind, and which was lined with long mirrors that concealed wardrobes, each of which had its particular use. There was a wardrobe for dress suits, a wardrobe for morning costumes, a wardrobe for riding and hunting suits, and another for shoes and hats and sundry toilet articles for which there was not room on the white marble shelves that encircled the huge bath-tub. "Well, colonel, you certainly are very comfortably fixed here!" cried Robert, in astonishment.

"Yes, tolerably," replied Louis de Mornac, laughing. "It is disgraceful, I suppose, for an old soldier to surround himself with so much luxury, but I spent so much of my life in dingy stuffy little rooms, when I was young, that I certainly have a right to indemnify myself for past sufferings. But you mustn't fancy that I am becoming completely spoiled. I ride horseback two hours every day, and when the time comes for leading another charge against the Prussians, you will find that I can wield a saber with the best of them. Unfortunately, there doesn't seem to be much hope of that just now, so we had better go to breakfast," he added, leading his young guest into a dining-room, which was even more elegant and complete in its appointments than the dressing-room.

"Sit down and help yourself," the host said, cordially. "The oysters are on the table, and there is some excellent sauterne at your elbow. I'll ring for my valet when we want him. What have you been doing since yesterday? Have you seen your usurer?"

"I called on him this morning, but didn't find him at home."

"And how about Mademoiselle Violette?"

"I am to see her this afternoon at three o'clock."

"In short, the situation of your affairs has undergone no change. I have some news for you, however."

Becherel felt almost sure that the communication was in some way connected with Violette, and he was right.

"I have no intention of repeating my lecture of yesterday in regard to a certain young lady and your plans concerning her," continued the colonel. "You are old enough to judge for yourself in such matters; but I promised to assist you in the noble and painful task you have imposed upon yourself. I am a man of my word, so allow me to say that on leaving you yesterday I went straight to the manager of the Fantasies Lyriques.''

'' And you spoke to him about Violette?''

'' I didn't talk of anything else; and I didn't waste my breath either. I found him in a very amiable mood; in fact he is not only willing but anxious to oblige me in every possible way. You see, I loaned him one hundred thousand francs last year, and he would be put to great inconvenience if I should ask him for the money, for the last theatrical season was a very poor one, and that upon which we are just entering doesn't seem likely to prove much better, so he is not only in great need of money but also of an *artiste* that will restore the prestige he seems to have lost. You will understand, too, that this *artiste* must not only be a marvel of grace and beauty but of talent and intelligence as well, when I tell you that she will have to learn a long and rather difficult rôle in three weeks. Of course I told him that I knew the very person he was looking for, so he consented to grant my paragon a hearing; and in order that there might be no time wasted he sent word to the author and composer of the operetta in question, and to the leader of the orchestra, that they must come to the theater this morning to decide upon the merits of the would-be star.''

'' Good heavens! and Violette knows nothing of all this!''

'' What do you take me for? I informed her yesterday. You told me her address, you recollect, so I wrote to her before I left Cochard's office, and at this very moment your protégée is probably showing them what she can do; and if the verdict proves favorable she will be engaged immediately and on very favorable terms.''

'' Is it possible? It seems to me that I must be dreaming! How delighted the poor girl must be. And it is to you that she owes this brilliant future!''

'' Don't boast too soon. It is by no means certain that she will please her judges; and even if she succeeds in that the public remains to be conquered, remember.''

"She will succeed in that, I am sure."

"I'm strongly inclined to think so myself; but there is one danger, and a very serious one, it seems to me. If she succeeds don't you think you are likely to be jealous?"

"What! jealous?"

"Yes. You love Violette now, and you are sure to love her still more fondly, for she is well worthy of your love, and like all young men in your condition you are sure to be in your seat close to the foot-lights every evening before the curtain rises. I can see you now in the first row of orchestra chairs gazing fondly at your divinity and rapturously swallowing every note that she utters."

"I shall try not to appear too ridiculous," said Robert, gayly.

"I presume so; but it will not do for Violette to have eyes for nobody but you. An actress belongs to the public and must divide her smiles equally among her listeners. How do you think you will feel when you see her casting sweet glances at some odious person such as Galimas, for example? He will be on hand, you may rest assured. He never misses a first night, I can tell you."

Robert colored and seemed unable to find any reply.

"Madame de Malvoisine, too, will be there," continued the colonel, "and her ward as well, and they will not come to applaud the *débutante*, I can tell you. What will you do if they venture to sneer or even to laugh at her? Will you publicly constitute yourself Violette's protector against her enemies, as well as against all admirers who are distasteful to you?"

"Really, colonel, one would suppose that you were resolved to discourage me—you who have just opened a theatrical career to this young girl, and who seemed to approve her determination to earn a livelihood in this way. Why should you disapprove to-day what you approved yesterday?"

"I disapprove no more than I approve. You don't

understand me, my dear boy. I simply wish to warn you
of the inevitable consequences of Mademoiselle Violette's
entrance upon a theatrical career, and to show you that
neither of you can long remain blind to the fact that
your situation with reference to each other must be
clearly defined. You are both deluding yourselves with
some absurd nonsense about friendship and platonic love;
and you cherish a vague hope of marrying her by and
by after she finds her relatives; but I have convinced
you, I hope, that this hope and the young lady's adop-
tion of a theatrical career are irreconcilable. The die
is cast, as she has probably been engaged by Cochard by
this time; and it is all for the best, perhaps, as she certainly has a decided talent for this calling, and a *prima-
donna* can easily dispense with ancestors and husband.
What does it matter whether she has a name and relatives
or not, provided she sings well?"

"So your conclusion, colonel?"

"My conclusion is that the trip to Havre, which I advo-
cated so strongly at first, has become entirely useless; besides, Violette would not have time to take it with us. On
and after to-morrow she will find herself obliged to be in
constant attendance upon rehearsals, and without a minute
she can call her own."

"I might go down to Havre alone."

"What good would it do? You could not find the house
in which her childhood was spent without her assistance.
Besides, there is nothing to prove that this house was in
Havre any more than in any other seaport town, so I advise
you to abandon the scheme altogether. Now let us speak
of another matter. You just told me that you did not find
the usurer at home. That being the case, you had better
write to him at once, for you must not remain under
pecuniary obligations to such a scoundrel. Before you go,
too, you must take the money to pay the note."

"As you please, colonel; but I would much rather leave

it with you until I am sure that Marcaudier is ready to receive it."

"Why don't you frankly admit that you are afraid of losing it, as you lost Monsieur Labitte's ten thousand francs the other evening. I think all the better of you for your prudence. I hope you have kept your word, and not touched the money made at the Bourse."

"I just met Gustave and told him that I would abandon my share of the profits to him. We had quite a stormy conversation on the subject, and the interview ended in a complete rupture."

"I congratulate you; and now we have settled all the questions of the day we can breakfast in peace. It won't take us long, as I've nothing but the classical *omelette aux rognons* and the traditional cutlet to offer you."

"That is enough and more than enough, colonel."

"Then you haven't the royal appetite of your father, who was one of the heartiest eaters in Brittany—and what a drinker he was! Ah! the young men of the present day are not to be compared with the men of my generation!"

The breakfast ended without any other incident of importance. Robert, who was overjoyed at Violette's probable triumph had very little to say, but the colonel's animated descriptions of Parisian life and of the ladies of his acquaintance amused his young guest immensely.

Nearly two hours had been spent in relating his achievements in love and war, for M. de Mornac, after lauding the charms of his divinities of days gone by, began to relate his campaigns in Africa and in the Army of the Rhine, when the valet entered to announce the arrival of a visitor; and Robert, who had not forgotten that Violette was expecting a call from him, promptly availed himself of this opportunity to take leave.

"Good-bye, my boy," said the colonel, pressing his young guest's hand affectionately; "go, but don't let it be long before you come again. I know you now as well as if

I were your own father, and can see that your good qualities more than atone for your faults, though they are not
trifling ones by any means. But you will be cured of
them; and if you will listen to me and follow my advice, I
feel sure that I shall succeed in making a man of you."

So Robert left the house very proud of M. de Mornac's
confidence in him, but only partially reassured in regard to
the probable consequences of his compact with Violette.
He perceived all the disadvantages of it—the colonel had
just pointed them out to him—and yet he did not once
think of breaking his promise, for he felt that he loved the
orphan too much to desert her.

He regretted, too, that he had not previously enlisted his
mother's sympathies in Violette's behalf, for Mme. de
Becherel, who might then have approved her son's generous scheme, would now certainly refuse him in constituting
himself the protector of an actress, no matter how worthy
of interest Marie Thabor, the infant prodigy she had seen
and heard at the convent at Rennes, might be.

These thoughts engrossed his mind so completely that as
he was walking up the Rue de la Pepiniére on his way to
the Rue de Constantinople, he turned into the Rue du
Rocher without even being aware of the fact; nor did he
become conscious of this blunder on his part until he
reached the house occupied by the Countess de Malvoisine.

A victoria was standing at the door, and Mme. de Malvoisine and Herminia were at that very moment descending
the steps with the evident intention of entering it.

Becherel hoped to escape their notice, but they had excellent eyesight, and it was very evident to him that they
had seen him.

" I am certainly very unlucky," he muttered, quickening
his pace. " They must have guessed that I am on my way
to see Violette, and they will not hesitate to proclaim the
fact to their friends, who will be sure to make all sorts of
ill-natured comments. It doesn't matter much, however.

I am prepared for almost anything on the part of these creatures."

He did not turn to see them enter their carriage, but hastened on to the intersection of the Rue du Rocher and the Rue de Constantinople. Violette admitted him herself, and by her beaming face it was very easy to see that she had good news to announce to him.

Ushering him into a little parlor which was very simply furnished but full of flowers, she said, joyfully:

" You will hardly believe what I am going to tell you, I am sure. I am engaged, and on the most liberal terms! It seems to me that I must be dreaming. I am to have five hundred francs a month to begin with, and the management is to furnish my costumes."

" Then the verdict was favorable?"

" How did you hear anything about it?"

" I just breakfasted with Monsieur de Mornac."

" The colonel! Ah! how can I ever prove my gratitude? But it is you I should thank, for had it not been for you he would not have recommended me to this manager."

Robert shared his protégée's joy, but he manifested less enthusiasm. The colonel's remarks upon the disadvantages of a theatrical career recurred to his mind, and he was a little surprised that Violette perceived only the sunny side of the new life that was opening before her.

" Yes," she continued, " they all congratulated me—the author, the composer, the leader of the orchestra, and the manager—I think *he* even embraced me. They tell me that I will play the part as no other person in Paris could play it, and that the very first performance will insure me the reputation of a star. And to tell you the truth, I was not so very much surprised, for I was really in splendid voice this morning. But how frightened I was when I found myself all alone upon the stage with four or five critics who did not seem to be very favorably disposed toward me. Fortunately I have more self-control than I thought, for I managed to conquer my terror, and by the time I had sung my third piece it seemed to me that I had done nothing else all my life."

"Which shows that you are a born *artiste*," replied Becherel. "You have certainly done well to follow your vocation."

"Are you really sincere in what you say?"

"Why do you doubt it?"

"Because you don't really seem to mean what you say. Do you blame me for accepting this offer?"

"I have not the right."

"You have the right, sir, for you are my best, in fact, my only friend; and if I had thought that I was displeasing you by presenting myself before this manager, I should certainly have remained at home."

"Then you would have done very wrong," replied Robert, quickly, for he saw that there were tears in his companion's eyes. "I am proud of your triumph, I assure you; and if I appear less delighted than I should, it is because I had dreamed of a different future for you—one that was less brilliant, perhaps, but filled with more lasting happiness."

"Yes, I know. You dreamed of restoring to me all I had lost—a name, relatives—perhaps a mother. But that was only a dream, alas! You would not succeed, and I should do very wrong to allow you to waste your time in such a hopeless undertaking. If I were able to give you any clew it would be very different; and yet I must admit that after I left you yesterday my recollection seemed to suddenly become clear upon one point, but only one. I know now the name by which I was called in my childhood, and which I thought I had entirely forgotten. And this awakening of memory was due to the merest chance," continued Violette. "As I was crossing the garden of the Tuileries, after leaving you, I encountered a party of children who were playing at Puss in the Corner under the trees. I love children, so I paused a moment to watch them. There was one who never succeeded in getting to a tree, and the others were continually calling her names to tease her."

"Well?" asked Robert, impatient to hear the rest.

"Ah, well! this name was the very name by which my mother used to call me. How had I happened to forget it, and why did it so suddenly recur to my mind! Doubtless, because no one had ever uttered it in my hearing since my infancy, for it is an old-fashioned name, and very few persons bear it nowadays."

"And this name is?"

"Simone. It is neither pretty nor musical, and—"

"Simone," repeated Becherel, greatly surprised, for it must have been this same name that he had heard while listening at the iron-barred door to the despairing appeals of Marcaudier's victim.

The mournful sound of the last syllable still rang in his ears, and he was surprised now that he had not guessed the beginning of the word. It was, doubtless, too, this same word that he had just seen on the paper wrapped around the apple thrown from the attic.

For an instant he was strongly tempted to draw this scrap of paper from his pocket and show it to Violette, but this similarity of names might be a mere coincidence; hence it would not be advisable to allude to it until the mystery of the Rue du Rodier had been cleared up, and as Violette could be of no assistance to him in that task, it was much better that she should remain ignorant of his intentions.

"What is the matter?" inquired Violette, who noticed her companion's evident perturbation.

"Nothing," stammered Robert. "It only seemed to me that I had heard the name before."

"You have seen it in Alfred de Musset's works, probably. One of the prettiest poems he ever wrote is entitled

'Simone.' You are surprised that I have read Musset's works, perhaps? Madame Valbert had them in her library, and I devoured them, though it was very wrong, I know. But I expiated that crime, and all the others I ever committed yesterday at Saint Maude. I told you, I think, that I intended to go and see Madame Valbert after leaving you. Well, she received me very coolly, and when I tried to explain why I left Madame de Malvoisine, she checked me by declaring that she knew all; that I had done very wrong, and that she should never take any further interest in me. The countess had been there before me. Though what she could have said against me I can not imagine.''

'' Some atrocious falsehood, of course. You might have expected it. Fortunately, you have no need of this Valbert woman's patronage now.''

'' No; but I was very much attached to her, and it grieves me to lose her esteem. I returned home almost heart-broken, and nearly cried my eyes out; but fortunately Monsieur de Mornac's letter came to console me.''

'' And you have fully determined to adopt the stage as a profession?''

'' Why should I abandon the idea? The mischief is done now. I have no friends left now.''

'' You have at least one.''

'' You? Yes, I know it. I hope, too, that Monsieur de Mornac will not desert me. Besides, I have the approval of my own conscience. I questioned that, after the rebuff I just told you about, and found that I had no cause to reproach myself. If I had a mother I could tell her every act of my life, and lay my inmost heart bare before her without a blush.''

''A mother!'' repeated Becherel, strangely moved. '' Have you renounced all hope of seeing yours again?''

'' Alas! yes. The Christian name I have succeeded in

recalling is too slight a clew for me to feel any hope of finding the mother whom I have lost, and whom I should have loved so tenderly. It would be a miracle if I did."

" But if this miracle should come to pass?"

" If my mother were restored to me, I should henceforth live only for her."

" You may rest assured that I shall do all in my power to discover the secret of your birth. I can not say any more now. I must even beg you not to question me on the subject. Forget that I entertain any hope of success, and think only of your *début*. When are you to see the manager of the Fantasies Lyriques again?"

" To-morrow morning. I have my part, and I am to learn the words to-night, and repeat them to-morrow. The other performers know theirs already, and Monsieur Cochard intends that the first performance shall take place in about three weeks."

" I shall be here at a quarter of five, mademoiselle."

" Call me Violette."

*" No, Simone—on condition that you will call me Robert."

" Simone? yes; that is my name. I am sure of it now. But I shall remain Violette to everybody except you. Now go, my friend: I must study my part."

Robert took the hand the young girl extended to him. She did not withdraw it when he imprinted a kiss upon it, and he went away firmly resolved to wage a relentless war upon Violette's enemies, and to solve the mystery of the Rue du Rodier at any cost.

CASH ON DELIVERY

CHAPTER V

ROBERT DE BECHEREL was perfectly right in supposing that Mme. de Malvoisine and Mlle. Herminia had seen him as they were descending the steps to enter their carriage.

It was the hour for their daily drive, and the weather being superb, they were not inclined to miss the opportunity to show themselves to all Paris in the Champs Elysées. Women who do not belong to the fashionable world are always anxious to see all they can of it, and never renounce the hope of eventually securing an entrance into it.

This was certainly the case with the countess of the Rue du Rocher, for it was the object of her life to gain a foothold in those aristocratic circles into which a person can not secure admission merely by proving that he is the possessor of great wealth, whatever people may say to the contrary.

Richer persons than Mme. de Malvoisine have implored admission in vain, and her persistent efforts had not yet been rewarded.

She had succeeded in securing a seat beside some of the leaders of fashion at the theater, and at charitable entertainments, but she had never been invited to set foot in any aristocratic drawing-room, and her own was frequented only by fast men and women of no social standing.

This was not because her past was generally known, however. Very few persons were as familiar with that lady's antecedents as Colonel Mornac; but no one really believed that her title of countess was genuine, and not a few suspected that her pretended ward was her daughter. Still, no one doubted that Mlle. des Andrieux was an excellent match, for inquiries made of Mme. de Malvoisine's notary had satisfied suitors that the handsome Herminia would bring the husband of her choice a dowry of four hundred thousand francs, to say nothing of the magnificent fortune she was sure to inherit from a childless uncle.

And yet, Herminia seemed likely to die an old maid, though she might have married well, in spite of the stain upon her birth, and the mysterious origin of her adopted mother's fortune.

It was all her own fault, however. She was dreaming of a marriage that would open a different world to her; besides, she wanted her husband to please her. Mme. de Malvoisine, tired of waiting, would willingly have abated something of her pretensions, but Herminia was obstinate, and that day, on account of dissensions which had been revived by a recent disappointment, they were both in execrable humor.

Their handsome victoria, drawn by two superb blooded bays, and driven by a majestic coachman in rich livery, reached the main avenue of the Champs Elysées before its occupants had exchanged a dozen words.

They attracted a good deal of attention, and they had already received a number of bows, but not one that flattered them, for the gentlemen who saluted them were much better known at the Bourse than at the Jockey Club;

and the great ladies they met on this fashionable thorough-
fare pretended not to see them.

Such isolation in the midst of this fashionable crowd was
not calculated to restore Herminia's serenity, and her sullen
air indicated that this *tête-à-tête* drive with the countess
was not at all to her taste.

" You look out of sorts," remarked Mme. de Malvoisine.
" What are you thinking about?"

" You wouldn't understand if I told you," retorted
Mlle. des Andrieux, dryly.

" Tell me, all the same. "

" I think I would like to change places with that flower-
girl who is running after us in the hope of selling us a bou-
quet. "

" Are you losing your senses?"

" No, I am in earnest. She is in rags, and probably
will have no dinner to-night, but she is free to come and go
as she pleases—and to love whom she pleases, and no one
thinks of sneering at her. "

" And who sneers at you?"

" Everybody, and not at me alone, but at both of us.
Oh! don't feign astonishment. You are perfectly well
aware of the fact. The Marquise de Charmière's landau
just passed us. "

" Well, what of it?"

" The other day, at the fair for the benefit of the Foundling Asylum, of which she was a patroness, you paid her
two hundred francs for a pin-cushion, and she was lavish
with her thanks. Ah, well! just now she turned her head,
so as not to be obliged to recognize us as we passed. "

" She did not see us. "

" Yes, she did; but she did not want to bow to us in
public. And look, here comes Claudine Rissler and Coralie
de Barancos; see them laugh in our faces as they pass.
Even such notorious women as these make merry at our
expense. "

"What is the matter with you?" asked her companion, evidently much annoyed. "Why are you so out of sorts to-day?"

"Because I am thoroughly tired of the life I lead," replied Herminia, promptly.

"I can't see that you have any reason to complain. I allow you to do as you like; in fact, your uncle often scolds me for letting you have your own way in everything; and if you are still unmarried, you have only yourself to blame. You are too hard to please."

"You think so; I think I am not. You have never introduced me to any one but *parvenues.* I want a gentleman for a husband, and I am going to have one."

"There was one at the house night before last, but you failed to make an impression. However, he is not worth regretting, a petty country squire that hasn't even a title to offer you. If you married him, you wouldn't even be a baroness."

"It's an easy matter to secure a title in Paris; besides, I don't care whether he has a title or not. I like him as he is."

"It remains to be seen if he likes you. I am inclined to doubt it. He had eyes only for Violette, and he must have seen her since I dismissed her, for I am satisfied that he was on his way to her house when we saw him just now."

"That is quite likely, but I intend to prevent him from going there again."

"You seem to be completely infatuated with the fellow."

"Yes," replied Mlle. des Andrieux, bluntly, "and I am determined that he shall marry me."

"I don't see how you are going to compel him to do it."

"You will see, however."

"I think it very strange that you haven't informed me of this decision before. I hope you will not carry things too far before consulting your uncle."

" My uncle! You know very well that he allows me to have my own way in everything. When will he return?"

" As soon as he finishes the business that called him to Marseilles. In two or three weeks, probably."

" I shall not wait for his return before ridding Monsieur de Becherel of that simpering Violette. Marcaudier will help me to do it."

" Marcaudier!" repeated the countess, in profound astonishment."

" Exactly. He is a man of infinite resources, and he will easily find a way to put an end to that affected creature's plotting and planning."

" What a strange idea! Marcaudier is devoted to us— to your uncle, especially—and he is a very shrewd fellow, but matters of this kind are rather out of his line."

" I have my reasons for consulting him, and at once. It is to his house that we are going now."

" What!"

" Yes, before getting into the carriage I told the coachman to drive to the Rue Mozart. It is four o'clock, and Marcaudier must have returned from the Bourse by this time, so we shall be sure to find him at home."

" What are you going to say to him?"

" You will hear. I shall say what I have to say in your presence."

Mme. de Malvoisine had long since discovered that it was useless to oppose Herminia. so she said no more. If Robert de Becherel could have heard this edifying conversation between the mother and daughter, he would not only have formed a more correct idea of the moral character of the ladies of the Rue du Rocher, but would also have realized more fully the dangers to which he had exposed himself by espousing Violette's cause.

It was to be a merciless war, a war to the death, that Herminia intended to wage upon her rival and indirectly upon him, and this unscrupulous woman was sure to find a powerful auxiliary in the person of Cash on Delivery, who was the willing tool of the pretended uncle whose millions would some day descend to Herminia.

Robert would not have recoiled, most assuredly, but he would at least have been better prepared to enter upon this unequal struggle; but he was far from realizing the dangers that threatened poor Violette, for at that very moment he was congratulating himself upon having concluded a treaty of friendship with her.

Colonel de Mornac, who was less interested in the sentimental side of the question than his young friend, would certainly have studied with great curiosity the effects of the training this young girl had received.

Reared by a worthy *bourgeoise*, Herminia would doubtless have turned out like other young ladies of that highly respectable class. She would not have dreamed of social distinction, and would probably have married some honest merchant, and made him a tolerably good wife.

But she had been taught from her earliest infancy to worship money. Her first gift had been gold coins, and though her supposed uncle lavished costly gifts upon her, he had never taken any pains to elevate her character or improve her mind, so it was not strange that the young girl soon became utterly spoiled. Accustomed from infancy to pay no attention to the advice of any one, her early years had been spent in tyrannizing over all around her—her mother as well as the servants. She entered the boarding-school at Saint Maude with a keen appreciation of her own beauty and her parent's wealth, but she had been an inmate of the institution only a short time before she began to understand her situation more clearly. She perceived that money was not everything, and that her birth closed against her doors that were open to much less liberally dowered girls, so she resolved to escape from her false position by means of a marriage that would insure her an *entrée* into the world of fashion, for she utterly failed to understand that such a marriage would lower the social standing of the man who made it without improving that of the woman.

Consequently nothing would satisfy Herminia but a young man of ancient and honorable lineage, and suitors of this class did not frequent the drawing-room on the Rue du Rocher. Robert de Becherel had come there one evening by the merest chance; his name pleased her, and she thought him charming, so she instantly resolved that he should marry her; but the idea of first making sure of Robert's consent never once occurred to her, for she did not suppose for a moment that any comparatively poor young man would refuse a large fortune, especially when it was accompanied with the hand of a handsome young lady.

The only obstacle, therefore, in her opinion, was Violette, and she felt sure of her ability to get her out of the way with the aid of the crafty Marcaudier, who was always ready to oblige her, provided it suited his interest to do so.

Even if M. de Becherel had taken a fancy to the musician, he would soon get over it. A few slanderous reports would probably be all that was needed to alienate him from her; but if these failed she would have to resort to stronger measures. She would reduce her rival to poverty by preventing her from earning a living, and then send to her some rich gentleman who would have no difficulty in enticing her from the path of virtue by promising her a comfortable maintenance. Robert, deserted for the sake of this wealthy capitalist, would become thoroughly disgusted with his former divinity, and it would only be necessary to get him embarrassed financially to make him ready and willing to marry an heiress.

It would be a compulsory marriage, it is true; but that mattered little to Herminia, provided she would have a right to call herself Mme. de Becherel. She would win her husband's love afterward—after the wedding.

Animated by these laudable intentions, and resolved to shrink from nothing to accomplish her object, she could not apply to a better person than Marcaudier. The countess had no voice in the matter, but it was necessary to consult the pretended uncle, and Marcaudier was the only person who had any influence over the person who held Herminia's financial destiny in his hands.

In the meantime, the two spirited bays had traversed the Avenue Eylau, and were already descending the rather steep Rue Mozart.

"I knew we should find him at home," said Herminia, at last breaking a silence that was beginning to alarm Mme. de Malvoisine. " Don't you see him there on the balcony, smoking a cigar?"

" Yes, but he is not alone."

" No. It is Julia Pannetier of the Fantasies Lyriques, who is with him. She has been living with him for more than a year. He will send her away, however. He is under too many obligations to uncle to refuse to see us."

" Your uncle is also under obligations to him," muttered Mme. de Malvoisine.

Herminia did not contradict this assertion. The victoria had just paused in front of the house, and Marcaudier was already on hand to assist his guests to alight.

" How do you do?" said Herminia, unceremoniously. " It was I who persuaded mamma to come to see you, for I wished to consult you on a very important matter."

" I was expecting you," replied the usurer, smiling. " Won't you come in?"

Their host ushered them into a drawing-room that opened upon the balcony and that commanded a view of the upper part of the Rue Mozart.

" What lucky wind blew you here, my dear madame?" he asked.

This question was addressed to Mme. de Malvoisine, who growled in reply:

"Herminia will tell you. I know nothing at all about it."

"I came to consult you upon a purely personal matter," said Mlle. des Andrieux, "and to ask your assistance."

"I shall be only too happy to serve you. What do you wish to consult me about?"

"About my marriage."

"I thought as much. Gustave Piton told me all about it. I have seen the young man."

"Monsieur de Becherel?"

"Yes. He has done me the honor to borrow ten thousand francs of me."

"What do you think of him?"

"I think he would suit you admirably, but he doesn't seem inclined to marry at present."

"I want to induce him to change his mind."

"That will not be a very easy matter, I think, but we can try. The moment is propitious, certainly. In debt to me, and dismissed by Labitte, whose private secretary he was, he probably hasn't a penny at his disposal."

"And yet you say that he would suit my daughter!" exclaimed the countess, indignantly. "We are not particular about a large fortune, it is true, but we don't want a pauper in the family."

"Pardon me, this gentleman is not a pauper by any means. I have made inquiries about him, and he has a very nice estate in Brittany, and belongs to one of the oldest and most highly respected families in his native province. His wife would be received anywhere—even in the Faubourg Saint Germain."

"That is all very fine," replied Mme. de Malvoisine, angrily, "but do you dare to assert that Herminia's uncle would approve this match?"

"I feel sure that Leon would not oppose it, particularly if he knew that Monsieur de Becherel pleased his niece,"

5

replied Marcaudier. "What are you laughing at, mademoiselle?"

"I always laugh when I hear you call my uncle Leon," answered Herminia. "It is all very well for children and young people to call each other by their Christian names, but it certainly does sound absurd in grown people."

"It is all a matter of habit, mademoiselle," replied Marcaudier. "Your uncle and I were together at an age and under circumstances when people are not likely to stand on ceremony, so he continues to call me Pierre, and I to call him Leon precisely as in the days when I was mate on board his brig, the ' Vulture.' "

"Have you heard from him?" inquired the countess.

"I received a letter from him this morning. He is well, and will return in about a fortnight. He spoke of mademoiselle in his letter, and expressed a wish to see her married this year. He says he is growing old, and has not time to wait."

"So my resolve to marry Monsieur de Becherel is an eminently sensible one," remarked Herminia.

"I think so, and I will do my best to bring the gentleman to your feet. I have a plan. Will you give me *carte blanche* to execute it?"

"Willingly."

"Then be kind enough to listen to me. In the first place, this young man is in my power to some extent, at least, by reason of a note that he has given to me, and that I can present for payment to-morrow, if I choose, for he signed it before it was filled out. He would not be able to pay it, for he supposes that it will not become due for three months, and it would take him some time to raise the money by means of a mortgage. I could give him a good deal of trouble, if I chose, you see, but I don't know that we should gain anything by it."

"On the contrary, it would only incense him against me, if he ever found out that you were a friend of mine."

" He knows that already, for I spoke to him about you when he called to see me on the Rue Rodier.''

" What did he say about me?''

" Nothing. He didn't seem inclined to commit himself in any way, and he appeared to hold marriage in holy horror. Yes, I think it will be best for me to abandon all idea of demanding the immediate payment of the note. He would find the money to pay me. His mother would give it to him; besides, he has other friends who would accommodate him—among them, one with whom we shall have to contend some time or other—a certain Colonel Mornac.''

" Colonel Mornac!'' exclaimed the countess. " He is a very honorable gentleman, and I consider that he honors my salon whenever he condescends to enter it.''

" I do not deny that, madame, but we shall have a dangerous enemy in him, nevertheless. I have already discovered that he is giving Monsieur de Becherel bad advice. Piton, whom I met this morning, tells me that the old soldier has urged his protégé to break off all connection with him, Piton—who is an old comrade by the way—and Becherel has done it. That doesn't matter, however. The great trouble is that the young man doesn't want to marry you, because he is in love with somebody else.''

" You have discovered that!'' cried Mlle. des Andrieux. " Marcandier, you are certainly a remarkably clever man.''

" No; I am a man who merely takes the trouble to reason, and to act upon the conclusion of his reasoning. The unsophisticated youth fell in love with your musician at first sight; so the first thing to be done is to break off a dangerous intimacy that has scarcely begun.''

" I have turned the hussy out of my house,'' said Mme. de Malvoisine.

" And you made a great mistake in doing so, in my opinion. By keeping her you would have been able to hold her in check, while out of your house she is free from your surveillance."

" Not so free as you suppose. It was I who rented and furnished the rooms she occupies on the Rue de Constantinople. I even paid the rent for a year in advance."

" This unfortunate generosity on your part does not give you the right to exercise any control over the young lady, however."

" Possibly not; but if I want the owner to give Mademoiselle Violette notice to leave I shall only have to say a word to the *concierge*."

" That would do no good, however. She could easily find other lodgings where Monsieur de Becherel would continue to visit her. There is only one way to alienate him from her, and that is to bring forward a rival—not a youthful rival, whose attentions would only increase Becherel's passion, but a protector who is able and willing to lavish every luxury upon the fair *pianiste*."

" The same idea has occurred to me," said Mlle. des Andrieux, smiling.

" Indeed! Well, we have this generous protector ready to our hand, and he will play his part to perfection, for he is really very much in love with the girl."

" You mean Galimas, I suppose?"

" Yes, he was talking about her to-day at the Bourse, where, by the way, he made at least three times as much as he lost yesterday, so he won't hesitate to spend several thousand louis to gratify his fancy; and however conscientious your former companion may be, I don't think she will turn a deaf ear to a man who is willing to place her at the head of an establishment costing one hundred thousand francs, though Violette sets a high value on herself, and she is right, for she is certainly very charming; besides, she will be worth more than twice as much a fortnight hence."

" What do you mean? Has she come into a fortune or

won the capital prize in some lottery?" asked Herminia, who was always thinking of money.

" No; but she is about to go on the stage; and as actresses are all the rage nowadays, Galimas will be willing to commit any folly for her sake when he sees her admired and applauded by the crowd."

" You certainly are not trying to make me believe that she has secured an engagement since day before yesterday?"

" It is a fact, nevertheless."

" Where?"

" At the Fantasies Lyriques."

" As a ballet-girl, then?"

" As the leading singer. She has a superb voice, you know."

Herminia bit her lip, and Mme. de Malvoisine, who seemed no better pleased than her daughter, said, dryly:

" She sings tolerably well; but where did the fool that engaged her hear her sing?"

" It's quite a long story. Colonel Mornac interested himself in the young lady's behalf at the request of Monsieur de Becherel, and as the manager of the Fantasies Lyriques—a man by the name of Cochard—would have been obliged to go into bankruptcy last year if the colonel hadn't loaned him a hundred thousand francs, it is needless to say that Monsieur de Mornac had very little difficulty in securing a hearing for any protégée of his."

" And the idiot expects Violette to retrieve the fortunes of his theater?" said Herminia, scornfully.

" He feels so confident of it that she is going to make her *début* in two weeks. He is staking his last card upon this *début*. He told me so himself this very morning when he called to pay some money that he owed me. He forgot that he has another account to settle with me, for he will have to pay dearly some day or other for having offended me by—"

"By dismissing your fair friend Julia Pannetier," interrupted Mlle. des Andrieux, with a merry laugh. She was delighted to learn that Marcaudier had a personal grievance against the manager who had just engaged Violette, for she felt sure that she would now have a zealous auxiliary, as they would both be equally interested in preventing Violette from succeeding in her new career.

"It is useless to try and conceal anything from you, mademoiselle," replied Cash on Delivery, smiling. "I have known Julia Pannetier a long time. I am deeply attached to her; and she has been set aside in order to make room for Mademoiselle Violette."

"How shameful!" exclaimed Herminia. "For a true *artiste* like Julia to be compelled to give place to a mere novice is an outrage; and I hope that Violette will fail as she deserves."

"I shall do my best to insure her failure, I assure you, and so will Julia. Everybody at the theater sides with Julia —the leader of the orchestra, the composer—everybody except Cochard. We have already made our preparations for the first performance. I shall have nearly a hundred men stationed in different parts of the house to hiss the *débutante*; and I have made a bargain with the leader of the claque by which it is agreed that his men are to applaud in the wrong places so as to annoy the other spectators. I will spend ten thousand francs, if necessary, to prevent the piece from being played through to the end. Julia knows all the ins and outs much better than I do, and she can tell you that Mademoiselle Violette is sure to be hissed off the stage, even if she possessed the talent of a Patti. A manager can impose a *prima-donna* on the public, but not upon other *artistes*, and all connected with the Fantasies will be leagued together against her, if only to please Julia, their former companion."

"I do not wonder!" cried Mlle. des Andrieux, "for Julia is charming. She sings to perfection, and dresses in

such exquisite taste that I never see her without longing to
ask the address of her *modiste*. Why do you not introduce
her to us?"

"Because—it would not be proper, mademoiselle," replied Cash on Delivery, gravely.

"Herminia!" exclaimed the countess, with an air of
outraged propriety highly ludicrous under the circumstances.

"And why not?" demanded Mlle. des Andrieux, not in
the least abashed. "A dramatic *artiste* is certainly as
good as the divorced women and grass widows that frequent
your salon."

Then turning to Marcaudier, she added:

"This is an excellent opportunity. Julia is here. She
was with you a moment ago on the balcony. Won't you
call her?"

Marcaudier, though he agreed with Herminia perfectly,
hesitated, for fear of offending the countess; but the question was settled by Julia herself, who having taken refuge
in the boudoir adjoining the drawing-room, had of course
heard every word of the conversation.

Timidity was not one of her failings, and thinking she
might venture to show herself she pulled aside the *portière,*
and putting her head into the room, she cried, archly:

"May I come in?"

Herminia ran to her, took her by the hand and led her
to Mme. de Malvoisine, who was choking with anger.

This fourth-rate diva was really a very pretty girl—a
brunette with a clear, colorless complexion, red lips, and
large black eyes. She had the confident air and cold smile
of a woman who is in the habit of exhibiting herself in
public; and it was without the slightest sign of embarrassment that she said to Herminia:

"I thank you, mademoiselle, for your good opinion of
me, and for all the harm you wish my rival. Pierre was
just telling me that Cochard had engaged her to fill my

rôles. She will not hold them long. Between us we will soon drive her off the stage."

Mme. de Malvoisine rose with an air of offended dignity, and stepped out upon the balcony through the open glass door. Marcaudier hastened after her in the hope of appeasing her wrath, and Julia was left alone with Uncle Leon's heiress.

"You must excuse her, she is full of prejudices," said Herminia, referring to her mother. "I haven't any myself, and will gladly be your friend if you will let me."

"I should be delighted. I like you already almost as well as if we had played together; besides, we are united in our hatred of that horrid Violette. You shall never regret having taken me into your confidence, I promise you that; and as I have had more experience than you have I may be able to give you some useful advice occasionally."

"Even if it is only on the subject of dress," laughed Herminia.

"You look very nice as you are. My style of dress wouldn't suit you. It is too loud. I am obliged to make myself conspicuous to please Marcaudier. He wants everybody to turn round and look at me when I drive in the Bois in his coupé. I serve as a sort of advertisement of his wealth, you see. Men are such fools!"

"All men are not."

"Fortunately! I have never seen Monsieur de Becherel, but I am sure that he is charming. In the first place he is young, and I hate old men."

"Marcaudier isn't old."

"Oh, no; and, of course I was very fortunate to meet him at the beginning of my career. It is so hard to make a start in life when one is poor. You who are in a position to choose, should marry only the man you love."

"That is what I am determined to do; but that creature is trying her best to take him from me."

"She will not succeed. After the downfall we are preparing for her he'll never want to set eyes on her again.''

"But will she fail? She has a superb voice, there's no denying it."

"I don't care how much talent a *débutante* has, she can't contend successfully with actors and actresses who are leagued together to insure her defeat. We have only one person to fear—Colonel Mornac—and as I live I do believe that is he coming down the street now."

It was indeed Colonel Mornac who was riding down the Rue Mozart on a chestnut horse which he had just purchased, and which certainly did honor to his knowledge of horseflesh.

Robert had left the colonel entertaining a visitor on the Rue de la Boëtie; but that gentleman had subsequently taken advantage of the superb weather to try his new purchase, and after riding in the Bois for an hour or two, was now returning to Paris by way of Auteuil.

So it was the merest chance that had brought him to the Rue Mozart where he little expected to see Mme. de Malvoisine, but he had excellent eyesight, and he recognized her while he was still some distance from her, talking on the balcony in front of a handsome private house with a gentleman he did not know.

He was not particularly surprised to see the lady so far from the Rue du Rocher, but being in rather a lively humor he decided to allow himself the mischievous pleasure of interviewing her in order to find out what she was doing there. Mme. de Malvoisine had not the same reasons for disliking M. de Mornac that her daughter had. On the contrary, she thought him a charming man, and greatly admired his lofty stature and martial air, so she did not leave the terrace on his approach, but on the contrary leaned smilingly over the balustrade to greet him.

Marcaudier knew the colonel, from having seen him at the theater, and was not sorry to have an opportunity to talk with Violette's defender and find out what kind of a person the *débutante's* enemies would have to contend with.

"Good-afternoon, my dear madame," began the colonel. "I did not expect to have the pleasure of meeting you to-day."

"I came here to call on an old friend," said the countess, glancing at Marcaudier, who bowed without speaking. "But why have you so unkindly deserted us?" she continued, reproachfully. "Madame de Carantoir was deploring your absence again last evening."

Mme. de Carantoir was the widow into whose good graces the colonel was trying to ingratiate himself.

"Ah, madame, one can not always go where one would like to go," the gentleman replied, gallantly. "I was obliged to spend last evening with some stupid old fossils who nearly bored me to death. I would greatly have preferred to be surrounded by fresh young faces—"

"Like that of Mademoiselle Violette."

"Like that of Mademoiselle des Andrieux," continued the colonel, without noticing the interruption. "How is she? I haven't seen her for three days, and I am really pining for a look at her."

"Indeed, sir?" said a voice that came from the open window, and almost at the same instant, the cameo-like profile and massive shoulders of the fair Herminia appeared behind her mother.

"I had no idea that you took such a deep interest in me," continued that imposing young lady, ironically; "but as you have been kind enough to inquire about me, I can, in my turn, take the liberty of asking what has become of the young lady who bears the name of a flower. You know who I mean."

"I haven't the slightest idea," replied the colonel, with unblushing effrontery.

"Ask Monsieur de Becherel. He hasn't forgotten *la belle* Violette. Ah! you recollect now!"

" Perfectly, mademoiselle. But I haven't met the person of whom you speak since the last evening I spent at Madame de Malvoisine's. "

" But you can hardly be ignorant that she is about to make her *début* at the Fantasies Lyriques, as it was you who recommended her to the manager. "

" So he engaged her this morning? How delighted I am to hear it! I wish her all the success she deserves!"

" And I hope she will fail ignominiously, if only to punish her for usurping the place of one who is not only a talented *artiste,* but also my friend. "

" I was not aware that you had any friends on the boards, " replied M. de Mornac, calmly.

" Yes; I have one. Come out, my dear Julia, and allow me to present to you the patron and protector of the creature who has usurped your place. "

Mlle. Pannetier, who had up to this time kept herself in the background, now came forward, with a smile upon her lips, very much as she would have responded to an *encore,* and began to stare at the colonel with rare impudence.

Mme. de Malvoisine, crimson with anger and shame, could hardly refrain from boxing the ears of the daughter who seemed to take so much pleasure in compromising herself; and Marcaudier was fairly boiling with rage at Herminina's imprudence in thus proclaiming herself Violette's enemy, for she might just as well have warned M. de Mornac then and there that they were plotting to ruin his protégée's future.

The only absurdity left for this simpleton to commit was to involve him in the quarrel, and this she immediately proceeded to do.

" Come, defend your friend!" she exclaimed, turning to the usurer. " Tell Monsieur de Mornac that you are deeply attached to Julia, and that you will not permit that fool of a manager to sacrifice her to an insignificant music-teacher.' "

This unexpected announcement completed the colonel's enlightenment, and he began to bestow more attention upon Marcaudier, who did not seem at all inclined to obey the injunctions of Mlle. des Andrieux, however.

Herminia once started, there was no such thing as stopping her.

"Tell him, too," she continued, "that Monsieur de Becherel is in your debt, and that you can give him no end of trouble if you choose, and that you will not deprive yourself of this satisfaction if our dear Julia is compelled to give place to a mere street-singer. It shall be peace or war, as he pleases."

Marcaudier devoutly wished that the earth would open and swallow him, but he did not open his lips, though he was resolved to give the imprudent girl a piece of his mind as soon as the colonel left; and the colonel did not compel him to wait long, for he now knew all that he wanted to know in regard to their projects.

"I must not keep you out in the open air too long, my dear madame," he remarked to the countess. "I fear you will take cold, so you must allow me to take leave of you."

And without waiting for any reply, he trotted briskly away with the intention of immediately warning Robert of the conspiracy that had been formed against his fair friend.

On reaching the door of his young friend's apartments on the Boulevard Poissonnière, he was admitted by Robert's groom, who recognized him from having seen him at Mme. de Becherel's house at Rennes, and immediately ushered him into the smoking-room, where he found Robert engaged in reading a letter.

"You here, colonel!" exclaimed Robert. "I am very glad to see you."

"You haven't that appearance, for you are certainly weeping. What! at your age! You are certainly nothing more nor less than a big baby!"

" No, colonel, I assure you. It is this letter. Read it, colonel.''

" I will, and I am going to read it aloud. "

And M. de Mornac began in a firm voice:

" Robert, my beloved, my only son, my heart is filled with profound grief by the knowledge of the grievous fault you have committed. I thank you, however, for not having concealed it from me, for it would have been still harder to learn the cruel truth through Monsieur Labitte alone. Your letter, fortunately, reached me at the same time that his did.

" I will not reproach you. You have, I am sure, suffered enough already. Do not grieve over the loss of the money. I will procure the amount, and send it to you in a few days.

" The money is nothing; honor is everything, and I trust you have not lost that. But I entreat you to spare me further grief and anxiety. I have suffered so much in the past that I beseech you to take pity on me in my old age, and as you are not proof against the temptations of Parisian life, return to me. You will be welcomed like the prodigal son in the Scriptures.

" We will live together, and not be separated from each other again until the day God summons me to Him, and you will not think with regret of the empty pleasures and frivolities of the wicked city that lured my son from me. I know that at your age, I can hardly expect you to be content with the quiet life I lead in Rennes; but I know a charming young girl who loves you, and who is ready to marry you. She will make you happy; she will bear you beautiful children that we will rear together, and bring you a magnificent fortune that will enable you to gratify the expensive tastes you inherited from your poor father.

" Write me that you consent, and come as soon as possible. Your betrothed is awaiting you. You can guess to whom I refer."

"Can you?" asked M. de Mornac.

"Yes," stammered Robert. "She refers to a young lady I met last summer."

"But you are in love with Mademoiselle Violette. We will speak of that presently, however. Let me finish the letter first.

"If you refuse, if you turn a deaf ear to my entreaties, I warn you, my dear child, that I shall not hesitate. I shall come to Paris. There is certainly a place for me in the little flat I took so much pleasure in furnishing for you. You will give me a cordial welcome, will you not? and let me pet and spoil you as in the days of your childhood? But you will not compel me to make such a complete change in all my habits, I am sure. I await your reply with confidence. I understand, of course, that you can not leave on the instant. Take your time, my son, but three weeks will surely be enough, will it not? Yes? ah, well! I shall expect you before the end of March. You will come with the spring-time.

"*From the mother who loves you more than ever.*"

"And more than you deserve," said the colonel, passing his hand over his eyes that had filled with tears in spite of him.

"Ah! here is a postscript!

"Would you believe it? poor Jeanette, who has served me for thirty years, and who was present at your birth, has offered me all her savings. Seeing me weep, she felt sure that you must have got into some trouble, and written to me for money. Everybody here is devoted to you."

"Well, what do you say to all this?" demanded M. de Mornac. "Shall I send your groom out for a carriage to take you to the railway station?"

"My mother doesn't ask me to leave Paris immediately."

"I see you going! You will be sorry to cause her pain, but you will not be able to make up your mind to desert Violette."

"I shall certainly wait until Violette has made her *début* at the theater at which she has just been engaged."

"I was sure of it, and I shall make no attempt to alter your decision. I shall only be wasting my eloquence, and I don't like to preach; but I bring you some news that may modify your plans. Just now, as I was riding down the Rue Mozart in Passy, I saw Madame de Malvoisine on the balcony of a very pretty private house, talking with a gentleman I did not know, but who seemed to know me."

"The Rue Mozart? Why, it is there that the money-lender, to whom Gustave sent me, lives."

"What kind of a looking man is this usurer?"

"Rather tall and stoutly built. He wears a full beard, and is from forty to forty-five years of age."

"That is the very man I saw. Ah, well! my dear fellow, he is conspiring with the countess and her daughter to have Violette hissed."

"I thought he was in league with them. But why is he so bitter against poor Violette?"

"Because she has usurped the place of an actress in whom he is deeply interested—a certain Julia Pannetier, whose friendship the proud Herminia does not disdain."

"I have heard of her before. She lives on the Rue Rougemont, not far from here, and doesn't bear a very enviable reputation in the neighborhood."

"Well, this is the charming quartet with which Violette will have to contend when she makes her *début*."

Robert was about to protest that he was not afraid of these people when M. de Mornac, springing up and rushing to the door at the further end of the smoking-room, exclaimed:

"What are you doing here? You are playing the spy on us, I believe."

As he spoke, he seized Jean the groom by the collar and dragged him into the presence of his astonished master.

"No, no; I was not listening, sir," protested the youth. "I swear I was not! When you seized me, I was just going to shake the dust out of the *portières*."

"Where did you pick up this fellow?" asked the colonel, turning to Robert.

"Near Rennes. He was born upon one of our estates, and I never had any cause to complain of him before."

Jean hung his head, but he did not appear much frightened. He was not more than eighteen years old, though he had the appearance of being over twenty, for he was a true Breton, with broad shoulders, a large round head, an intelligent face, and large brown eyes that usually met yours unflinchingly.

"Very well; get out of here, and don't let me catch you prowling around again," said the colonel, pushing him into the adjoining room, and closing the door upon him.

"I can't rid myself of the impression that he was listening to us," he remarked to Robert. "If I were in your place, I wouldn't keep him."

"He is devotedly attached to me, I assure you, colonel. I have noticed, though, that he has been going out rather too much for the past two or three months, and I shouldn't be surprised if he had made a conquest of some shop-girl in the neighborhood."

"Well, to return to the subject of which we were speaking a few moments ago; you seem to think yourself capable of defending Violette from the attacks of this usurer and these unscrupulous women, but I intend to second you in your efforts, and as a man who has been warned is equal to any two, I shall immediately see Cochard, and take measures to prevent any disorder on the night of the first performance. Now, what are you going to say to your mother?"

"I shall tell her that she will see me before the end of March."

"And you will promise me to take no decisive step without your mother's knowledge and consent?"

"I give you my word of honor that I will not."

"Then you can count upon me. Come and see me as soon and as often as you can, and do try not to get into any more scrapes. If you are tempted to do so, reread the letter of the sainted mother who lives only for you. It will make you a better man, and save you from being again led astray. I will now leave you to your reflections, for I must go and see Cochard to warn him of the dastardly trick those people intend to play upon him. I am almost as deeply interested in the *débutante's* success as you are, for if she fails, Cochard will go into bankruptcy, and I shall never see my hundred thousand francs again."

With this farewell, the colonel went out to remount the horse that was waiting for him in the court-yard, and Becherel made no attempt to detain him.'

CHAPTER VI.

ROBERT DE BECHEREL was grateful to the colonel for having warned him of the plot against Violette, but he was not sorry to see him take his departure, for he wanted to be alone.

After his visit to the Rue de Constantinople, Robert had made up his mind to explore the mysterious building on the Rue Rodier that very evening—the building in which a woman who might be Violette's missing mother, was pining.

A single word had given him this new clew. Violette had suddenly recollected that her real name was Simone, and this was the word the prisoner had written with her blood on the paper she had thrown into the street through one of the openings in the roof of her prison. This was enough, and more than enough, to make Robert resolve to reach her if such a thing were possible.

He had not said a word to Violette about his plans, however, for he feared he would arouse hopes that might not be realized, but he had hastened home, where he found a letter from his mother awaiting him—a letter that had only strengthened him in his resolution, for, though he understood perfectly well that his mother would never consent to his marriage with an actress, he flattered himself that she would not refuse a poor but worthy orphan.

If Violette should succeed in finding her mother, she would cheerfully abandon all idea of going on the stage. She had just assured him of this, in accents that dispelled all doubt of her sincerity, and now he was convinced of this, the dangers she would incur at her *début* at the Fantasies Lyriques troubled him much less, for he had reason to hope that she would not be subjected to this ordeal.

The possibility of treachery on the part of his groom very naturally troubled Robert a little under the circumstances. He had trusted the boy implicitly, and any betrayal of his confidence would be specially unfortunate at a time when he was more than ever in need of a faithful servant, if only to assist him in his preparations for the exploring expedition he had resolved to undertake that very night.

And, as a person always finds it easy to believe what he wishes to believe, Robert finally came to the conclusion that M. de Mornac must have been mistaken, especially as Jean had been selected by Mme. de Becherel from among many other applicants for the position, because she knew he was honest and industrious: so Robert confined himself to scolding him, and the youth defended himself so stoutly that his employer, convinced of his innocence, concluded to give him his instructions for the evening.

Robert had carefully considered the means to be employed in accomplishing the object, and his plans were completed even to the minutest details.

The first thing to be done was to procure two knotted ropes with a hook at each end—one rope very long, and the other much shorter; a dark-lantern, a small chisel, and a strong pair of pincers; and M. de Becherel could hardly purchase these articles himself, while Jean could perform the commissions without the slightest impropriety or inconvenience, as a servant often needs tools that a gentleman would hardly be expected to use.

Jean was naturally cautious, and even taciturn, like all Bretons—when they have not been drinking—and he received the order to purchase these articles without making any comment or evincing the slightest surprise.

"I am going out now," Robert said to him; "but I want you to put all these articles in a small trunk, with a change of linen, and a suit of clothes. I shall return here about nine o'clock, and you must then procure a carriage for me, and put my trunk on it. I intend to leave the city this evening by the Northern Railway, but I shall probably return some time to-morrow."

"Monsieur may be sure that everything will be in readiness," said Jean, laconically.

"Very well; go and make your purchases, and try not to forget anything."

The groom started out on his errand without replying, and Robert immediately sat down to write to his mother. His letter was affectionate, for he really adored his fond parent; but he said nothing definite about his plans. He casually remarked that there were some matters that might detain him in Paris for awhile, and gave her to understand that he did not despair of finding a situation quite as desirable as that he had lost. All these matters, however, would be decided between now and the latter part of the month, and his mother would soon see him again, in any

case. It is needless to say, however, that he carefully
avoided any allusion to his possible marriage with the heiress.

The letter concluded, he hastened out, jumped into the
first empty carriage he met, and alighted at the intersection
of the Rue Milton and the Rue Rodier, for he wished to
present himself on foot at the door of the Hôtel de la
Providence, where he proposed to spend the night, if he
found the room that overlooked the roof of the back building was vacant.

The entrance of this hotel was not imposing, by any
means; but it was much more respectable in appearance
than the old barrack guarded by Mother Rembriche, and
the proprietor of the establishment was much more court-
eous and obliging than the majority of his *confrères*.

He rose instantly, when Becherel told him that he would
like to engage a room for a fortnight, and replied:

"I have only one that is unoccupied just at the present
time, and that is on the fourth story; but in a few days I
shall have a better one to offer monsieur."

"In the fourth story" thought Robert. "Why, that
must be the very one I want."

But he only said:

"Very well: I will try to make it do for the present;
but I should like to see it before I engage it."

"Certainly, sir. I will show it to you, of course. Have
you much baggage? I ask, because the room is rather
small."

"Only a small trunk that is now at the Northern Railway Station, and that I shall call for this evening if the
room suits me."

"Very well, sir; I will now show you up, if you like."

The room was very small, and contained only a curtain-
less bed, two cane-seat chairs, and a pine table, adorned
with a broken wash-bowl and pitcher; but Robert was not
in pursuit of luxury now. He was interested only in the

view, and without even stopping to glance at the furniture, he walked straight to the window through whose dusty panes only a small amount of sunlight could force its way.

"I will have it washed," the proprietor made haste to say.

He might have dispensed with the promise, however; for Robert had perceived that the window overlooked the roof of the building Marcaudier had converted into a prison.

Robert opened the window, and leaning over the sill, remarked as if casually:

"The view from here is not bad."

"In the direction of Montmartre it is obstructed to some extent by the houses opposite, but you have a view of a very pretty garden, and it is a rare thing to get a glimpse of a bit of verdure in Paris; besides, the ground being high here, the air is excellent."

"I know it, and I should judge, too, that it must be very quiet here. I have to work at night sometimes, and I don't like to be disturbed."

"Oh, monsieur could not have chosen a better place in that respect. The noises of the city do not reach us here; besides, there is hardly any travel on the Rue Rodier. The building you see before us is unoccupied, and the owner of the house at the other end of the garden is away from home. Monsieur might suppose himself a hundred leagues from Paris, and if monsieur happens to be engaged in literary pursuits—"

"Precisely" interrupted Robert, delighted at this opportunity to attribute to himself some plausible profession. "I have written a play, and I came to Paris to submit it to the judgment of a celebrated author who resides on the Avenue Trudaine, not far from here. I shall probably have to make some changes in it, and am, therefore, anxious to secure quarters where I shall be free from interruption."

"Monsieur may be sure that no one will enter his room,

except at his request. I will give orders to that effect. Will monsieur take the room?"

"That depends upon the price," said Robert, the better to personate the rôle of traveler.

"Sixty francs a month, payable once a fortnight, in advance."

The dingy little room had never been rented for more than twenty-five francs a month before, and not often at that price; but Becherel would willingly have given five times the rent asked for the privilege of occupying it; so he immediately handed thirty francs to the proprietor, who pocketed the money with evident satisfaction, and said:

"If monsieur will now go down with me to the office, I will enter monsieur's name upon the register. It is a formality required by the police, as monsieur is doubtless aware."

Some of the difficulties of this rash undertaking were already becoming apparent; but this was not of a nature to daunt Robert, for there was nothing to prevent him from getting out of the difficulty by a slight prevarication.

The innkeeper, at his dictation, inscribed the name of Roberts in the column of names, and farmer in the place reserved for the profession or business of the guest.

Becherel's name was really Robert, and he did own several farms.

"I will be here with my trunk between nine and ten this evening," he remarked, when the formality of registering was concluded.

"Monsieur will find his room ready. There is no fireplace in it, but if monsieur desires a fire, I will have a portable stove carried up."

"That is not necessary. A table to write on, and a couple of candles will be all I shall need."

And Robert went away, well satisfied with the opening of his campaign. He might have obtained further information from his host, but he thought it more prudent not to make any inquiries in regard to the neighbors, for an imprudent question might excite suspicion.

Everything was now in readiness, but several hours must elapse before Becherel could begin operations, so he thought he might as well employ the time pleasantly.

He accordingly strolled leisurely down the Boulevard des Italiens, and seated himself in front of Tortoni's, to smoke a cigar and watch the passers-by.

While thus engaged, he saw Gustave Piton enter the establishment in company with two other brokers, but as they showed no sign of having seen him, he concluded to remain. Gustave seemed to be in the best of spirits, and from this fact Becherel concluded that he must have devised some means of securing possession of the fruits of his fortunate speculation.

However this may have been, the gentlemen left the place after a stay of about twenty minutes, and soon after their departure, Robert crossed the boulevard to get his dinner at the Café Anglais.

He was not in the habit of taking his meals at this expensive restaurant; but it was not the first time he had entered it, and he felt none of the embarrassment that assails so many provincials when they venture into a public place frequented by wealthy and aristocratic Parisians.

He ordered a dinner that did honor to his knowledge of gastronomy, and wines suited to his situation—a bottle of old Musigny to give him strength, and a half bottle of excellent champagne, to bring about that confidence and that nervous energy so necessary when one is about to embark in a difficult undertaking; and this twofold result was so far attained that when he rose from the table about half past eight o'clock he felt ready and able to achieve wonders.

He then directed his steps homeward, and on arriving there, found that his orders had been judiciously and intelligently carried out, and that nothing had been forgotten;

so, after placing a revolver and a box of cartridges in his pocket, and buckling a belt like those worn in gymnasiums around his waist, he sent Jean out in search of a carriage.

When the vehicle arrived, and his trunk had been placed upon it, he went down-stairs, bade Jean take good care of the rooms until his master's return, and then loudly ordered the coachman to drive to the Northern Railroad Station.

On arriving there, he had his trunk carried into the waiting-room, and dismissed his carriage. A quarter of an hour afterward, he took another, had his trunk placed upon it, and gave the coachman the address of the Hôtel de la Providence.

A criminal or an outlaw would not have taken more pains to throw the police off the scent; but Becherel had several reasons for adopting this course. In the first place, he did not want Jean or the *concierge* to know where he was going, for he desired his nocturnal expedition to remain a secret, and in the second place he thought it possible that his new host might question the coachman in order to ascertain where his guest really came from.

The drive from the station to the hotel was not a long one, and his change of quarters was effected without any incident worthy of mention. The proprietor of the house received his new guest very cordially, and escorted him up to his room himself, followed by a shabbily dressed servant with the trunk.

The wash-bowl and pitcher had been removed from the table, and it was now furnished with writing materials, including a quire of foolscap and two candles.

As soon as these last had been lighted, Becherel thanked his host for his attentions and dismissed him, after which his first care was to satisfy himself that the door had a bolt on the inside, and finding there was one he both locked and bolted the door, placing the key on the inside so as to prevent any one from looking through the key-hole.

Thus protected alike from any sudden intrusion and from

espionage, Robert proceeded to unpack his trunk, removing from it everything except the suit of clothing, for which he had no immediate use and which he had brought with him chiefly to convince Jean that he was really going to the country; and after placing the other articles on the bed he cautiously opened the window.

The moon, which was in its last quarter, had not yet risen, and the night was very dark. Not a star glimmered in the sky and there was not a breath of air stirring.

Becherel consequently ran very little risk of being seen while he was making his way over the roof; but on the other hand the darkness made it impossible for him to calculate the exact distance that separated him from the field of his explorations.

Fortunately he had measured it pretty accurately with his eye during the day and knew that the roof to which he wished to descend was only seven or eight feet below his window, though it extended some distance beyond the hotel; but the only windows in this roof were on the side next the alley, so the great difficulty consisted in making his way up one side of the steep roof, over the comb, and then sliding down to the openings on the other side, which had probably been closed at nightfall.

The first part of the undertaking was much the easiest; for Robert, if he had not been obliged to regain his chamber again could have jumped down upon the roof without the slightest difficulty.

One question, however, remained to be decided. At what hour should he begin work?

Of course the longer he deferred the undertaking the less danger he ran of being troubled by inquisitive neighbors, provided he allowed himself time to complete it before daylight; but on the other hand if he deferred it too long he might become nervous and possibly discouraged, hence it would perhaps be advisable for him to profit by his present ardor. Besides, the quiet residents of that neighborhood probably retired at a very early hour. Even now, though a neighboring clock had struck ten only a few minutes before, all the inmates of the Hôtel de la Providence seemed to be asleep.

The proprietor had not exaggerated when he extolled the remarkable quietness of the place. No sound reached Robert's ears; and as he leaned from the window he could see no light except the reflection of the street lamps on the Rue Milton. Marcaudier's house concealed those on the Rue Rodier from him. This profound stillness and the total absence of light in any of the surrounding houses made him decide upon immediate action.

It was not very cold; and his coat would only hamper his movements, so he took it off, buckled his belt more tightly around him, put the chisel and pincers in his pockets, lighted his lantern, lowered the shade so as to conceal the blaze of the candle from view, and hung it around his neck with a chain provided for that purpose. This done, he twined around his chest the longer of the two ropes, and after thus equipping himself he fastened the short one securely to the window-sill; he then crawled out upon the window-ledge feet foremost, and seizing the first knot in the rope with both hands, he lowered himself to the roof below. It took him only an instant to reach it; but the next step would prove a much more difficult one, as it would consist in dragging himself up to the comb of the roof—no easy matter, when this roof is covered with slates closely overlapping one another, and presenting no projections to serve as points of support.

Robert did not hesitate, however, and by dint of strength and perseverance finally succeeded in reaching the comb of the roof. This feat accomplished, he paused to take breath and also to examine the side upon which he must next venture.

As he had foreseen, the small windows in the roof were closed, and no ray of light was visible through them; but this might be due either to their extreme thickness or to the fact that the interior of the garret was shrouded in darkness. In either case Robert's task was now rendered more difficult by the necessity of prying open one or both of these windows with his chisel, and the danger of slipping during the operation.

Robert was about to venture upon this inclined plane when he saw a light suddenly appear in the second story of the private house fronting on the Rue Milton; but the light vanished almost instantly, to appear a moment afterward in the story below, only to again disappear; and Robert felt sure that this light was carried by some one who was descending to the basement of the house and from there perhaps into the garden.

To satisfy himself of this fact he crawled cautiously to the end of the building, and then stretched himself out at full length, with his head projecting beyond the gable end; but though his position was by no means comfortable he was soon well repaid for his trouble, for only a minute afterward he saw a man with a lantern coming slowly down the garden and straight toward the building on which he was perched. Certainly this person, whose features were concealed from the anxious watcher's gaze by the darkness, had not left the house at this hour of the night merely to stroll about the garden; so Robert felt very little surprise when he saw the man, when directly beneath him, open a door and enter this same mysterious building. The inmates of the house on the Rue Milton also had access to this extension of Marcaudier's house, that was evident.

Were they, then, the usurer's accomplices, or was there really, as Cash on Delivery declared, a party wall that divided the building into two parts? It seemed more than probable, however, that the prison in which the woman was confined had two doors, one opening into the house on the Rue Rodier and the other into the garden; and in that case there could be no doubt of the neighbor's complicity.

However this might be, the mystery was certainly deepening; and Becherel, though greatly perplexed, was obliged to wait for the man to emerge before taking any further action in the matter, for it was not impossible that the man was with the prisoner at that very moment. He had, perhaps, come to bring her food; and in that case his visit was not likely to be a long one.

Robert continued to watch, therefore; but he had seated himself astride the comb of the roof a little further back from the gable end of the building, and was now dividing his attention between the garden and the windows in the roof.

Soon it seemed to him that the panes of glass became a little more brilliant, as if there was a light beneath them, but a very faint light, like that of a lantern. He did think strongly of satisfying himself of the fact, but he said to himself that he would probably be unable to see anything by reason of the thickness of the glass, and that he had better remain where he could command a view of the garden.

It was well that he did, for in about five minutes the windows became dim again, and a few minutes afterward the man reappeared in the garden still carrying his lantern; and Robert, who was watching him, saw him re-enter the house and extinguish his light before closing the door.

That was all. The house remained dark and silent, so the man probably departed as he had come—by way of the Rue Milton—so he did not live in the house, and everything seemed to indicate that he would not return again that night.

The aspect of the situation had suddenly changed. The jailer who was guarding the prisoner was probably not Marcandier after all, for Marcandier would hardly have taken the trouble to make such a long détour.

But if Robert intended to rescue the victim, the moment had now come to make the attempt.

Becherel proposed to lower himself into the garret with the aid of the long knotted rope; and he did not altogether despair of inducing the prisoner to leave it with him and make her way over the roof to his room in the Hôtel de la Providence, where she would be safe until he could take her elsewhere, for her tormentor would not think of coming there to look for her.

If she refused to attempt a journey that was certainly rather difficult and dangerous for a woman, he could at least have a conversation with her and induce her to tell him her story; and when he had learned her history he would go, in company with Colonel Mornac, and inform the nearest commissioner of police of the facts and request him to put an end to this state of affairs.

Robert accordingly made his way cautiously along the comb of the roof until he reached a point directly above the nearest window, then lying flat upon his stomach, he slid down the roof, feet foremost, steadying himself as well as he could with his hands. A professional tiler might have attempted this feat without much danger; but Becherel, who had no experience in such matters, certainly ran a great risk of losing his life.

Fortunately the slope was more gradual than on the other side of the roof, and though it took Robert fully ten minutes to make the descent he finally succeeded in securing a position directly under the window, and where the space left by a broken slate furnished him with an insecure foothold.

He began work by unrolling the rope coiled around his body; he then detached his lantern, which had been greatly in his way in the descent, placed it on the roof within reach, surrounding it with a coil of rope to hold it in place, and then drawing the chisel from his pocket he inserted the slender end of it under the lower corner of the window-sash.

The window was heavy, and Becherel had a great deal

of difficulty in starting it, for it had not been made to open outward, but it was provided on the inside with two iron supports that worked in a piece of notched iron and prevented the window from falling.

After the first slight raising of the sash was accomplished, Robert placed both hands upon the chisel and bore all his weight upon it. Soon a grating sound warned him that the iron arms had caught in the notches, and that the sash, sustained by these supports, would remain open.

The opening was quite large enough for a man to pass through; but before venturing he cautiously put his head in to see what he could see, but he could distinguish nothing in the dark depths below, nor could he hear the slightest sound.

Nevertheless the prisoner must be there, as her jailer had left the house alone; so Robert concluded she was asleep. He did not think for an instant of abandoning the undertaking so fortunately begun, however. There was a steel hook at each end of his rope, one large and one small, and he fastened the largest to one of the iron supports that upheld the window and which was quite strong enough to sustain the weight of his body.

But he did not want to descend until after he had secured a look at the depths below, for it was by no means improbable that the prisoner was guarded by an assistant jailer, who would attack Robert as soon as he reached the floor and before he had even time to assume an attitude of defense. So he attached his lantern to the small hook at the other end of the rope, and he was about to lower it into the garret when the broken tile upon which his feet were resting gave way.

He felt himself sliding down the roof with the swiftness of lightning, and thought he was lost. To say that he did not lose his wits for an instant would be doing him too much honor; but the instinct of self-preservation remained and supplied the place of the missing will.

Involuntarily Becherel stretched out his arms to clutch something, and his right hand coming in contact with the rope that had been fastened to the iron support, he clung to it with all the energy of despair. It was a fortunate thing for him that he had seized it not more than a yard from its point of attachment, for if he had caught hold of it lower down it might not have successfully resisted the strain caused by the sudden jerk, which was much less severe under the present circumstances.

This fact is perfectly understood by all mountain explorers and Alpine travelers. Four tourists, one of whom was an English nobleman, perished a number of years ago simply because they had allowed the rope that bound them to one another to become too slack, and a misstep made by the last person in the line dragged them all down a frightful precipice.

Becherel was more fortunate; but his descent was so rapid, and the window was only such a short distance from the eaves, that before he could stop himself his legs were beyond the spouting.

The lantern, too, was dangling quite a little distance below him; and as the light in it was still burning, it might attract the attention of pedestrians on the Rue Rodier.

But no one seemed to be passing; besides, such a possibility was the least of Becherel's troubles. He was thinking only of escaping from his perilous position, so the first thing he did was to seize the rope tightly with both hands, for he knew that he would not be able to sustain himself long with the right.

When he had done this, and succeeded in raising himself enough to get one knee on the spouting, he thought himself virtually saved, though he realized that the frail support might give way beneath him at any instant. He did not remain on this dangerous perch long, however, but slowly and laboriously raising himself, hand over hand, he

at last reached the open window again, and then drew up
the rope that had saved him from death.

The candle in the lantern was still burning, and the
time had come to make use of it in lighting the depths below, so Becherel cautiously lowered it, and found that the
ceiling of the room in which the unfortunate woman he
had come to deliver was confined could not be more than
ten feet high. The floor was bare, and Becherel not only
saw no furniture, but no sign of the prisoner.

Still, the light must have woke her, even if she was
asleep, so why was she crouching in some corner of her
dungeon instead of approaching the lantern? Did she not
understand that this light, descending from above, indicated that succor was at hand?

Becherel perceived now that the light with which he had
provided himself would be of very little service to him
unless he descended with it, but he was unwilling to do this
until he had satisfied himself that an enemy was not lying
in wait for him below, so he deferred action yet a little
longer.

His patience was finally rewarded.

After about five minutes of attentive watching he saw
something moving within the lighted circle. One might
have supposed it the bottom of a swaying curtain appearing and disappearing at regular intervals—a fragment of
material that certainly did not move itself, and that must
be the bottom of some garment, doubtless of a trailing
dress, and Becherel rightly judged that the recluse must
be walking around the lantern, as a moth, attracted by the
light, circles around it without daring to approach it.

"She will finally make up her mind to touch it," Robert
said to himself, and he was right, for after revolving
around it a number of times, she suddenly knelt down and
examined the light.

It was certainly a woman, and she was enveloped in a
long wrapper that covered her from her neck to her feet.

She was bending so low over the light that Becherel could not even catch a glimpse of her face, but he hoped that she would finally pick up the lantern and hold it up over her head for the purpose of ascertaining where it came from, and who had lowered it.

He was disappointed in this hope, however, for the prisoner after a short halt, hastily retreated, and again became invisible. She had probably taken refuge at the other end of the garret.

Robert could scarcely hope for her return now, and if he desired to carry the investigation any further he must certainly venture down himself. The chisel he had used was still lying on the roof fortunately, for it might have fallen into the street, and Becherel, who did not want to leave any trace of his visit, hastily replaced it in his pocket, and then turning, he introduced his feet into the opening and began to descend with the aid of the knotted rope.

This was mere child's play in comparison with the difficulties he had already overcome, and he soon reached the floor below. As soon as he set foot upon it he unhooked the lantern from the rope, and started in search of the prisoner. He did not see her at first, but he perceived that the only article of furniture in the room was a cot bed with a tick filled with straw upon it. There was not even a chair or a table, nothing but a long shelf fastened to the wall, a stone pitcher, and in one corner a torn screen.

Upon the shelf were the remains of a hermit's repast, some decayed fruit and a morsel of moldy cheese. The prisoners at Mazas fare infinitely better, and Becherel wondered how a human being could manage to subsist upon such a diet.

Where was the victim of this barbarity? She could not have left the garret, so Robert immediately proceeded to explore the dungeon, which was but imperfectly lighted by the lantern.

Robert rather expected to find the recluse hiding behind

the screen, but he did not expect to find her crouching
upon the floor with her face buried in her hands. He did
not see her at first, but on moving the screen he nearly
stumbled over her, and warned by this sudden collision, he
lowered his lantern until the light fell full upon the bowed
form of the unfortunate woman.

"Rise, madame," he said, kindly, touching her lightly
upon the shoulder.

Her only reply was a low moan.

"I have come to release you," he added, gently.

On hearing these words she straightened herself up a
little, and partially revealed a face emaciated by privations
and distorted with terror.

"Do not harm me," she murmured, imploringly.

"You have nothing to fear. I am a friend," replied
Becherel.

And as she did not move, he took her by the hand and
raised her to her feet. She offered no resistance, and
Becherel could examine her at his leisure, for she remained
as motionless as a statue. It was evidently fear that thus
petrified her, for she gazed at Becherel with such terrified
eyes that she looked like a prisoner who sees her execu-
tioner suddenly appear before her.

She was clothed in a long loose gown of coarse gray flan-
nel, very like a monk's robe in shape. Her head was
covered with a mass of disheveled gray hair, and her face
was wax-like in its pallor.

Still she must once have been very handsome, for her
features were remarkably regular and delicate. It was
difficult to decide upon her age. By her wrinkled and
haggard face one would have supposed her at least sixty,
but she might have been much younger. Solitude and
cruel treatment age prisoners very rapidly. When Latude
left the Bastile he looked like a centenarian.

Becherel endeavored to discover some resemblance between this woman and Violette, but he utterly failed, and

he soon perceived that the light of his lantern troubled the unfortunate woman, who was undoubtedly accustomed to live in comparative darkness. The light dazzled her, and to escape it, she closed her eyes like an owl surprised by a ray of sunlight.

Robert, who had not let go of her hand, perceived that she was trembling violently, so he led her to the cot and placed his lantern on the shelf that served her as a table.

She seated herself mechanically on the side of the cot, and sat there without moving or speaking.

Robert thought she was waiting for him to question her.

" I had a great deal of difficulty in reaching you, madame," he said, gently, " and we have no time to lose. The man who was here just now may take it into his head to return—"

" No, he will not return until to-morrow night," murmured the prisoner.

" He will not find you if you will consent to follow me."

" Follow you?"

" Yes, and immediately. It is not an easy road to travel, it is true, but I will help you."

She did not appear to understand him, so Robert pointed to the opening overhead. She glanced up at it, but dropped her head again, almost instantly, and did not utter a word. Becherel saw her shudder.

" You are afraid to venture?" asked Becherel.

She made a sign of assent.

" Ah, well! even if you are afraid to make the dangerous journey I can save you all the same. Tell me who you are. Tell me your story, and I swear that you shall be free to-morrow. I will inform the authorities that you are detained against your will, and at their order the doors of your dungeon will be opened, and the wretches who have immured you here will be punished. Tell me all, I beseech you. You must understand what I say to you. I am awaiting your response."

The response did not come, however, and Becherel began to wonder if he was not dealing with an idiot; still, he did not lose heart.

"You can not have lived here always," he continued. "You must have lived somewhere before you were confined in this horrible place. You must have had a name. Tell me what it was."

"A name!" repeated the woman, vacantly.

"Yes. What were you called?"

"I don't know; I have forgotten."

"Make an effort to recollect, and your memory will surely return."

"I can not."

Robert could scarcely credit this total obliteration of a faculty that becomes impaired with age, but that is never entirely lost. Old people do not remember facts of recent occurrence, but they recollect those of a remote date very plainly; and even idiots and lunatics retain some recollection of their past.

Robert, who was aware of this fact, did not abandon all hope, but he adopted another means of ascertaining what he wanted to know.

"You lived in a seaport town, did you not?" he asked, abruptly.

"The sea—yes, I have seen it. It is beautiful."

"You lived in Havre, I believe."

"Havre? No, I know no such place."

"The deuce! it seems that I must have been mistaken," thought Becherel. "In fact, all maritime towns have piers."

"But you, at least, know who Marcaudier is," he added, aloud.

This new attempt proved no more successful than the first, however. The recluse looked at him with a bewildered air; she had evidently never heard of Marcaudier before.

The further Becherel proceeded with his investigation the more convinced he became that he had been mistaken in his suspicions, and already he was inclined to believe the usurer innocent of the crime of which he had formerly accused him.

It might be, after all, that Cash on Delivery was not the culprit. Indeed, from what he had seen on the roof, Robert was inclined to think that this woman's persecutor resided in the house on the Rue Milton.

"Do you know where you are?" continued Robert.

The prisoner shook her head.

"You are in Paris—in a house that fronts on the Rue Rodier and extends to a garden on the Rue Milton."

These names seemed to make no impression on the prisoner, but she exclaimed:

"A garden? I love gardens! There are flowers in them?"

"You had one years ago, probably."

"Yes, it was full of roses."

"Why did you leave it?"

The light that had shone in the unfortunate woman's eyes a moment before suddenly became dim, and she again relapsed into the torpor that so disheartened Becherel.

Had she really lost her mind, or was she only playing a part—answering unimportant questions, but ignoring all of a compromising nature.

An idea that in spite of his protestations of friendship she might take him for an emissary sent by her jailer occurred to him.

"She is so afraid of him that she dares not commit herself," he said to himself. "Perhaps she is even afraid that he is listening at the door by which he entered and left the room. She fears that he is setting a trap for her, and that he will kill her if she complains of his ill treatment."

The supposition seemed plausible enough certainly, for the scoundrel's victim still maintained the submissive, cringing attitude of a dog that is in the habit of being beaten. It was necessary, consequently, to reassure her, but this was no easy matter, as all the protestations in the world would have very little weight with her.

Still the matter must be settled one way or the other, for he was still in doubt whether he was in the presence of Violette's mother or not. But he had in reserve a final test which he fancied must prove decisive. If this did not solve the mystery, there would be nothing left for him but to go away as he had come. The mystery of the recluse interested him only so far as it concerned Violette, and if it did not concern her he cared very little about delivering a stranger—a mad woman too, who ought perhaps to be kept in confinement.

This feeling was not very generous perhaps, but it was at least excusable in a person in Robert's situation.

"You misunderstand my intentions, perhaps," he continued, after a pause. "I am your sincere well wisher, and though I do not know all the events of your life, I at least know that you have a daughter."

Robert was by no means sure of this fact, however, but the well-known maneuver of telling a falsehood to get at the truth seemed at first likely to prove successful.

The prisoner gave a violent start; her eyes sparkled and she lifted up her head. One might have supposed that the maternal feeling had suddenly revived in her crushed heart.

"Shall I tell you her name?" asked Becherel, in even gentler tones. "Her name is Simone."

"Simone!" repeated the unfortunate woman, passing her hand over her brow; "yes, I know the name. I have heard it before, but I have no daughter. No, I have none."

The memory of the recluse had evidently received a shock, but the shock had not been sufficiently severe to render it lucid, and Violette's lover saw that he would have to begin over again.

" She is nineteen years old," he continued, " and she is a beautiful blonde, with dark eyes. She must have been lovely even in her infancy. You surely can not have forgotten her—if she were here, you would recognize her I am sure."

He received no reply, but he could see that the blow had told.

The drawn features of the recluse showed plainly enough that she was making a desperate effort to recover the almost broken thread of her ideas. The swelled veins stood out like whip-cords under her wax-like skin, and the big drops of sweat that covered her forehead betrayed a violent mental struggle.

It might be that solitude and privations had caused this loss of reason in her case. This was more than probable, indeed, for Robert could no longer suspect her of feigning madness to conceal her secret, for it was evident that she was suffering terribly.

" If I should take you to see her, you would be very glad, would you not? And the poor child who has mourned your loss for so many years would bless me for restoring her mother to her."

" Simone? Did you say that her name was Simone?"

" Yes, and this name must certainly remind you of the time when you held her in your arms. You can now enjoy that happiness again. There is nothing to prevent you from seeing her again if you will only summon up courage to leave this horrible place with me."

" But how?" asked the prisoner, brusquely. " He locked and barred the door to-night as he always does."

" Who is he?"

" My persecutor—the cruel man who keeps me here to die of cold and starvation. I have implored him a hundred times to kill me, and end my sufferings, but he will not."

" Why does he torture you thus?"

" I do not know."

" But you must know who he is."

" No."

" But you can certainly describe his face to me, as he comes here every night."

" He always comes masked. I have never seen his face."

" That is very strange, but it is conclusive proof that you must know him. If you had never seen him in former years, when you were free, he would not take this precaution. He must speak to you, however—"

" Very rarely. He throws my food to me as if I were a dog; and when I complain he never even answers me."

All this shed no light upon the mystery Becherel was trying to solve, but it seemed to him that the prisoner was beginning to understand better what was wanted of her. If the poor creature was mad, as he had good reason to fear, she certainly had her lucid moments by which he must endeavor to profit, if possible.

So Robert lost no time in reverting to the name that had made a fleeting but very strong impression upon the prisoner, judging by the change in her countenance.

" You pretend that you have no daughter," he remarked, " but you know very well that you had one, and that she disappeared. You think she is dead, probably, but she lives, I swear it! She is looking for you, and I have promised to find you for her."

He paused, for he saw that she had ceased to listen to him. Her mind seemed to be in the clouds, and she closed her eyes like one in a dream. How was he to arouse her from this lethargy?

A new idea suddenly occurred to him. The apple and the paper in which it had been wrapped were still in his pocket, and he decided to make use of them.

" You are silent when I speak of Simone," he said, " and you seem to have forgotten her; and yet you remember her sometimes, as you summon her to your aid, for it was certainly you who threw me this."

As he spoke he showed her the apple and the paper on which she had written with her blood the name he had just uttered.

The effect was instantaneous, but exactly contrary to what he had hoped, for she had scarcely glanced at the articles held out for her inspection, when she suddenly sprung to her feet, exclaiming:

"It is false! I have written nothing! I have thrown nothing! You lie! You have invented this story to get me beaten. You are a cruel man. Go away! I never want to see you again. If you speak to me again I shall not answer you."

And before he had time to prevent it she fled to the other end of the garret, and again concealed herself behind the screen. It was certainly madness now, and frantic madness, for she began to utter wild and despairing shrieks.

Becherel was utterly at a loss what to do, and he began to ask himself if his undertaking was not as insane as this woman, for how was he to calm her and induce her to listen to reason? He could not flatter himself now that he would be able to resume the conversation at the point to which he had conducted it prior to the unfortunate resolve that had spoiled everything.

The worst of all this was that the cries did not cease. She was uttering incoherent words now, and he recognized the voice as the same he heard when he lost his way in the passage on his first visit to Marcandier; but now it was raised to such a pitch that it must almost reach the street.

The situation was becoming extremely critical, for passers-by or neighbors might hear the sound, and imagining that a woman was being murdered, insist upon the interference of the police.

For the first time since the beginning of the adventure

he thought of beating a retreat before he had conducted it to a successful termination. It was a great disappointment to him to be obliged to leave before he had solved the mystery, but there seemed to be no help for it.

He waited, however, with a faint hope that the recluse would become quiet and consent to listen to reason. Human strength has its limits, and one can not shriek on indefinitely. The woman would certainly be obliged to cease when her voice failed her, and that was already becoming weaker.

A few moments more and these alarming cries must cease, and Robert was about to approach the unfortunate creature, so as to be able to take immediate advantage of the first opportunity to make himself heard when he was deterred by a loud pounding on the outside of the door.

Who was rapping? Certainly not Marcaudier, for he was not likely to be at the house on the Rue Rodier at that hour of the night.

"Will you stop your noise, you hussy?" cried a voice that Becherel thought he recognized as the voice of Mother Rembriche.

The effect of this coarse order was instantaneous. Not another sound escaped the prisoner.

But though the rapping ceased, there was nothing to prove that the hideous old portress was not standing there still, with her ear at the key-hole, and this possibility decided Robert. He said to himself that if he should attempt to talk with the prisoner, or even to approach her, the cries might begin again, and Rembriche, who seemed to possess her employer's entire confidence, undoubtedly had a key to the iron-barred door, and might enter for the purpose of punishing the prisoner for the disturbance she had made, and in that case Robert, on finding himself face to face with the old hag, would have no alternative but to take the stranger's part.

He was strongly tempted to do this now, but such an act

might only make her situation still more intolerable, for if every door was standing open, he was by no means sure that the unfortunate woman would consent to follow him out of the house; and even if she did, what would he do with her, for it was very doubtful if he could succeed in finding a carriage, and if he did it was not unlikely that she would absolutely refuse to enter it. Under these circumstances it would probably be better to leave her where she was, and make another attempt to rescue her at some future day.

Hastily extinguishing the lantern for fear that a ray of light might make its way through the key-hole, and warn Mother Rembriche that the prisoner was not alone, he again fastened it around his neck, and seizing the knotted rope, made his way nimbly to the window in the roof, pulled the rope up after him, unhooked it, and then closed the window, though not without considerable difficulty, for the supports were rusty and did not move very readily. He succeeded in lowering the sash, however, and everything having been put in place, he undertook his return journey.

This was made without any accident this time, and he soon found himself in his poorly furnished chamber safe and sound, but far from satisfied with the result of his expedition.

He had seen with his own eyes that a woman was confined in that gloomy attic, but there was nothing to prove that this woman was Violette's mother. She had evinced some emotion on hearing the name of Simone, but she had speedily recovered from it, and he had been unable to extort any definite information from her.

The unfortunate woman was mad; Robert was convinced of that, but she was certainly none the less worthy of interest on that account, as she was detained there by force and was certainly very cruelly treated. But Becherel was beginning to get over his chivalrous notions. He said to himself that the poor creature's relatives might have good

reasons for guarding her themselves instead of placing her
in an insane asylum—private reasons that did not justify
them in maltreating her, but that certainly did not concern strangers.

Who were these inhuman relatives? The occupants of
the house on the Rue Milton probably. Marcaudier must
be their accomplice, or at least their confidant, as his portress guarded the prisoner.

But there was no apparent connection between this unfortunate affair and Violette's history.

" And even if I should discover for a certainty that this
unfortunate woman brought Violette into the world,"
thought Robert, " what would Violette do with an insane
mother—a mother who could not even tell her the secret
of her birth, as she has lost her memory as well as her reason. It would only be a fresh disappointment for Violette,
and a heavy responsibility, to say nothing of the fact that I
should only incense Marcaudier still more deeply against
the poor child by wresting the victim from her persecutors.
It would certainly be better for me to abandon for the
present a project that would only increase the dangers of
Violette's situation. I had better consult Colonel Mornac
perhaps before abandoning the undertaking, but I don't
much like the idea of telling him about my unfortunate
expedition; he would be sure to laugh at me. I know
too, the advice he would give me. He would advise me to
let the matter drop, I am sure, and I think he is quite
right. ' Don't run after two hares at the same time,' the
proverb says, and I shall have quite enough to do to defend
Violette against the enemies that have leagued themselves
together against her."

So with the fickleness that was one of his greatest faults
Robert de Becherel suddenly abandoned the scheme upon
which he had based all his hopes. He had dreamed of restoring a mother to Violette, who would then abandon her
plan of going on the stage, and whom he could subsequent-

ly marry with the approval of his mother—his dear mother, who might arrive in Paris at any moment—and now this fine scheme had all ended in smoke, and Robert was thinking only of insuring the *débutante's* success, without asking himself to what his increasing love for the fair Violette was likely to lead.

Having come to this conclusion, he felt strongly tempted to return to his comfortable rooms on the Boulevard Poissonnière, but he could hardly depart in the middle of the night without exciting the suspicion of his host; besides, he was unwilling to leave his trunk filled with compromising articles behind him. It would be much better for him to defer his departure until the next day, and then announce that a telegram received that morning compelled him to return home immediately, to his very great regret.

After smoking an incredible number of cigars, and walking up and down his room a hundred times, Becherel finally concluded to go to bed.

He had considerable difficulty in getting to sleep, but fatigue coming to his aid, he finally succeeded in closing his eyes, muttering:

"The deuce take the mad woman! The deuce take Marcaudier! Live Violette and the Fantasies Lyriques!"

CHAPTER VII.

THREE weeks had elapsed and Robert de Becherel had made no attempt to repeat his visit to the garret on the Rue Rodier.

For a few days the poor woman he had left to the mercy of her persecutors was ever in his mind, and more than once he was on the point of relating his discovery to the commissioner of police of that precinct. Had he been in his native town he certainly would have done so, but being a comparative stranger in a large city, such a step on his part would be likely to involve him in considerable trouble.

To excuse himself in his own eyes, he told himself that it would not be too late to deliver the prisoner after Violette had made her *début*. That, if this *début* proved a success, Violette would have no further need of him; and that if she failed, there would still be a chance of his finding her relatives in Havre or elsewhere, as it could not be her mother who was languishing in the den on the Rue Rodier; but all this specious reasoning was, in reality, only an excuse for his indifference in regard to the fate of the recluse.

The plain truth was that he was madly in love with Violette, that he now lived only for her, and that it mattered very little to him whether she found her relatives or not, provided she returned his love.

He saw Violette at her own home every day, after her return from rehearsal, for he would not go to the theater for fear of compromising her.

Their conversation would have bored the colonel almost to death, as he was not of a sentimental turn of mind, but they enjoyed it immensely, and Violette, without absolutely revealing to Robert the secret of her heart, had allowed him to divine it. In fact, she no longer attempted to conceal that she loved him, and she troubled herself very little about the future. She was seriously imperiling her peace of mind, it is true, but she had confidence in herself, and in her own sense of right, and believed Robert incapable of taking advantage of the love he had inspired; nor had she had any cause to complain, or to regret the course she had pursued, for up to the present time everything had gone on as smoothly as heart could desire.

Cochard, feeling confident that her *début* would prove a brilliant success, spoiled and petted her as the owner of a racing stable pets the horse with which he expects to capture the Grand Prize. The composers of the opera rubbed their hands as complacently as if they had discovered a gold mine, and even the other performers were obliged to admit that the fair Julia's successor was an accomplished musician and a *cantatrice* of the first order.

She had learned her rôle with extraordinary ease, and now knew it so thoroughly, and was so sure of her effects, that she felt none of that fear of feeling afraid that generally troubles *débutantes*.

Colonel Mornac attended most of the rehearsals. He, too, felt confident of Violette's success, and he did not conceal his opinion from Becherel who frequently breakfasted with him, but he did not think it advisable to remind the protégé of the disadvantages of his infatuation for an actress. A young man twenty-four years of age rarely listens to this kind of sermon, and M. de Mornac did not like to waste his breath.

Of his recent adventure, Robert had said never a word, and as the colonel had never thought his young friend really in earnest in his intention of searching for Violette's relatives, he never alluded to a subject in which he took very little interest.

Marcaudier had given no sign of life. Becherel had written to him, announcing his desire to take up the note, but the usurer had made no response, so Becherel had concluded to wait until the note became due.

The prodigal son had written frequently to his mother, and from the letters he received in reply, Robert could see that his parent's patience was nearly exhausted, and that she might make up her mind to start for Paris at any moment.

Violette often inquired about Mme. de Becherel, and looked forward with delight to meeting her, little suspecting the greeting the aristocratic and devout lady was likely to bestow upon a singer at the Fantasies Lyriques.

A few weeks before she had been less sanguine about the result of this meeting, but her happiness imparted a rose-colored hue to everything.

There was one matter of an extremely annoying nature that Violette had not mentioned to her lover, however. For the last fortnight she had been receiving anonymous letters from a gentleman who offered her, not his hand and heart, but his protection and fortune.

The young girl had paid no attention to the first letter, but in those that followed he had been more explicit. He offered her a cozy little establishment of her own—that dream of all *débutantes*—thirty thousand francs in bonds, and a monthly allowance almost equal to one twelfth of a cabinet minister's yearly salary.

And in return for this unparalleled generosity, he asked nothing, at least for the present, not even an interview. He did not even say where he had seen Violette, but he promised to reveal his identity on the evening of the first performance.

Violette, of course, had no intention of accepting the offers of this unknown adorer, but she foresaw that she would have considerable difficulty in avoiding his attentions; and she feared that Robert, if he discovered the truth, would challenge this man as he had challenged Galimas at the house of Mme. de Malvoisine. She did not want her lover to imperil his life on her account, so she resolved not to ask his aid, but to protect herself.

To the great relief of both Robert and Violette, the day on which the first performance was to take place dawned at last. Everything had been in readiness for more than a week, but the manager, who was an adept in the art of advertising, had excited public curiosity to the uttermost by deferring the *début* of the young and beautiful Mlle. Thabor from day to day, upon divers pretexts; and every morning there appeared in the papers a few cleverly written lines announcing that a star of the first magnitude was about to appear upon the stage of the Fantasies Lyriques.

Violette had not been willing that her own pretty name should figure in these notices, and upon the posters, so she had taken for her *début* the name of Marie Thabor, that had been given her years before, in Rennes. All sorts of rumors were rife in relation to her. Some said that Cochard had discovered her at the house of a spurious countess, where she played the piano at so much a month, and that she was remarkably pretty.

Every seat in the house had been sold for more than a week, and the colonel, who had an extensive acquaintance, had aided not a little in spreading the report that a paragon of beauty and talent was about to display herself to the admiring gaze of the public.

M. de Mornac had not thought it worth while to tell the manager why he took such a deep interest in Mlle. Thabor, and Cochard was not even aware of Robert de Becherel's existence, and supposed the old soldier's evident desire for the success of this venture was a very natural aversion to losing his one hundred thousand francs.

He had heard that the *débutante's* enemies had formed a cabal against her, but he counted upon the benevolence of the public and the beauty and talent of his new actress to avert this danger.

He depended, too, upon his leader of the claque.

The colonel had also given his instructions to this dispenser of applause, the important personage upon whose tact and address the success or failure of a play and of an actress not unfrequently depends.

The colonel had taken the matter deeply to heart, and had devoted all his time and influence to it. He had also purchased a large number of seats in which he intended to place his friends of both sexes.

Nor had he missed a single rehearsal. On the contrary, he had been ever on hand to encourage and advise Violette, and to conciliate the other performers, who had not been very favorably disposed toward her at first, especially the women.

Robert had sedulously refrained from any act or attention that would compromise Violette in the least, but he had no intention of carrying his self-sacrifice so far as to absent himself from the first performance, though he had sworn not to go behind the scenes. He had merely purchased a well-located orchestra-chair, and he had resolved not to leave it until the end of the performance.

The final rehearsal had taken place with closed doors. Even the newspaper critics had not been admitted, this unusual precaution being only another ruse of Cochard's to excite the curiosity and eagerness of the public to the highest possible pitch.

On the morning of the eventful day, Robert breakfasted with the colonel, who seemed more and more confident, though the subject of Violette's *début* was scarcely broached. On the eve of a duel, the man who is to fight is not much inclined to talk with his second about the approaching encounter.

After leaving the colonel, Robert went straight to the Rue de Constantinople, for Violette, who was obliged to be at the theater some time before the rising of the curtain, would not be able to see him at five o'clock, as usual. She even insisted upon shortening this interview, and after twenty minutes of confidential conversation they parted, with the agreement that Robert was to wait for Violette in a carriage at the artists' entrance, after the close of the performance, and escort her home, but that they were to exchange no sign of recognition while she was on the stage.

On leaving her, Becherel went straight home to dress.

He was obliged to dine earlier than usual, as the performance began at eight o'clock, and he wanted to take a short walk before dinner to quiet his nerves, for he was more uneasy and excited than he would have been willing to admit.

On reaching his lodgings, he found Jean engaged in brushing his clothes, and making preparations for his master's toilet. Since the reproof that M. de Mornac had administered to this youth, whom he had accused of listening at doors, Becherel had been very well satisfied with the conduct of his groom.

He had sent him to the Hôtel de la Providence for the trunk left there, and Jean had performed this rather delicate mission very satisfactorily, and when he gave an account of the expedition, he had evinced no surprise at the fact that his master, who had ostensibly left the city by the Northern Railway, should have sent his trunk to a second-class lodging-house on the Rue Rodier.

Jean was certainly a valuable servant, whatever the colonel might say. He continued to go out rather too often, but as Robert spent most of his time away from home, his servant's absence caused him no inconvenience.

He had never mentioned Violette's name, in the youth's presence, so he supposed, and with reason, that Jean must be ignorant of her existence.

Though Robert had not announced his intention of going to the theater that evening, it was not difficult to divine it, so he was not surprised to hear Jean ask permission to remain out until midnight, in order that he might be able to pay a visit to a compatriot who had just arrived in Paris. At the same time, Jean handed him a letter that had been received by post. It did not bear the Rennes postmark, nor was the handwriting that of Mme. de Becherel; still, there was nothing peculiar in the appearance of the missive. It was in a neatly sealed square envelope, and there was nothing to prevent Robert from opening it at once, but he liked to divine the name of the writer by studying the superscription. This was a sort of mania with him, when he did not recognize a handwriting at the first glance, and he was sure that he had never seen this before.

It was not without something like a presentiment that he finally broke the seal, and drew out the letter, and he had scarcely glanced at the unfolded sheet when a peculiarity struck him. There was no address like " Sir," or

"My dear friend," standing out in bold relief, nor was there any signature below the ten or twelve lines that filled half the page.

His presentiments had not deceived him. It was indeed an anonymous letter, and it read as follows:

"Violette is a pretty girl, and Monsieur de Mornac is a shrewd man. They are enjoying themselves hugely at your expense. He has been her lover for a fortnight, and, of course, wishes her well, but he hasn't the slightest desire to marry her. He wants to find a man who is enough in love with the girl to do that. He has found him in you. You are a good match for her, and Monsieur de Mornac is your best friend. Marry without delay. You three will form a united household, and you will be the happiest of them all. Not this evening, however. This evening, after the performance, you will find yourself in a very unenviable frame of mind."

When Becherel looked up, after perusing this letter, the face he disclosed to view was so distorted that Jean asked him if he was ill.

"Leave me; I will dress without your assistance," replied Robert, brusquely. "I give you leave of absence for the whole evening, and when you return, you need not wait for me."

Jean disappeared, and his master sunk heavily into an arm-chair. The blow he had just received was as severe as it was unexpected, for Becherel had never had the shadow of a doubt of Violette's honor or M. de Mornac's loyalty. His first thought was that the accusation was absurd, and that the anonymous correspondent was a wretch whose calumnies should be treated with silent scorn, but, as usual, in such cases, upon reflection, there were circumstances that seemed to substantiate this charge.

Robert asked himself for the first time why the colonel,

who was essentially worldly in his nature, had suddenly taken such an interest in Violette, and so warmly espoused her cause. And why, since Cochard had engaged her, had M. de Mornac ceased to preach wisdom to his young friend? Why had he seemed, by his silence, to encourage him in his infatuation for Violette? Why had he refrained from any allusion to a scheme in which he had at first taken such an interest—the attempt to discover the orphan's relatives? To these questions, and others of a similar nature, Becherel could find no satisfactory response.

Fortunately it was not long before a reaction began, and he bitterly reproached himself for his weakness and credulity. How could he suppose for a moment that a brave soldier could so lower himself as to shamefully deceive the son of an old friend, and that a pure and artless girl could be guilty of such base treachery?

"Those wretches are the writers of this letter, unquestionably," muttered Becherel. "It is to them that I must look for redress; and I shall have it, for I know where to seek it."

This letter could in fact have come only from one of Violette's enemies—one of those who were plotting her ruin. There were at least three of these enemies—Herminia, Marcaudier, and Julia Pannetier—but Robert's suspicions fell chiefly upon Herminia, for the letter sounded like that of a jealous woman.

"This evening, after the performance, I will show this outrageous production to Violette," he thought, "and to-morrow to Monsieur de Mornac. I love them both, and I esteem them both too highly to conceal it from them. After they both have seen it, we will talk the matter over, and decide what measures we had better take to suppress the whole set."

Nevertheless, he read the letter over again, and he now noticed one sentence that had not struck him particularly at first.

"This evening, after the performance, you will find yourself in a very unenviable frame of mind."

This rather obscure prediction ended the letter like a sort of threatening postscript. What could it mean? Becherel after racking his brain for some time, finally concluded that it was merely an allusion to the hisses that were to assail the *débutante*.

The explanation was not altogether satisfactory, but he was unable to find a better one, so he finally placed the letter in his pocket-book and proceeded to dress himself.

His toilet completed, he sent Jean out for an open carriage, and ordered the coachman to drive down the Champs Elysées.

It was nearly sunset and the avenue was thronged with carriages, for the weather was delightful, and Robert had the pleasure of meeting the ladies of the Rue du Rocher who were returning from the Bois in their victoria. He very naturally refrained from bowing to them, but he fancied that the fair Herminia bestowed a defiant look on him as she passed, accompanied by a mocking smile; but this mute declaration of war made very little impression upon him, for he was already aware of that young lady's intentions. He continued his drive as far as the Arc de Triomphe, then returning by way of the Place de la Concorde, he dismissed his carriage and stepped into a neighboring restaurant to get his dinner.

A stay of an hour at a well-served table restored him to a more cheerful frame of mind and dispelled his few remaining doubts.

He became thoroughly convinced of the absurdity of the accusation, and firmly resolved not to give the unpleasant subject another thought until the next day.

It lacked only a few minutes of eight when he alighted from his carriage on the Boulevard du Temple in front of the theater in which Violette's fate was about to be decided —and his own as well.

The façade was a blaze of light. Long lines of glittering gas-jets festooned the cornices, and above the principal entrance the name of the operetta appeared in letters of flame.

It was a brilliant affair, this reopening of the Fantasies Lyriques, which had been closed for six months—and the pit and upper galleries were already crowded, though the fashionables were but just beginning to arrive. Private coupés were dashing up to the door laden with gentlemen in evening dress, so it was evident that the colonel had excited the curiosity of his friends among the club men to the highest pitch, since they had shortened their dinners for fear of missing the new diva's first appearance on the stage.

The operetta that was to retrieve Cochard's fortunes was the work of a talented composer, but the plot, unfortunately, was rather old-fashioned. It was a sort of spectacular drama—one of those that occur in an imaginary country ruled by a Queen Tohubohu XXV., or by a King Potiron XXXVI. The author of the libretto had entitled it the " Isle of the Birds," and the plot even surpassed other productions of the same kind in silliness and absurdity. It was a wonder that the composer had succeeded in finding pretty airs to accompany such nonsensical words.

Robert had heard all this through M. de Mornac, and also through Violette, who was not altogether pleased with her rôle, nor with her costumes, but who hoped that the music would redeem the words; and the colonel did not doubt it.

Becherel was less confident, however; and some remarks he heard as he entered the theater did not tend to reassure him.

" The ' Isle of the Birds,' " sneered one of the fashionable gentlemen who crowded by him. " What an absurd title! Why didn't they call it the ' Isle of the Partridges '?"

At any other time Robert would probably have agreed

with the speaker, but he was thinking only of Violette
now; and anything said against the theater in which she
was about to sing affected him like a personal insult.

The house was small, but it had been freshly painted
and decorated; and none of its *habitués* had ever seen it
graced by an equally brilliant audience. Robert had considerable difficulty in reaching his seat, which was in the
third row of orchestra-chairs; and to do so he was obliged
to crowd by Gustave Piton, who was sitting beside a fellow
speculator and talking at the top of his voice as usual.

The former comrades exchanged no sign of recognition,
however. The breach was final.

Several *loges* on the right of the stage were already occupied by fashionably dressed gentlemen who evidently belonged to the *upper ten*. These must be friends of the
colonel, who had come to applaud; but on the other side of
the stage were several members of the *demi-monde*, and
Robert, who knew two or three of them by sight, strongly
suspected them of being hostile to the *débutante*, and he
could not doubt their intentions when he discovered Julia
Pannetier among them in a gorgeous toilet.

In the dress circle there was a neutral assemblage, made
up of respectable citizens attracted by the advertising that
had been bestowed on the piece and the actress, a number
of young men proud of witnessing a first performance, and
a large number of ladies. Upon this now neutral party,
which was much more numerous than either of the others,
the success of the piece really depended, for it would fail
or succeed according as these persons joined the friendly or
hostile factions.

Becherel next devoted his attention to the occupants of
the orchestra-chairs. Galimas sat enthroned in the first
row—Galimas in full evening dress, with his hair elabor-
ately curled.

Had he come to hiss Violette? Robert almost hoped so,
for that would give him an excellent opportunity to revive

their old quarrel; but he suspected, on the contrary, that the broker intended to applaud, and in such a manner as to attract the attention of the young singer he had previously met in the Countess de Malvoisine's drawing-room.

Robert could not prevent him from doing so, but he mentally resolved to watch him, especially after the performance, and to compel him to leave if he ventured to lie in wait for Violette at the private entrance.

The colonel's predictions were verified. Robert was already jealous of his neighbors, and felt strongly inclined to watch the manner in which Violette's smiles were distributed among the audience.

The signal for the rising of the curtain was given. The orchestra began a lively overture and the curtain rose upon a stage setting intended to represent the Isle of the Birds. Upon the sea-shore in the shade of some superb tropical trees, sat his majesty, King Vulture I., surrounded by his court. His prime minister, the grand duke, and the chief of the powerful Owl tribe was kneeling before the throne awaiting his royal master's commands.

Queen Guinea Hen was seated beside her august spouse; and guards in the shape of red and blue peacocks, and maids of honor in the form of doves surrounded the royal couple. The costumes were original; the doves were all pretty girls, and the odd *mise-en-scène* was greeted with a murmur of approval.

The *débutante* was not on the stage; but Robert knew that she would soon make her appearance, and his heart throbbed violently.

It is needless to say that he hardly heard King Vulture when that winged monarch advanced to the front of the stage to explain the cause of his troubles to his wife and subjects. The music at his palace had been completely disorganized by the flight of his chief singer, a volatile Titmouse, who had just eloped with a disreputable Goldfinch.

A substitute must be found at once, and all the birds in
the kingdom were commanded to give an immediate exhibi-
tion of their vocal powers, to the great dismay of Queen
Guinea Hen, who feared that her royal husband would fall
in love with the successful candidate.

Suddenly the door of one of the most conspicuous boxes
opened noisily, and everybody turned to glance at the new-
comers. The first to appear in sight was Mme. de Malvoisine, blazing with diamonds, and outrageously *décolleté*.
Mlle. des Andrieux followed her closely, and they both seated
themselves in the front of the box, spreading out their
dresses and overturning chairs and foot-stools, to the great
annoyance of the other spectators.

Becherel turned pale on seeing these ladies. He had
almost hoped that they would not come, but now he could
no longer blind himself to the fact that Violette would
have their bitter animosity to contend with. He noticed,
too, that instead of devoting their attention to the stage
they began to gaze about the hall as if in search of the
friends they had convoked to hiss the *débutante*. Herminia even distributed little nods here and there among
the audience; and Becherel saw that the most friendly of
all was addressed to Julia Pannetier, who sat enthroned in
a box nearly opposite. Evidently there was a complete
understanding between the two ladies; they had their devoted adherents, too, among the audience; and Herminia
was looking for them through her lorgnette as a general
reviews his soldiers before a battle to satisfy himself that
each man is in his place.

In the meantime King Vulture had resumed his tirade,
but it was soon interrupted by the hurried entrance of a
sea-gull who announced that two unknown birds, that
sung very sweetly, had just been driven by a tempest upon
the rocky shore of the island. His majesty gave orders
that they should immediately be brought into his presence,
and four superb parrots left the group of guards only to

reappear almost instantly, escorting the strangers—a nightingale and a linnet.

The nightingale was, of course, the tenor of the Fantasies Lyriques, the idol of the Boulevard du Temple, who had formerly been on excellent terms with Julia Pannetier.

The linnet was the *débutante*, and a murmur of admiration greeted her entrance.

Her costume became her well, and though it was very modest, it displayed her beauty to great advantage. Her large dark eyes sparkled brilliantly from beneath her black velvet hood, a closely fitting gray bodice revealed her lithe and graceful form, and the skirt was just short enough to show a neat ankle and a dainty little foot incased in gray boots with tiny bird claws at the ends.

Led by the nightingale, she came forward with bowed head as befitted a linnet who had ventured into a strange land without a passport; but when King Vulture asked, " What brings you to my kingdom, young strangers?" she slowly lifted her head and her eyes fairly illuminated the hall.

The leader of the claque had no need to give the signal for applause. It burst forth simultaneously in every part of the hall, and it lasted so long that Violette almost lost her self-possession. She had not expected such an ovation, and her joy overcame her.

Herminia turned green with envy, and Julia pretended to sneer.

Robert was delighted with this triumph, but he realized that it was, as yet, only a triumph of beauty; and he asked himself anxiously what effect her voice would produce—the clear and melodious voice that stirred the depths of his inmost heart whenever she spoke.

She had only two or three sentences to utter before she sung, and she said them without the slightest embarrassment.

She explained to the king that she had come from a distant land with the nightingale, the companion of her childhood; that they were traveling about the world together, earning their living by singing, and that having ventured upon the sea the vessel had been driven ashore by a terrible storm, and they had escaped death only by a miracle.

Then the good-natured king of the island, having asked her to give him a specimen of her vocal powers, she began her grand *morceau* of the first act, upon which her whole operatic career probably depended.

It was a highly original and very difficult *aria* that the composer had written expressly for her—a sort of *romanza* in which she related her misfortunes with a series of trills and runs in which she imitated the song of the bird she represented at the end of each couplet, and ending with a prayer addressed to Vulture I. "Pity, pity the poor linnet."

It was a grand success. The applause was so loud and so prolonged that the tenor who impersonated the nightingale was obliged to wait at least five minutes before he could sing in his turn. At last, the applause having abated, he had opened his lips to begin, when a loud hiss resounded, as a clap of thunder sometimes resounds in summer from a cloudless sky. It came from the upper gallery, that is to say, from one of the cheap seats, but Becherel trembled lest this hostile demonstration would encourage some of Violette's other enemies below to hiss her.

Everybody looked up to see who the offender was. Robert did the same, and had the unspeakable satisfaction of hearing cries of "Put the rascal out!" "Out with him!" and of seeing a shower of blows fall on the delinquent, who defended himself stoutly, but was finally hustled out.

Before he disappeared, however, Becherel had had time to catch a glimpse of him, and, to his profound astonishment, he fancied he recognized his groom, Jean, in the delinquent. He was probably mistaken, however. Jean had asked his permission to remain out late this evening, it is true; but how very improbable it was that the boy would have paid to attend the theater instead of spending the evening in a wine-shop with his friend. Besides, even if he had taken it into his head to enter the Fantasies Lyriques, he certainly would not have ventured to interrupt the performance.

The audience seemed resolved to atone for this act of discourtesy, however, for the applause burst forth again, though it is needless to say that Herminia and her friend, Julia Pannetier, took no part in it.

On the contrary, they were eagerly gazing up in the gallery, as if hoping that the disorder there was going to continue, and that the young man's example would be followed by his neighbors.

Galimas had taken the *débutante's* part, and was now applauding in the most vehement manner, partly to show his enthusiasm, but principally to attract Violette's attention.

She was not even thinking of him, however; though she had not lost her wits, by any means. On the contrary, she waited with wonderful calmness for the confusion to subside, and her eyes meeting those of Robert, she smiled to reassure him.

It was a violation of their compact; but he was not offended. He thanked her, indeed, with a slight nod of the head, and the telegraphing stopped there.

The tenor now sung his air, which was less rapturously received than that of Violette, however. The king immediately appointed the linnet chief court-singer, and a stormy conversation ensued between Vulture I. and his queen, who was already jealous of the young stranger. The first act ended with a chorus by the doves, accompanying the refrain of a short song rendered by Violette with exquisite taste, and the applause it elicited was interrupted by no hostile demonstration this time.

The *débutante's* success was assured. Robert, who was overwhelmed with joy, went out to get a breath of fresh air, and the remarks he overheard in the corridor only increased his delight.

"The piece will run for at least a hundred nights," remarked one gentleman.

"Thanks to the *débutante*, for the piece itself is stupid. I never saw a prettier girl. And what an exquisite voice. It's as clear as crystal."

"A new diva is born to us," said a noted critic, gravely.

Becherel longed to embrace him, but he restrained himself, and ascended to the *foyer*, in the hope of meeting M. de Mornac, for the suspicions that had haunted him before he came to the theater were now entirely dispelled, and he no longer doubted that the anonymous letter was a tissue of impudent falsehoods and atrocious calumnies.

Seeing no familiar faces, however, he left the *foyer*, and was about to descend the stairs to resume his seat in the orchestra, when in the corridor leading to the first tier of boxes, he found himself directly behind a gentleman who had a lady on his arm. He did not recognize them at first, for he could see only their backs, but it seemed to him that this was not the first time he had heard the gentleman's voice.

He did not think of trying to listen to what they were saying, and it was almost in spite of himself that he heard a few words that aroused his suspicions.

"How enraged I am!" said the lady. "This affair will cause me an attack of illness, I do believe. Have the asses that applaud her no ears? A simpleton that doesn't know how to carry herself on the stage, and who flats atrociously! Men are idiots, upon my word!"

"It has taken you a long time to find it out, my dear," replied the gentleman, coolly. "I predicted all this, you remember."

"But you promised me that the piece should not go on to the end, recollect."

" Well, we have only reached the end of the first act, and there are three of them. "

" The other two will be just like the first. They will yell themselves hoarse every time she sings, and throw bouquets at her and recall her a dozen times! And the famous cabal on which you counted. What about that? Not a hiss—yes, just one; and I know who gave that. He did it to please me; but the others don't dare to open their mouths for fear they'll be put out, chicken-hearted creatures! They are all cowards, even Florimond, the tenor. He swore to me that he would make her miss all her effects, and he is evidently as big a fool about her as all the rest."

" What else could you expect, my dear? She is very pretty, and has a great deal of talent, unquestionably. Mademoiselle des Andrieux pretends to the contrary; but—"

" So the girl is to succeed, I suppose, and all the newspapers will be chanting her praises to-morrow, and indulging in all sorts of odious comparisons. They will say that Cochard has done wisely to engage her in my place. If this is all you can say to console me, you had better go back where you came from, but I warn you that I shall not remain until the close of the performance. I have had enough of hearing them yell and clap their hands. "

" Come, come; don't be foolish! You know very well that I don't intend this girl to take your place, if I can help it, and that I've a grudge against Cochard. To close his theater, and insure the failure of his new singer, I am ready to employ strong measures, if necessary—"

" What measures? What do you intend to do?"

" I will explain. In the first place, I—"

Robert did not hear the rest of the sentence, however, for they had reached the head of the staircase, and the crowd had divided into two currents, one of which continued in the direction of the boxes, while the other made its way down the rather steep staircase.

In less than ten seconds, Becherel found himself separated from the lady and gentleman, and as they had seen him, and as he knew what to expect now, he did not think it worth while to follow them.

Chance had placed him directly on the heels of Marcaudier and his lovely Julia. He had had the pleasure of hearing them deplore Violette's success, and bitterly as they hated her, Robert did not believe that they had it in their power to do her any serious injury now.

It was with a tranquil mind, consequently, that Robert resumed his seat. Galimas was already in his, casting complacent glances around him.

Herminia and her mother were still occupying their box, and in a few moments Becherel saw Marcaudier enter it.

The ladies received Cash on Delivery very graciously. Herminia made him take a seat beside her, and was soon engaged in an animated conversation with him; but just then the leader of the orchestra rapped on his desk to announce the beginning of the second act and Robert forgot everything else in thinking of Violette.

When she reappeared upon the stage, there was such a frantic burst of applause that the ceiling seemed about to fall. The *débutante* had changed her costume; she was still dressed as a linnet, but as a court linnet—in silk and velvet, and with diamonds everywhere, on her neck, in her ears, and in her hair—the superb paste jewels furnished by the manager, and they enhanced her beauty wonderfully.

The second act was only one long triumph for her. She was on the stage all the time—now singing an aria that she rendered with charming *abandon* and perfect taste—now carrying on a lively conversation with Vulture I., who wished to seat her upon his throne—and with Queen Guinea Hen, who was plotting to deliver her into the hands of the owls, the executioners of the Bird Kingdom. Violette played her part with wonderful skill and vivacity. Her acting was as good as her singing. She was evidently born for the stage.

In the midst of the transports excited by the brilliant successes of the girl he loved, Becherel was disturbed by the sound of subdued talking on his right, and, turning, he was not a little surprised to see one of the ushers standing in the next aisle beckoning to him, and calling attention to a bit of paper that he held in his hand.

Irritated by this pantomime, the spectators in the same row with Robert were beginning to give unmistakable signs of displeasure.

The words, " Silence!" and " Hush!" uttered by some of the least patient among the spectators seemed to intimidate the young man, and, seeing that Becherel showed no inclination to move, he devised another way to fulfill the commission which had been intrusted to him, and for which he had doubtless been liberally paid.

Whispering a few words in the ear of the gentleman who occupied the seat nearest the aisle, he handed him the paper, and this gentleman passed it in turn to his next neighbor, who did the same, after glancing at the superscription, and so the note passed from hand to hand until it reached Becherel, who took it with some hesitation, and saw that it bore, not his name, but these words written in pencil:

" For the gentleman occupying seat No. 89 in the 3d row of orchestra-chairs."

Who could have sent this missive? Evidently some one who was in the hall or in the theater, Violette, perhaps; that is, unless the sender was Galimas or Marcaudier.

Becherel, who was rather alarmed, opened it, and had some difficulty in deciphering the following lines:

" Your mother has just arrived in Paris. It seems that she has written to you, but that you have failed to receive her letter. Finding no one at the station to meet her, or in your lodgings on the Boulevard Poissonnière, she sent
7

your porter to my rooms in search of you, and my valet
advised him to come here. I have just seen him, and told
him that you would return home immediately. Your
mother is waiting for you in the porter's lodge, for he
hasn't the key to your rooms, and your groom has gone
out. You must not keep her waiting there. Hasten home
without a minute's loss of time, and return as soon as you
have installed her comfortably there. Tell her some story
that will convince her it is necessary for you to absent yourself for an hour or two.

"You will be able to return to the theater before the
close of the third act. Violette is counting upon your escort home, after the performance; in the meantime, she
begs me not to leave her for an instant, so it is impossible
for me to get away from the theater, even for a few moments. To-morrow, I will see Madame de Becherel, and
speak a good word for you.

"Everything here is progressing as favorably as heart
could desire. Your little friend's success is assured, and
what a success! In less than two years she will be engaged
as *prima donna* at the Grand Opera House. You ought
to be well pleased. I am jubilant."

For a signature there was only an initial, an M, but this
note could have come only from the colonel.

Well pleased? The poor lover was hardly that! The
inopportune arrival of his mother had spoiled all the joy
caused by Violette's triumph, but it is only just to say that
he did not hesitate to follow M. de Mornac's advice.

His darling was on the stage, but the colonel would, of
course, tell Violette why her lover had left in the middle of
the act, and he knew her well enough to feel sure that she
would forgive him for this apparent breach of courtesy
toward her; so he rose to make his way to the door.

This was no easy matter, however, for he was some distance from the aisle, and he was obliged to crowd by at

least a dozen gentlemen. Indeed he was scarcely upon his feet before cries of "Down in front!" and "Sit down!" resounded behind him. Such a commotion was created that the actors paused for a moment, and Robert, before reaching the door, had the misery of seeing Violette turn pale and pause in the song she had just begun, but it was too late to recoil now, so he hastened on, followed by the black looks of the audience.

On reaching the street, he jumped into a carriage, promising the coachman a princely *pourboire* if he would drive like mad, and, stimulated by a hope of receiving the promised reward, the driver whipped up his horse so energetically that he was not ten minutes in reaching his destination.

Robert, without stopping to pay him, rushed into the hall, and was not a little surprised to find his porter seated by the fire, quietly reading his evening paper.

On being questioned by Robert, he declared that no lady had been there, that he knew nothing about M. de Mornac, and that he had not left his lodge that evening. Becherel was so sure of the truth of the statements contained in his letter that it was a long time before he could be convinced that some one had played a trick on him. When he did come to this conclusion he ceased to attribute the letter to the colonel, for M. de Mornac was a perfect gentleman, who would have scorned to play such a trick upon any one, and above all to drag in the name of Mme. de Becherel, for whom he entertained a profound respect.

Finally it occurred to him that the perpetrator of the joke might be his former friend, Gustave Piton. Gustave knew that Mme. de Becherel thought of visiting Paris, and was quite capable of one of those rough practical jokes so common among brokers; and the mere suspicion so exasperated Robert that he resolved to insult him at the very first opportunity, and as one might present itself that very evening at the theater, he jumped into the carriage and ordered the driver to take him back to the Fantasies Lyriques with all possible speed, unmindful of the astonished face of his porter, who evidently suspected him of having suddenly lost his mind.

"There is one good thing about it," Becherel said to himself; "I shall not miss the third act, and my return will reassure Violette, who must be wondering what has become of me. After the performance I shall show this note to the colonel at the same time with the other anonymous letter. Two anonymous letters in one day are certainly a little too much. I no longer do him the injustice to believe that he wrote either of them, but I want to show them to him nevertheless."

Becherel reached the theater just as the *ent'racte* was ending, and hastened to his seat so as not to excite the displeasure of the audience a second time.

The countess and her daughter were in their box, but neither Marcaudier nor Gustave were anywhere to be seen. Julia Pannetier, on the contrary, was parading her charms in her *loge*, surrounded by her friends, and Robert fancied she wore a triumphant air; so triumphant in fact, that he began to wonder if Violette had not been hissed at the close of the second act.

He also perceived that the audience was murmuring because the curtain did not rise, and Robert, surprised at the delay, began to fear that there had been some accident. Certainly something of an extraordinary nature must be going on behind the curtain, for the musicians were all in their places only waiting for their leader to give the signal to begin.

Becherel noticed, too, that the fair Herminia was smiling maliciously, and exchanging signs with Julia Pannetier. These amiable creatures were doubtless rejoicing over a *contretemps* that would be almost sure to make the audience less favorably disposed toward the *débutante*, but they showed no more astonishment than if this incident had formed a part of the evening's programme.

At last, just as Robert was beginning to feel seriously alarmed, the signal resounded. It was greeted with general applause, but as the curtain slowly rose the hubbub gave place, as if by enchantment, to a profound silence.

There appeared before the eyes of the breathless audience a superb stage setting, representing the palace of the king of the birds—a stage setting that cost poor Cochard a small fortune—but great was the surprise of the audience on beholding there neither Vulture I., surrounded by his guards, nor Queen Guinea Hen, attended by her maids of honor. Not an actor nor an actress was to be seen; the stage was deserted, and magnificent as was the palace, that alone would not satisfy the already irritated audience.

In a moment there advanced from one of the flies to the foot-lights a gentleman dressed in black, whose face wore the grave and contrite expression of a stage manager who is obliged to make an unpleasant announcement.

Robert, though greatly agitated, flattered himself that he must have come to ask the public's indulgence for an artist seized with a sudden hoarseness, and fondly hoped that the victim was not Violette.

The stage manager began as follows:

"Ladies and Gentlemen—We have the misfortune to announce that the management finds it absolutely impossible to continue the performance."

There were exclamations of disappointment, but before breaking into imprecations the crowd waited for an explanation.

"With an unpardonable forgetfulness of her duties as an artist, and of the respect she owes the public, Mademoiselle Thabor—"

"Oh, oh! what? What is the matter with her? Is she ill?" cried eager voices.

"Mademoiselle Thabor, dressed, and all ready to go on

the stage, hastily left the theater without warning any one, and in spite of our efforts, we have been unable to find her."

The bursting of a thunder-bolt in this handsomely decorated hall would not have caused greater confusion and excitement than this startling announcement. The close of it was drowned in the uproar, and very few persons among the audience heard that the management were willing to return the money unless purchasers of tickets would prefer to hear the rôle of the Linnet given by another actress.

The spectators rose *en masse*, and projectiles of every sort fell thick and fast upon the unfortunate stage manager, who had barely time to make his escape before the curtain fell. And really the audience had abundant grounds for dissatisfaction, for never before in Paris had an actress been known to disappear during a performance, above all during a first performance. Such things may happen occasionally in foreign countries or in distant provinces, but Parisians do not take kindly to jokes of this kind, and if the interior of the Fantasies Lyriques escaped demolition that night it was only because the kind Providence that watches over the destinies of theatrical managers interposed in Cochard's behalf. As it was, the policemen and guards on duty had all they could do to check the disorder, and prevent accidents while the public was boisterously vacating the hall.

Robert could think only of the missing Violette. What madness had seized her? Had she become frightened, or had she suddenly lost her reason? And above all, what had become of her? His first impulse was to fly to the assistance of the woman he loved. He forgot that he would arrive too late, so he rushed madly toward the door. By jumping over the seats he succeeded in reaching the corridor, and from there fought his way fiercely through the crowd to the street, which he reached without his overcoat, but not without many bruises.

He did not stop to hear what people were saying there. He knew where the private entrance was, and he rushed frantically toward that.

At the door he encountered a crowd of machinists and *figurants* who were anathematizing the artist whose flight threw them out of employment; but he forced his way through them by dint of blows that were returned with interest, and finally reached the greenroom where Cochard, his stage manager, Florimond, and several others were raving and tearing their hair like men demented.

The name of Marie Thabor was upon every lip, accompanied by very unflattering epithets, and when they saw Becherel appear—Becherel, who was a stranger to all of them—they rushed upon him to drive him from the room.

He shook them off, however, and said, turning to the manager:

"I am a friend of Colonel Mornac's. Where is Mademoiselle Thabor?"

"Go and ask your friend the colonel," replied Cochard, who was nearly frantic. "He left about a quarter of an hour before she did. He has met her perhaps. Ah! he can surely boast of having got me in a pretty scrape. I am ruined! He will lose a hundred thousand francs, but that doesn't do me any good."

"But what has happened?"

"This is what has happened. That creature thought it would be a fine joke to allow herself to be enticed away by some man in the audience, some enemy of mine undoubtedly. Ah, well! they shall both pay dearly for it, for I will find her, and bring suit against her. I will place my damages at three hundred thousand francs, and the gentleman shall pay it."

"What is the man's name?"

"How do I know? Do you suppose she made me her confidant? She had more than one lover, I suppose. You must hunt for him in the crowd. But I have something else to do than stand talking with you. Clear out of here!"

Becherel, frantic with rage, was about to leap at the manager's throat when the colonel entered just in time to prevent it; but, unfortunately, Becherel's wrath was not appeased, but only diverted into a new channel.

"You must know where she is," he cried, savagely.

"What do you mean?" retorted the colonel, straightening himself up, "and why do you venture to address me in such a tone?"

"Violette left the theater with you."

"Are you mad?"

"And I call upon you to tell me where you have taken her."

"And I advise you to be silent."

"So you do not even deny that you are her lover?"

"This is really going a little too far, and if you think I will allow a boy like you to insult me, you—"

Robert, now quite beside himself, raised his hand to strike his supposed rival, but the colonel seized it in mid-air and checked the movement that was about to terminate in a blow.

"I consider it received," he said, coldly. "You will now come with me, and we will settle our differences. My dear Cochard," continued the colonel, without departing from his usual calmness, "I am truly sorry for what has happened, and I consider myself bound to indemnify you for the loss my protégé has caused you. Forgive me for having recommended her to you. I might have foreseen what has happened. The devil really seems to have had a hand in it. I had gone out for a few minutes to smoke a cigar when the girl decamped. Had I been here I could have prevented her from going, I am sure, but the mischief is done now, and I repeat that I will do my best to repair it."

"If she had only waited until after the close of the performance!" moaned the unfortunate manager; "but a fit of madness seems to have seized her. The woman who dressed her tells me that just as the girl was leaving her dressing-room to go on the stage a note was handed her. She read it, and walked straight on, without saying a word —only instead of entering the flies she went down into the street. The *concierge* saw her pass out, and two mechanics, who were smoking their pipes on the sidewalk, saw her enter a carriage that was waiting for her."

"And she entered it just as she was—in her stage costume. I just questioned them, and also the woman who dressed her. There is only one point upon which I am still in the dark, and that is the cause of her sudden departure."

"The cause! It is not difficult to guess that. She was the mistress of some enemy of mine, who offered her a large sum of money to play this trick on me. It was this same scoundrel who sent the carriage for her, and wrote to her that the moment had come for leaving the theater. He knew very well what he was doing, the villain!"

"Do you suspect any one in particular?"

"No, I have a host of enemies, but I have no idea which of them it was."

"We shall find out, never fear! and I will see that he is punished as he deserves. In the meantime, my dear fellow, you had better take the thing philosophically. I will see you again to-morrow."

Then turning to Becherel, who looked crest-fallen enough, M. de Mornac said, coldly:

"Now, sir, I have an explanation to ask of you. Will you have the goodness to follow me?"

The witnesses of this scene had not uttered a word, and they gladly beheld the colonel depart with the young stranger, whom they took for one of the missing artist's jilted lovers.

Robert followed the colonel in silence. He was beginning to see that he had made a great mistake in accusing M. de Mornac, and to deeply regret his rashness.

"Sir," began the colonel, as soon as they reached the street. Then, with a sudden change of tone, he continued: "No, it was all very well to address you in that formal manner before those people, but it is not worth while when we are alone. I prefer to talk to you just as I am in the habit of doing. You will gain nothing by it, however, for your insolence is likely to cost you dear. I now propose to walk home by way of the boulevards, and you can accompany me as far as the Faubourg Poissonnière, as that will give me plenty of time to say what I have to say to you."

"As you please, colonel," replied Becherel, meekly.

"In the first place," remarked the colonel, "you are not to suppose that I bear you no ill will for your insult just now. I am more than twice your age, and you are the son of an old friend, but that will not prevent me from fighting with you. You need a lesson, and you shall have it. You will receive a visit from my seconds to-morrow. Now will you have the goodness to explain why you ventured to publicly accuse me of a most infamous act? The absurd idea that I was that girl's lover never entered your brain unaided. Some one must have insinuated as much to you."

"You are right. I received an anonymous letter, and—"

"I suspected as much. And you were fool enough to believe it!"

"I did not believe it at first; but during the performance I received another letter announcing that my mother had just arrived in the city, and that she was waiting for me at my rooms. I thought this note came from you."

"Indeed! Couldn't you see that the handwriting was not mine?"

"You have never written to me."

"That is true. Well, after you received this letter—?"

" I left the theater before the conclusion of the second act, and taking a carriage, drove home with all possible speed. On my arrival there my porter assured me that no one had called in my absence. I saw that somebody must have been playing a practical joke on me, so I drove back to the theater, where I arrived just as it was time for the third act to begin. You know the rest."

"" No, I do not."

" Well, when the stage manager announced that Violette was missing I lost my senses, and rushed out of the hall and around into the greenroom, where I found Cochard, who told me that you left the theater about the same time that Violette did."

" And from that you unhesitatingly concluded that I had carried her off. You are rather rash in your conclusions, young man."

" I was so frantic with grief and rage that I had lost the power to reason."

" Then you are now convinced that you made a mistake, and that I had nothing to do with your divinity's disappearance, I suppose?"

" I am so sure of it that I beseech you to assist me in finding her."

" You certainly amuse me! You must be pretty well acquainted with your Dulcinea, and know whether she is capable of being enticed away by any man who is richer than yourself."

" No, I am sure she is not! I would stake my life upon her honor."

" You talk like the fond lover that you are! One can never answer for a woman. I am convinced, however, that this one, like yourself, has been made the dupe of some scoundrel who was resolved to ruin her. She, too, received a letter, it seems."

" Yes; and she saw me leave the theater while she was on the stage."

"Then all is explained. You were enticed out so she would notice your departure; and then she was probably informed that you had been run over by a carriage, or that you had broken your leg, or something of the kind, and wanted to see her immediately."

"And it was Marcaudier who wrote all three of the letters. I understand now why, in the one received before going to the theater, he told me that the evening was going to end badly for me."

"It is quite probable that he was the writer; but he certainly had accomplices—male as well as female. First, Herminia and her mother, and also some gentleman who had taken a fancy to Violette."

"Yes, Galimas!" exclaimed Robert. "He was in the hall. But what makes you think so?"

"Because Marcaudier, though he is certainly a scoundrel, did not entice Violette away in order to murder her. He must have made a bargain with Galimas to take the young lady off his hands, and they both hoped that she would allow herself to be tempted by the broker's brilliant offers. They are even capable of keeping her a prisoner until she decides; but they will have to release her some day or other unless she concludes to accept the dishonorable proposals of this rich speculator."

"Oh, colonel!"

"Not that I think she will; but it is well to be prepared for the worst; and if that should come to pass there will be nothing left for you to do but forget her. But if, on the contrary, she refuses, they will find themselves obliged to release her; and in that case she had better enter no complaint against them. You will even be the first to recommend silence. I even think that the best thing you can do for the present is to remain perfectly quiet."

"And you will do nothing. You will allow—"

"I will make inquiries about all these people. A former non-commissioned officer in my regiment now holds

an important position in the secret service, and through
him I can find out all about this Marcaudier and the capitalist who backs him—that pretended uncle of Herminia,
whom no one has ever seen.   When I have secured this information I will not refuse to lend you a helping hand,
though you must not forget that you owe me reparation for
your insult just now!   I shall content myself with wound-
ing you in the arm, however, so you will get off quite
easily, after all.   But I see that you lost your overcoat in
the crowd.   It's as cold as Greenland; and I don't want
you to have an attack of pleurisy.   I have said all that J
have to say to you, so you had better take a carriage and
get home as fast as you can.   You will hear from me to-
morrow."

Robert watched M. de Mornac walk away without daring
to offer him a hand.   After doubting the loyalty of his
best friend, he now began to doubt Violette's innocence.

CHAPTER VIII.

AFTER her arrival at the theater, about the same time
that Robert de Becherel was finishing his dinner on the
Champs Elysées, Violette passed successfully through all
the tribulations that await a *débutante*.   She endured with
heroic patience the encouragement of the manager—encouragement that is entirely superfluous at the last moment
—the recommendations of the author and composer to take
particular care about such and such a passage in her rôle—
the premature and rather ironical congratulations of the
other performers, the grumbling of the costumer, who
positively insisted upon shortening the skirt of her dress,
and the slowness of the hair-dresser, who seemed determined never to finish her task.

The colonel had had the good sense to hold himself aloof
until she left her dressing-room at the call of the prompter,

and even at that trying moment he uttered only a few affectionate words, so she retained her presence of mind to such a degree that she instantly recognized Herminia in her *loge,* and Robert in one of the orchestra-chairs.

The applause had not agitated her, nor the hiss that resounded from the upper gallery; and at the conclusion of the first act she was the recipient of an enthusiastic ovation in the greenroom; an ovation in which M. de Mornac took part. But she did not seem unduly elated, and her modesty won all hearts, even those of the other performers.

The next act passed off equally well, and her success was no longer doubtful, when Violette saw Robert rise and hurriedly leave the hall. Then, for the first time, she became slightly agitated; but the curtain fell to the sound of enthusiastic " bravas!" which failed to calm the anxiety of the *débutante,* however, for she could not imagine why Robert had left the theater so suddenly, and she already began to feel a presentiment of impending misfortune.

She was anxious to confide her misgivings to Colonel de Mornac, but that gentleman was nowhere to be found. He had just left the theater, telling Cochard that he was going out to smoke a cigar, but that he would return before the curtain rose for the third act, so Violette finally consented to go up to her dressing-room.

She was just leaving it when one of the call-boys handed her a note which she tore open with a trembling hand, and which contained only these lines, written in pencil, like the communication Becherel had received:

" Robert has just met with a serious accident. I have had him taken to the house of a lady friend. He insists upon seeing you. Come immediately. My carriage is in waiting to take you to him."

The trap was apparent, and yet the girl allowed herself to be caught in it.

She did not doubt for a moment that this message came from M. de Mornac. She did not ask herself how the accident could have occurred, or how the colonel had happened to be on hand just at the right moment to pick up the injured man. She thought only of hastening to the bedside of the man she loved, and to see him once more before he died, if die he must.

It did not even occur to her that she ought to inform the manager of her intentions. What good would it do? He would only try to detain her; and she was firmly resolved to respond to M. de Mornac's summons.

Rushing down into the street, she was met only a few steps from the private entrance by a servant in neat livery, who said, lifting his hat respectfully:

"The carriage is here; and if mademoiselle will have the goodness to follow me—"

"What has happened to Monsieur de Becherel?" interrupted Violette.

"A terrible accident, mademoiselle. He was knocked down and trampled upon by a pair of runaway horses. He was picked up unconscious, and they fear that his leg is broken."

"Where is he?"

"Only a short distance from here, mademoiselle. Monsieur de Mornac witnessed the accident and had Monsieur de Becherel taken to the house of a lady who resides on the Quai de Valmy. We shall be there in five minutes."

Violette had never heard of the Quai de Valmy, but she knew that the colonel had a large circle of acquaintances, and supposing that the carriage and servants were his, she entered the well-appointed coupé which was standing a little way off without the slightest reluctance.

The footman closed the door, climbed upon the box beside the driver, and the horse started off on a swift trot through the Rue d'Angoulême, in the direction of the Canal Saint Martin.

Just before he came to the bridge the coachman turned to the left, and Violette saw, without being really conscious of the fact, that she was rolling along a nearly deserted quay, lined with warehouses and a few dimly lighted dwellings. She could think only of Robert, and it seemed to her that the horse, though he was really moving at a very rapid pace, only crawled.

Soon the carriage passed under an arch and into a courtyard, but so swiftly that Violette had only time to catch a glimpse of a two-story house and a tall gate that closed noisily as soon as the carriage passed.

The footman opened the door, assisted the young lady to alight, ushered her into a brilliantly lighted hall, and said:

"Will mademoiselle have the goodness to walk upstairs?"

Violette needed no urging, but rushed up the white marble steps in breathless haste. On reaching the landing she saw an open door directly in front of her.

She crossed the threshold, and was not a little surprised to find herself in a cozy dining-room that seemed intended only for a *tête-à-tête* repast, it was so small, and contained so few chairs.

A Venetian glass chandelier, in which all the candles were lighted, hung over an exquisitely decorated table, where wines that rivaled the topaz and amethyst in hue sparkled in cut-glass decanters.

This dainty feast spread in a house where a dangerously injured man was lying astonished Violette, and a vague feeling of alarm took possession of her.

Hastily traversing the dining-room, she entered first an exquisitely furnished salon and then a dainty boudoir, hung with pale-blue satin.

All these rooms were brilliantly lighted, but they were empty.

"The servant was mistaken," thought Violette. "They must have carried Monsieur de Becherel to a room on the floor above."

So, returning to the hall, she hurried upstairs. There

she found more lights and another open door leading, this time, into a library handsomely furnished in ebony and gilt. Violette did not pause even to glance at the richly bound volumes that filled the book-cases, but hastened on into a bed-chamber, which was no more reassuring in its aspect. There were mirrors everywhere, even at the foot of the bed, which stood in a lace-draped alcove. Opening out of this chamber was the bath-room, a marvel of luxury. The bath-tub, table and vases were of onyx; the toilet articles were ivory or silver.

The very sight of this retreat convinced Violette that she had been basely deceived, and she now thought only of making her escape before the man who had decoyed her here presented himself. But how was she to do it? She had heard the *porte-cochère* close behind her, and she felt sure that the scoundrel's hireling would refuse to open the gates at her bidding.

She ran to the window to call for help, but unfortunately the window opened upon an inner court-yard where she saw only the coupé that had brought her here. The horses had already been unharnessed, and the coachman had disappeared.

"Ah, well! my dear, how do you like your new quarters?" asked a voice behind her.

Violette started as if a serpent had stung her, and, turning, found herself face to face with a man she both hated and despised.

Galimas was standing before her, eying her insolently, with his hat on his head and a smile on his lips, an evil smile that made the girl shudder.

"What the deuce are you doing there by that open window?" continued the broker. "You will certainly catch cold. Close it, and come and take a seat in this easy-chair. You will be much more comfortable, and we can have a talk. I have a host of things to say to you, for we have not met since you left Madame de Malvoisine's."

"Leave the house!" said Violette, in a voice husky with emotion.

"Leave the house? Yes; I acknowledge that you have a perfect right to order me out, as you are in your own house. Yes, mademoiselle; this house and all it contains shall be yours to-morrow. You have only to go to my notary and sign the deed that puts you in possession of a piece of property that cost three hundred thousand francs, and that is really worth a good deal more—for it was purchased, at a great sacrifice, of a bankrupt merchant who built it and furnished it for his lady-love. The neighborhood is not all that could be desired, perhaps; but, as you will have your horses and carriages, there will be nothing to prevent you from going to the Bois every day. You will have an allowance of five thousand francs a month besides; but you know my intentions, as you have received my letters."

"So it was you who wrote to me?"

"Of course. I am surprised that you didn't guess the truth at once. There are not many men in these days who offer a woman a handsome establishment and an income of sixty thousand francs—a fortune in itself, but you are worth it."

"Wretch!" muttered Violette.

"What! you call me hard names? You make a great mistake, my dear. But perhaps you are angry with me for having enticed you away in the middle of the performance. A nice trick I played on your manager, didn't I? Well, you needn't worry about it. If you want to try the stage again, you can secure a dozen engagements on much better terms than those offered by that sneaking Cochard. And I sha'n't oppose you, I promise you that, for you have an immense amount of talent; and it would really be a pity not to profit by it. Besides, I understand women, and know that they must be allowed to follow their inclinations in such matters. You are a born actress, so you

ought to follow your vocation. I only ask a little gratitude. I shall not be exacting, by any means, and when
you come to know me better, you will see that I'm not a
bad fellow at heart, and you will get used to me. Come,
don't be so shy!" he continued, coming a step nearer.
"One would suppose you were afraid of me."

"If you come a step nearer, I will dash my brains out
on the stone pavement below."

Violette's tone and gesture convinced Galimas that this
was no idle threat; so he paused, though he did not yet acknowledge himself defeated. He told himself that he had
to deal with a very excitable nature, and that if he attempted to carry matters with a high hand he would only exasperate Violette; so it would be much better to try to win
her by gentle means.

"Be calm, I entreat you, mademoiselle," he said, in an
entirely different tone. "You misunderstand my intentions, I assure you."

"Then will you allow me to leave this place?" asked
Violette, coldly.

"Leave this room? Why, certainly. I would even like
you to see that the home I have prepared for you is well
arranged. It will please you, I am sure."

"I wish to leave this house, and immediately."

"You are not a prisoner here, I assure you. To-morrow you will be perfectly free to go and come as you please.
But at this hour of the night it would be a positive crime
to allow you to depart. Remember that we are on the
banks of the Canal Saint Martin, in a locality infested by
vagabonds, who would certainly molest you."

"That makes very little difference to me. I would rather
be murdered than remain here."

"You are very hard on me; but I bear you no ill-will,
for I am sure you will think twice before deciding upon a
step that you would certainly regret afterward. The night
brings counsel, you know; so make up your mind to spend

it in your own house. I did hope to take supper with you
here, but if my presence annoys you, I will leave you—and
return to take breakfast with you to-morrow morning, if
you will allow mé.   When you feel inclined to rise, you
will only have to ring, and your maid will answer the summons. I thought it best to give her leave of absence this
evening. You will find some dresses in the wardrobe to
make a selection from, for I presume you won't care to remain dressed as you are, though your costume is extremely
becoming."

Violette had not expected to hear this man talk to her in
this strain. It was very evident that he did not believe
she could possibly refuse the brilliant destiny he offered
her. This unscrupulous broker was not in the habit of
meeting women he could not dazzle with his gold, and
sure of triumphing eventually, he very willingly consented
to wait; so Violette asked herself if she would not do well
to take advantage of the respite offered her, and seek a
means of escape in the meantime.

" And now, to convince you that I am not quite so bad
as I appear to be, I will bid you good-evening," continued
Galimas. " We will resume this conversation to-morrow
morning, and with me, I repeat, you will be as free as air,
for I am satisfied that you would not abuse your freedom.
It is agreed, is it not?"

" I am grateful to you for going, but I will promise
nothing," replied Violette, proudly.

" I ask no promise from you," answered Galimas. " I
know what promises are worth. I would rather rely upon
your voluntary conversion."

And without waiting for a reply, he left the room, closing the door behind him, but without locking it, for Violette heard no key turn in the lock.

The poor girl's first impulse was to prevent his return
by pushing the bolt, but she searched in vain for this pro-
tecting bolt. There was none.

In despair, she ran to the window. It was her only resource, not for flight, for she would certainly be killed if she attempted to leap from it.

What had become of the coarse *parvenu* who was aping the customs of the *grands seigneurs* of the old *régime?* Had he left the house to give her time for reflection, or was he hiding in some corner of this hateful house, like a tiger that is only watching for an opportunity to spring upon his prey?

She little suspected that he had gone to consult his accomplice.

Galimas was utterly corrupt at heart. He belonged to that class of wealthy men who firmly believe that money is the real king of the world, and he never hesitated to gratify a caprice, whatever it might cost him. And why should he hesitate, when he did not believe there was such a thing as virtue? Still, he had his doubts in the present instance. No woman had ever gone so far as to threaten to throw herself out of the window before in order to rid herself of his presence; besides, he had never been obliged to abduct any one by force before. And, though he had allowed himself to be persuaded into these rather violent measures, he had no idea of compromising himself or of getting himself into serious difficulty with the authorities; so before going any further he wanted to know what the originator of this conspiracy thought of the state of affairs.

This adviser was in the basement, waiting for Galimas to report. This basement contained the kitchen pantries and servants' rooms, but as the household of the new mistress was not yet organized, the allies ran no risk of being disturbed.

"Well?" asked Marcaudier, on seeing the broker appear.

"Well, I haven't been able to extort even the vaguest kind of a promise from her. She talks of nothing but killing herself. Of course, I don't believe she means it, but it's not a very promising beginning."

" I warned you, remember."

" Oh! she'll become tamer by and by."

" Are you sure of it?"

" Not absolutely; and if I thought she would always be as savage as she is now—"

" What would you do?"

" I would let her alone. I've no desire to have my eyes scratched out, and I shall be sure to if this girl's mood doesn't change."

" But in that case you will have to release her."

" Of course; though I should hate most mortally to do it, for she's as pretty as a pink; but I can't detain her by force."

" And do you fancy that would be the end of the matter?"

" Why not? She would have no special cause to complain of me, I am sure."

" I differ with you. You have done her a very serious injury. She was on the eve of a great success, and now her career is ruined."

" Nonsense! her mysterious disappearance will only serve as an advertisement."

" And how about Cochard? What will he say when he finds out that it was you who carried off the *prima donna* who was to retrieve his fallen fortunes?"

" I'm not afraid of Cochard. He hasn't a penny."

" And you're not afraid of the girl's lover, I suppose? Or, perhaps, you think she'll refrain from telling him what has occurred?"

" That country bumpkin I met at Madame de Malvoisine's? No; I'm not afraid of him. If he thinks he has any just cause of complaint, I'll fight him; besides, we have an old score to settle."

" Oh, the fellow won't fight with you. He will go to his friend, Colonel Mornac, who is a very influential man, and they will call on the government attorney and enter a formal complaint against you. Violette is not of age, recollect. She is certainly not over nineteen, and the Penal Code punishes the forcible abduction of a minor very severely. You're almost sure to bring up in the Court of Assizes."

Galimas was beginning to be thoroughly frightened, but he was so angry that he replied, savagely:

"This is a fine way for you to talk, upon my word If I've got myself into a scrape it is all your work. I hadn't even thought of such a thing as abducting the girl. I only intended to send an intermediary to her to try to convince her that it would be better to live a life of ease than earn her bread by giving music-lessons. Then you come and suggest that I resort to a highly romantic expedient that will be sure to make an impression on the girl's imagination, you say. You even offer to carry the scheme into execution. It was you who wrote the anonymous letter; it was you who furnished the carriage and servants. And now you talk to me about the Court of Assizes. It's a nice time to do that, truly. You had better tell me what I must do to escape it, for if I go there you'll go too."

"There is no need of either of us going there, if you will only listen to me. But, first, let me prove to you that I was sincere in advising you to abduct the girl. I have never concealed the fact that I had my reasons for wishing to separate her from this Monsieur de Becherel, who is so much in love with her that he really thinks of marrying her. I should have accomplished my object, dear sir, if she had decided to accept your proposals. I hadn't much hope of it, however. I knew her too well. But I said to myself: Let us make the experiment. When she sees the beauties of the house on the Quai de Valmy she will succumb, perhaps. Well, we have tried the experiment. What do you think of it? Do you honestly believe that you will ever succeed in overcoming this prude's scruples?"

"I'm afraid not."

"So you think of allowing the bird to escape from the

cage, and that is precisely what I don't want to do. I want also to prevent the possibility of her injuring us."

"But how? I hope you don't think of wringing her neck?"

"Of course not. Only brutal idiots resort to such measures as that."

"I wouldn't let you do it, if you wanted to. But what is your plan?"

"I want to rid you of her by gentle means, but effectually. You can not possibly do it without my assistance."

"I want to know the means you intend to employ."

"Why? So that you may share the responsibility with me. It would be greatly to your advantage for me to act alone. You certainly don't think me fool enough to burden my conscience with a murder? I'll take entire charge of the whole affair. All you will have to do is to keep quiet, and send about their business any persons who take it into their heads to question you. No one saw Violette enter the house; at least no one but the men who brought her here; and I can depend upon them, so the rôle you have to play is not a difficult one. You must go upstairs again and tell the young lady that on reflection you have decided not to detain her against her will, and that she is consequently at liberty to leave immediately. You can even offer to take her home in a carriage. She will refuse your offer, but she will accept her freedom. While you are talking with her I will go and open the *porte-cochère* so she can leave whenever she pleases."

"But—"

"Oh, don't insist upon an explanation. I sha'n't give you any. You can accept my offer or not, as you choose. If my proposal doesn't please you, I'll decamp and leave you to settle the affair with your prisoner as best you can."

"The deuce take her and you, too," growled Galimas. "I'll say a word or two to her, and then—well, I'll leave the whole matter in your hands."

" That is the best thing you could possibly do, my dear fellow. Now I will leave you. After your interview with the fair damsel you can remain here or return home, as you prefer. You won't see me again to-night, but to-morrow, at the Bourse, I'll give you some news that will ease your mind, I trust."

As he spoke, the originator of the conspiracy took leave of Galimas, who made no attempt to detain him. The broker had had quite enough of this unpleasant predicament, and was anxious to put an end to it without delay, so he went up to the room where he had left Violette.

On entering the apartment where the girl was waiting for her destiny to be decided, Galimas saw that she was still standing close to the window; so, without making any attempt to approach her, he said:

" I have reflected, mademoiselle, and I do not wish you to retain an unpleasant recollection of me. You would do well to remain here until to-morrow morning, but you are not obliged to do so. You are at perfect liberty to leave this house. You would not make use of my carriage, I know, if I offered it; you would prefer to leave on foot. It would be an act of the greatest imprudence, though. Permit me, however, to tell you that you will probably find a carriage on the boulevard. Permit me also to add that I am entirely at your service, whatever happens. I should deem myself very fortunate if you should write me that you had changed your mind. My address is No. 31 Rue du Quatre Septembre."

And Galimas disappeared without even giving Violette time to thank him. She could not understand why this man had so suddenly abandoned his pursuit of her; but this was no time to deliberate, for he might change his mind, so it was advisable to take advantage of this opportunity. She listened and heard him descend the stairs. When the sound of his footsteps had died away, Violette waited a few minutes longer in order to allow him ample time to leave the house.

After five minutes, which seemed well-nigh interminable, she decided to make the venture; and slipping out into the brilliantly lighted hall, she reached the vestibule without meeting any one.

The *porte-cochère* was standing open. She rushed out and found herself on the deserted quay. She did not know where she was, or which way to go; but the all-important thing was to place a long distance between her and the house she had just left, so she began to run with all her might, keeping close to the houses. The black waters of the canal terrified her; but she said to herself that she should soon reach a more frequented locality or meet a carriage, so she hastened on.

After a few minutes she heard the sound of carriage-wheels behind her, and glancing back she saw a fiacre approaching at a very leisurely pace. If the vehicle was empty it was certainly Heaven that had sent it to her, she thought.

She paused and waited until the shabby vehicle, driven by a coachman who seemed to be more than half asleep, overtook her; then darting out into the street she called loudly to the driver, who was muffled nearly to the eyes in the big cape of his old-fashioned overcoat.

" I'll give you ten francs to take me to the Rue de Constantinople!" she cried.

" All right, my little lady," replied the man, stopping his horses. " I'll have you there in less than no time. Jump in!"

Violette did not need to be told twice. She opened the door, and bowing her head, hastily sprung into the carriage.

Before she had even time to seat herself, however, she was seized by strong hands and a large leather gag was applied to her mouth, while some one tied her feet and hands with ropes; and as if to increase the horrors of this abduction, so much more frightful than the other, her eyes were immediately bandaged with a large handkerchief.

All this was done with marvelous dexterity and rapidity; and the perpetrators of the outrage did not utter a word.

There were at least two of them; one who was sitting beside her and the other opposite, on the front seat of the carriage.

Violette was utterly unable to move or to cry out; indeed, it was only with the greatest difficulty that she could breathe.

She felt that she was lost, and she commended her soul to God, for she had retained all her clearness of perception, and she asked herself what these wretches intended to do with her. Why had they subjected her to this fresh outrage when she had been completely in their power before, and where were they taking her?

The horses were now moving at a rapid trot, making the vehicle clatter and bound as it traversed the badly paved street; but soon the jolting became much less violent, and Violette knew that they must be on the asphalt; but it was impossible for her to tell the direction in which they were going. She thought, however, that they must be taking her outside the city limits to murder her in the open fields or throw her into the Seine.

Death had no terrors for her; but she did not want to die without seeing Robert again; nor could she bear the idea that he might suspect her of having consented to the abduction, as actresses sometimes suddenly abandon the stage to follow some Russian prince who is ready to cover them with gold.

And this was the fate that inevitably awaited her, for she could not hope that Robert would ever guess the truth?

It would be impossible to describe her sufferings during this terrible drive which, although comparatively short, seemed to her a century long.

At last the carriage stopped, the door was opened, and Violette was taken out and carried across the pavement by the head and feet exactly as if she had been a bale of merchandise.

She knew that she was taken into a house—for the air was much warmer—but only to be carried directly through it, and by the grating sound of gravel under the feet of her captors she suspected that they next traversed a garden walk.

Any doubts on this point were speedily dispelled, for the branches of a shrub wet with dew grazed her face, and the smell of freshly stirred earth greeted her nostrils. She heard, too, the fluttering of a suddenly awakened bird.

Then the air became warmer again. Her captors had left the garden and were now slowly ascending a staircase. The man who held her head was walking backward, and Violette received a slight jolt at each step. She had the presence of mind to count them; there were twenty-two of them.

On the twenty-second they paused and set her upon her feet without letting go their hold, however.

A key grated in a lock, a door creaked as it turned upon its hinges, and Violette was gently pushed forward by one of her persecutors.

Bound as she was, it was only with the greatest difficulty that she could walk at all. She did manage to take a few steps, however, and almost immediately some one unbound her ankles and then her hands.

She waited for them to remove the bandage from her eyes and the gag from her mouth, but she waited in vain. Again she heard the door turn upon its hinges, and the key grate in the lock.

Her persecutors had departed.

In what kind of a place had they left her? Why had they not killed her then and there? Could it be that they were reserving her for a still more horrible fate, that of slow starvation? She could not implore their compassion, for they had disappeared. An oppressive silence reigned around her—the silence of the tomb—and in this frightful solitude she could distinctly hear the beating of her own heart.

There was nothing to prevent her from removing the gag from her mouth and the bandage from her eyes now, but she dared not. She feared some appalling sight would meet her gaze; for the air she inhaled was so foul and nauseating that she asked herself if she had not been placed in some charnel house.

But however horrible her surroundings might be, she could endure this suspense no longer, so she slowly began to remove the gag. She succeeded finally, though not without considerable difficulty, for it was held in place by wires behind the ears like a fencer's mask. Then she had only to remove the bandage from her eyes. This done, she opened them, but could see nothing, the darkness that surrounded her was so profound.

Where was she? She could not imagine; and she dared not make any attempt to explore her dungeon for fear that any step she took might bring her to an open trap-door and precipitate her into a pit below.

She said to herself that she could not be very far from the door by which she had entered, and that there was consequently no danger that the floor would give way beneath her feet if she moved in that direction, so she retreated instead of advancing.

Soon she reached the wall, and leaning against it she listened breathlessly, for she fancied she heard a strange sound—a faint moaning, that ceased only to begin again a moment afterward. Her blood curdled in her veins at the thought that some other human being was languishing in this dungeon; her limbs gave way beneath her, and she sunk upon the floor.

Her physical strength was exhausted, and her mental

powers were beginning to desert her. The blood rushed to her head, and she gradually relapsed into a state of partial unconsciousness. Robert's image appeared before her; she fancied she could hear him cursing the perfidious creature who had deserted him to follow the infamous Galimas. Robert must have noticed the scoundrel's maneuvers during the performance, and supposed that he had won Violette with his promises of gold; and now, Robert, instead of making an attempt to find her, was swearing that he would never set eyes on her again.

This thought broke the poor girl's heart, and deprived her of her only hope. There was nothing left for her but death now, and she longed for it with all her heart.

At last sleep came; the leaden slumber that follows great crises.

How long she slept she never knew; but when she woke she was utterly unable to recall what had passed. She opened her eyes, but only to instantly close them again.

Day had dawned, and the light that stole through the windows above dazzled her, dim as it was.

Suddenly she fancied she felt some one's breath upon her cheek. The idea aroused her from her lethargy, and opening her eyes they met those of a woman who was kneeling beside her—a woman whose face was almost touching hers, and whose lips were murmuring incoherent words.

A cry of astonishment escaped Violette, and she hastily raised herself upon one elbow; still the woman did not move, but continued to devour her with her eyes.

" Who are you?" asked the girl, in a trembling voice. " Are you a prisoner like myself?"

She received no reply; but this time she heard the words the stranger was repeating:

" Simone!" she was saying. " Simone, where are you?'

" Simone! that is my name!"

" That is false! Simone is dead. You are saying this

just to try me—like that man who came here and tried to get me away.''

'' But what if I should be the Simone you believe dead?''

'' You look like her, but you are not Simone.''

'' What would you do if you should find her again?''

'' What would I do? How dare you ask me that? Do you not understand that she for whom I mourn was my daughter?''

'' Your daughter!'' exclaimed Violette, beginning to scrutinize the face of the stranger in her turn. Those features, haggard with suffering, aroused no recollection in her mind. They were entirely strange to her, but it seemed to her that she had heard this sweet and well modulated voice in the days of her childhood.

'' Now tell me your name in your turn,'' she said at last.

'' My name? I have forgotten it. I try to recall it sometimes, and there are days when it suddenly recurs to me.''

'' Well, try now, I beseech you. ''

The woman bowed her head upon her hands, and sat for a long time silent and motionless.

Then suddenly straightening herself, she said:

'' Years ago they used to call me Bertha. ''

Violette turned pale. She, too, had suddenly recalled the name.

'' Did you live in a sea-port town?'' she asked.

'' Yes, I lived near the sea. But how did you know that?''

'' You lived in Havre, perhaps?''

'' No, in Ingouville. ''

Violette knew enough of geography to be aware that the pretty village of Ingouville was in the suburbs of Havre.

'' Did you live near the water?'' she asked, quickly.

'' Yes, we could look on the sea from the windows of our house.''

"And there was a large garden full of flowers, was there not?"

"Yes. Oh, those flowers! I loved them so. I wonder if there are any flowers now?"

The tears rose to Violette's eyes.

"You had a daughter, had you not?" she asked.

"Yes; and I idolized her, but they took her from me."

"Who took her from you?"

"I do not know. She was stolen. She was playing in the garden one evening; I left her for a moment, and when I returned, she was gone."

"And you have never seen her since?"

"No, never. My grief at her loss destroyed my reason. They shut me up in a ship, and I was on the sea a long time."

"And afterward?"

"I can not remember what happened afterward. Where are we?"

"You are in Paris. That is all I know, for I, too, was dragged here last night by force, after my captors had bandaged my eyes. Your daughter was taken from you; my mother was taken from me. I was scarcely four years old when I was found asleep on a bench in a public park in Rennes—a long way from the city of Havre, where I was born."

"Why do you say that you were born in Havre?"

"Because I am sure that I was. I recollect that my nurse carried me out on a long pier—and that garden full of flowers at Ingouville. I can see it yet."

The stranger listened with breathless eagerness, and her eyes sparkled with extraordinary brilliancy. It was evident that both intelligence and memory were returning.

Suddenly she sprung toward Violette and seized the frightened girl by the fair shoulder, for the corsage of the costume she wore was moderately *décolleté*.

" This mark?" demanded the recluse, touching a small dark spot that marred the whiteness of the soft skin.

" I have had it ever since I was born," replied Violette.

" My daughter! for you are indeed my daughter," exclaimed the poor woman, smothering her with kisses.

For some minutes the mother and daughter embraced and wept over each other in silence.

" Ah! I felt sure that you were my mother," exclaimed Violette. " It is God that has united us."

" Yes, we will die together—for it must have been with the intention of killing you that they threw you into this prison. Do you know who your persecutors are? Tell me all about your life. What were you doing when they seized you, and why did they treat you as they have?"

" I was reared by charity, in a convent. Afterward I became a music-teacher in a boarding-school near Paris, and afterward companion in the household of a lady called the Countess de Malvoisine."

Violette paused. She could not bear to tell her mother that she had afterward sung in a theater, though she fully expected to be questioned about the singular costume she wore. But the recluse did not seem to notice it. Since she had been pining in Marcaudier's prison house the unfortunate woman had had time to forget how young girls usually dress.

Nor did the name of Malvoisine seem to make any impression upon her. She had never heard it before evidently.

" Listen," she said, pressing Violette to her heart, " I do not know what they intend to do with you. Perhaps they intend you to perish of cold and hunger. I have managed to endure these privations for years, but you could not endure them long, so we will try to make our escape. A man came here one night, not very long ago. He entered by way of the roof. He wanted to save me, but I refused to go with him. I thought that my perse-

cutors had sent him here to set a trap for me. He showed
me a paper on which I had written your name, and which
I had thrown through that window up there. I hope he
will come again; but if he does not, we shall perhaps be
able to make our escape without his assistance."

"It must have been Robert," thought Violette. "I
understand now why he promised to restore my mother
to me about a fortnight ago."

CHAPTER IX.

AFTER his brief conversation with the colonel, Robert de
Becherel returned home in a state of mind closely border-
ing on frenzy.

He no longer suspected M. de Mornac of treachery, but
he still doubted Violette, and the mere thought that she
might have allowed herself to be tempted by the proposals
of a man like Galimas caused him the most poignant suffering; and, though he tried hard to convince himself that
such a thing was an impossibility, he did not succeed.

Very unfortunately, too, he found himself condemned to
a state of inaction. What could he do? Galimas and
Marcaudier would laugh in his face if he went to demand
Violette at their hands. Besides, the colonel had advised
Robert to take no action in the matter until he heard from
him. He had even promised that he should hear from
him the next day, so there was nothing for Robert to do
but wait.

The poor fellow passed a frightful night. He locked
himself up in his room, and even forgot to ascertain if his
groom had returned—the groom he thought he had seen
kissing Violette in the upper gallery.

This strange incident recurred to his mind when he
woke, however, and ringing for Jean, who promptly appeared in answer to the summons, wearing a decidedly
shame-faced air, he proceeded to question him.

The youth denied the charge at first, but on being pressed, finally admitted that he had entered the theater on a ticket purchased at the door, and that he hissed because the piece bored him. This explanation did not satisfy his master, however, and Jean's discomfited mien showed plainly enough that his conscience was not clear; and when Robert announced his intention of sending him back to Rennes, he hung his head and wept, instead of protesting.

The morning passed quietly. Becherel had resolved not to go out for fear of missing M. de Mornac's visit, and on leaving the table, after going through the form of break-fasting, he went into the smoking-room and stretched himself out on a sofa to once more review the situation.

It seemed inextricable, and after racking his brain in vain to solve the mystery of Violette's disappearance, he began to think of his mother, and to wonder if he had not better join her at Rennes without delay. He had not received a letter from her for several days, and she might arrive in Paris at any moment; but why should he keep her waiting any longer, now that he had no hope of ever seeing Violette again? All his dreams of happiness had vanished, and he now began to think with something like regret of the quiet, uneventful life he had previously disdained.

He was engrossed with thoughts like these when a vigorous pull at the bell announced the arrival of the colonel, who was immediately ushered into the smoking-room, and who began as follows, without preamble of any kind:

"Last evening I promised to give my attention to the matter that interests you so deeply, and I have kept my word. I have just left police head-quarters, so I am now in a position to give you some definite information in regard to the persecutors of your lady-love, and in a quarter of an hour you will know as much about their past as I do. Galimas is a *parvenu* in every sense of the word. Born of poor but dishonest parents, he acquired his education at a public school, where he learned to read and write, and above all, to count. At sixteen years of age he was sweeping out a broker's office; at eighteen he was filling the responsible position of messenger; at twenty he was acting as clerk for another broker. Where he got the money that first enabled him to speculate on his own account the devil only knows. This much is certain; he is worth four or five millions to-day, which he has made dishonestly, of course, but without ever doing anything that would render him liable to prosecution by his victims. As for Marcaudier, his history is more complicated. It is closely connected with that of the ladies on the Rue du Rocher. The Malvoisine, as I think I have already told you, was at the head of a large dress-making establishment twenty-five years ago."

" Here in Paris?" asked Becherel.

" Yes, on the Rue Vivienne. She had a large and fashionable *clientèle* in those days, and was very handsome, though by no means virtuous. Among other male acquaintances she made that of a gentleman whose reputation was of a very doubtful kind, but whose wealth was incontestable, judging from the style in which he lived. This gentleman, who resided in Paris only at intervals, answered to the name of Morgan, and was the owner of a number of vessels, which he sometimes sailed himself. The fruit of his *liaison* with Josephine Lureau, now known as Madame de Malvoisine, was a daughter."

" Herminia?" exclaimed Becherel.

" The same, though she bore her mother's name until the day when the *modiste* after a long eclipse reappeared in Paris as the Countess de Malvoisine. That was about fifteen years ago, and everybody has forgotten Josephine Lureau now. The only traces that remain of her are on the archives of the prefecture."

" And Marcaudier, colonel?"

" I was just coming to him. This Morgan, who is Herminia's father, but who never acknowledged her—probably because he was a married man—reappeared in Paris at the same time, purchased a house for his daughter and her mother, and one for himself, and has since led a very retired life, absenting himself for months at a time, never showing himself at the house of the pretended countess, and indulging in no luxury or display, though he has a balance of at least twelve million francs in the Bank of France. He brought back to Paris with him a man who doesn't seem in the least inclined to bury himself, however, and who has made himself quite famous by some very successful speculations at the Bourse. This man is your usurer, Pierre Marcaudier, *alias* Cash on Delivery.''

" Who is doubtless in the employ of Herminia's father —an atrocious scoundrel, apparently—and as that young lady took it into her head that she would like to marry me, Marcaudier invented a plan to get Violette out of the way in order to eventually bring me to the feet of his master's illegitimate daughter.''

" That is exactly my opinion.''

" But what has he done with her?''

" I am inclined to think that he entered into a compact with Galimas to entice her to some house where the gallant broker hides his lady-loves. My friend has promised to find this house, and in the meantime he has carried his courtesy so far as to place at my disposal two detectives who are now waiting for me in the street below. I was anxious to see you before I started out after Galimas, so—''

" But how about Marcaudier? Nobody can convince me that he was not the originator of the conspiracy; Galimas was only a tool.''

" That is very possible; but even admitting you are right, we are not much better off. Where could Marcaudier have taken Violette? Certainly not to his own house in Passy?''

"I do not know."

"I do," said Jean, suddenly appearing before them.

It was a scene for a painter.

The groom had dropped the *portière* behind which he had been hiding, and now advanced tremblingly; M. de Mornac, furiously angry, made a movement as if to spring at his throat, exclaiming:

"So you have been listening again, you rascal? This is a little too much, and I'm going to give you a sound thrashing."

"Don't touch me," said the Breton, squaring himself for the encounter.

He was strong, like all his countrymen, and if the colonel had undertaken to correct him he would probably have had a lively time of it.

"It is to my master that I wish to speak, and to him alone," continued Jean.

"Well, speak then," said Becherel. "Vindicate yourself, if you can; but tell the truth. You will gain nothing by trying to deceive me. I have dismissed you, and I shall not take you into my service again."

"Monsieur did perfectly right to dismiss me. I deserved it; but I do not want to return home until monsieur has forgiven me."

"Forgiven you for what? For listening at doors?" retorted Robert, angrily. "Go and ask absolution of your father-confessor. He will give it if you have no other sins to reproach yourself with."

"What! you stand here and waste your time in talking with this fool, instead of kicking him out-of-doors? You can not wonder that I leave you in disgust."

"You will make a great mistake, then, sir," said Jean; "for I have several things to tell my master—things that you, too, ought to hear, for—"

"Explain quickly, then," interrupted Robert, glancing at the colonel as if to beg him to remain.

"About three weeks ago," began Jean, "I unintentionally overheard you talking of a lady who resides near here, on the Rue Rougemont—Madame Julia."

"Ah! so you are a lover of hers!" exclaimed M. de Mornac. "I might have known it."

"I was, but that is all over now. In the first place, she has another, and that doesn't suit me. Besides, after what she did yesterday—"

"Do you propose to entertain us with an account of your love affairs?" thundered M. de Mornac.

"Let him alone, colonel," said Becherel, who was beginning to see the drift of his groom's remarks.

Then, turning to Jean, he added:

"You went to the theater last night, you told me."

"Yes, monsieur," replied the youth, promptly; "and I was very sorry that I did, when I saw you there, seated behind the musicians. It was Madame Julia who gave me the ticket."

"And who ordered you to hiss, I suppose?"

"That is true; and I assure you I had no desire to; the young lady dressed like a bird was so pretty, and sung so sweetly. But Madame Julia motioned me to do it, and I didn't dare to disobey her. I was sorry for it afterward, though, for the men around me beat me and turned me out."

"And what then?"

"I had had enough of the theater, and would have been glad to return home, but Madame Julia had made me promise to wait for her in a *café* on the boulevard, so I waited."

"Did she come?"

"Yes; and she was in high spirits. She told me that it had been a hard matter to prevent the audience from breaking up everything in the theater. They were so mad because the singer couldn't be found. I said I was sorry to hear that, and she laughed and made fun of me. She said that the young lady had taken her place, so she hated her, and was glad to get rid of her, and she added that the girl would never give her any more trouble, for she had been put in prison.''

" In prison?'' exclaimed Robert.

" Yes; and when I asked her what the poor young lady had done that she should have been arrested by the gendarmes she told me that I was a fool—that the gendarmes had had nothing to do with this affair—that it was a friend of hers who had carried the girl off.''

" Did she tell you where he had taken her?''

" Yes; to a house that belongs to him, and where he intends to detain her by force. I thought it an abominable shame, but I didn't say so, because I wanted to find out if all this was really true; and when she had given me proofs that it was, I told her that she was a good-for-nothing hussy, and walked off and left her.''

" But why did you say nothing about all this when I returned last night?''

'' I didn't know that monsieur was acquainted with the young lady they had treated so badly. Still, the story I had heard worried me. I saw, too, that monsieur was in trouble; but I didn't dare to ask him what the matter was. But when I heard monsieur speak of the singer and how she had been kidnapped, I confess that I hid behind the curtain so as to hear more.''

" I forgive you.''

" I even thank you,'' added the colonel, '' especially as you were shrewd enough to get some useful information out of the hussy. Was it to a house of the Rue Mozart that they took the young lady?''

" No; she told me the name of the street, but I don't remember it very well. It seems to me that it was something like Martin or Morton.''

" The Rue Milton?'' exclaimed Becherel.

" That is it.''

"Why, it is there that Herminia's father lives," remarked the colonel.

"The mystery is solved!" cried Robert. "Morgan's house is connected by a garden with the house on the Rue Rodier, in which Marcaudier receives his clients. Jean, my boy, you have rendered me a service I shall never forget. Leave us now. I want to be alone with the colonel."

Jean disappeared, and Becherel immediately began to tell M. de Mornac all about his expedition of a fortnight before. M. de Mornac listened to the story with all the attention it deserved, but seemed to draw a rather startling conclusion from it, for he said, coldly:

"You certainly did very wrong to keep this adventure from me. If you had told me about it, we should not be where we are now."

"Yes; I did very wrong," replied Becherel, promptly; "but now you know all about it, I think you can not doubt that Violette has been taken to the place I speak of."

"I am not altogether sure of it, for this reason: if it was really Marcaudier that committed the outrage, there was no necessity of his associating Galimas with him in the affair. Besides, if it is really Violette's mother Marcaudier keeps shut up in his garret, he would commit a great imprudence by imprisoning the daughter there too."

"You forget that Marcaudier knows nothing of Violette's history, colonel. The Malvoisine and her daughter are equally ignorant of it, you recollect. They know that Violette was a foundling, but that is all."

"That is a sound argument, and we run no risk by acting on the supposition that you are right, and acting immediately. I have almost *carte blanche* from the prefecture. My two detectives are in the street below, and I have a carriage in waiting. We will enter it with them. I say we, because I am going to take you with me. You know the ground, and you may be of service to me."

"And we are going where?"

"To the Rue Milton, of course. But, after we get there, you must let me operate alone. I don't know how I shall manage it, but I assure you that I shall succeed in getting into the house some way or other. Are you ready?"

It is needless to say that Robert did not keep the colonel waiting, even for a moment, and the whole party were soon driving rapidly in the direction of the Rue Milton. It was not until they had gone a short distance beyond the suspected house that the colonel ordered the coachman to stop.

They all alighted, but the detectives remained near the carriage, while M. de Mornac and Becherel proceeded toward the house.

"I'll give you my instructions now," remarked the colonel. "Morgan has been away, but I am sure he has returned, for all the shutters are open, as you see. You are to wait for me on the other side of the street, directly opposite the house, and not move until you receive further orders from me."

"What, colonel, you are going into the house alone?"

"Yes; if I need you I will call you."

"But this Morgan must be a scoundrel of the deepest dye, and his servants are probably no better than he is, so you run no little risk of personal violence."

"I'm not afraid of that. I have a good revolver in my pocket. Besides, I have taken my precautions, and at the very first signal from me the detectives will rush to my aid. The signal is to be a pistol-shot."

"But they may not hear it. They are so far off."

"But you will, and you can call them. It will not be necessary, however. I know how I can keep Monsieur Morgan on his good behavior."

"And you think he will see you?"

"I am sure of it, and he will listen to me, too. I haven't time now to explain how I intend to proceed, but you surely have sufficient confidence in me to allow me to be guided by my own judgment."

And, without giving Becherel time to make any more objections, M. de Mornac crossed the street and gave the door-bell of Morgan's house a vigorous pull.

The servant who answered the summons was in his shirt-sleeves, and had a feather duster in his hand. His appearance was by no means prepossessing, and it was in a rough, almost insolent manner that he said, gruffly:

"Who do you want to see?"

"Monsieur Leon Morgan," replied the colonel.

"My master is not seeing any one to-day."

"He will see me, however. Tell him that I have called at the instance of Monsieur Pierre Marcaudier, to see him on a matter of grave importance."

The servant hesitated. In fact he seemed to be on the point of shutting the door in the visitor's face, when a harsh voice cried from the end of the hall:

"Let him in!"

Colonel Mornac pushed by the servant, and found himself face to face with a man whom he recognized as Morgan from the description that had been given of him at the prefecture of police.

The man was tall and stout, with very broad shoulders. He had a brick-red face, closely cropped gray hair, and shaggy eyebrows. He looked like a sailor, or rather like a pirate. His eyes were sharp, and his face stern and even forbidding in its expression, though his features were regular, and he must even have been quite handsome when he was young.

He wore a loose blouse that exposed his neck to view.—a thick, bull-like neck, and had a short black pipe in his mouth.

"Did you say that you called at Pierre Marcaudier's request?" he asked, brusquely.

"Yes, Monsieur Leon."

"How did he hear that I was in the city? I arrived only this morning, and I wrote him that I should not return until to-morrow."

"That is true, but he bade me call at all hazards. I want to speak to you on an important matter. He will call himself this evening."

"Very well; step out into the garden with me."

This proposal was eminently satisfactory for many reasons. An interview in a room would have had its dangers; in the open air the colonel ran little if any risk.

So he followed Morgan, who finally paused in the middle of a path some distance from the house, and said, bluntly:

"We are alone now. What do you want with me? But, first, tell me who you are. I don't know you."

"But Pierre Marcaudier knows me."

"That is very possible; but what is your name?"

"My name would have no significance to you. It is enough for you to know that I was sent here by the prefect of police."

"A detective! *Mille tonnerres!* We'll see about this. Jean Marie!" shouted Morgan, at the top of his voice.

But before the servant he summoned had time to respond to the call, the colonel drew a revolver from his pocket, and said, coolly:

"If you do not send your servant back, I shall fire in the air, and the policemen who are waiting for me in the Rue Milton will rush in."

The threat proved effectual, for Jean Marie had scarcely shown his face in the door-way, when his master cried:

"Remain in the hall, and don't let any one in."

"That order is entirely useless," remarked M. de Mornac, coolly. "If I summon my men, they will burst the door open if necessary. It will be greatly to your interest, however, to create no scandal, for I have merely come to ask an explanation of a certain fact. If this explanation appears satisfactory to me, you will be subjected to no further annoyance."

Morgan's face just at that moment was a curious study. He was evidently trying to decide whether he should spring upon the colonel and strangle him with his brawny hands or hear him to the end. He would not have hesitated, probably, if he had had a clear conscience.

"I have never had any dealings with the police," he said, at last. "I was formerly a large shipowner; I am worth fifteen million francs, and I made my money honestly."

"I know who you are," interrupted M. de Mornac; "and I also know that since you took up your abode in Paris, about fifteen years ago, your life has been irreproachable. I can not say as much, however, of the man you honor with your confidence, for frequent complaints have been made to us of Marcaudier's usurious practices."

"That is no concern of mine. Pierre sailed with me years ago; he has had an interest in some of my commercial enterprises, and in that way has made a great deal of money. What he does with it is no business of mine. It is hardly probable that you came here to talk to me about these matters, so tell me just what you want and have done with it."

"Very well. A complaint has been made against you, and the investigation of the charge has been intrusted to me. You are accused of unwarrantable and forcible detention."

"Detention!" repeated Morgan, in the tone of a man who did not comprehend the meaning of the word. "What do you mean?"

"In other words, you are accused of having imprisoned a person against that person's will, and of detaining the person by force; and you are doubtless aware that the law severely punishes any outrage of individual liberty."

"Who accuses me of this?"

"Neighbors, who complain of being annoyed by the cries of that person, who, they say, is so continually shrieking and screaming for help that they are unable to sleep at night."

" I have no neighbors, and there is no sense in the complaint. Those who made it must have some object in thus endeavoring to injure me, and their charge is utterly unworthy of credence. You can search my house from top to bottom, however, if you like. I will show you through it myself."

The pretended agent from the prefecture was silent for a moment, but he did not seem to be convinced.

" Pardon me," he said, at last, " but doesn't that house I see at the further end of the garden belong to your friend, Monsieur Marcaudier?"

" I am really unable to say."

" We are not, however. And it is from that very house that the cries and moans proceed."

" Then apply to the owner of it for the information you desire."

" We shall be obliged to do that eventually, I do not doubt; but in the meantime will you allow me to broach another side of the question? The information we have received is full and explicit. We are sure that some one is confined in that building, and a warrant for an examination of the premises will soon be issued—probably to-morrow, and the result will doubtless be extremely unpleasant for Monsieur Marcaudier. If he were the only person concerned in the matter this search-warrant would have been issued long ago, for he does not bear a very enviable reputation with us; but he is an intimate friend of yours, and it is well to think twice before involving a person like yourself in such an affair."

" I am extremely grateful to you, I am sure," said Morgan, with an ironical grimace; " but pray finish what you have to say."

" If you know the truth I assure you that it would be greatly to your interest to tell it before any further action is taken in the matter. I should add that we are perfectly willing to admit that there may be no real crime at the bottom of all this; that is, in the ordinary sense of the word. Forcible detention is considered a grave offense, particularly when it is practiced upon an individual whose existence troubles the person committing the offense; for example, when the victim is a person who has a right to property that is in the possession of the offender; but there are circumstances which render such an act almost pardonable. Suppose, for instance, that some member of a family should be afflicted with insanity. That is a great disadvantage, and, in fact, a positive affliction to children, and even near relatives. When one belongs to such a family marriage becomes difficult and sometimes impossible; so not a few persons endeavor to conceal the disgrace, and instead of sending their afflicted relative to an insane asylum they keep the victim in their own custody, and sedulously conceal the fact from their friends and acquaintances. This is very wrong, certainly, but after all it is natural, for we are none of us perfect.''

'' No; and there are many more scoundrels than honest men, in my opinion. But what are you driving at?''

'' I want to say to you—I am authorized by the prefect of police to say to you—that if the person forcibly detained there is an insane person and has been confined there for the reasons I have cited, it would change the aspect of affairs entirely. The motives that led to the detention would be considered, and if it could be proved that it had not been done in the interest of an avaricious relative, no prosecution would ensue, but the authorities would confine themselves to ordering the transfer of the demented person to a private lunatic asylum.''

'' That is your private opinion, I suppose?''

'' No; it is the opinion of my superiors; and they would not only carefully refrain from making the matter public, but would assume the whole responsibility—as they have an undoubted right to do.''

Morgan did not utter a word. He seemed to be reflecting.

"I tell you all this, sir," continued M. de Mornac, "because the affair is sure to create a great scandal if the authorities should be compelled to resort to legal measures. Of course all this would affect you more or less directly, as Marcaudier is a protégé of yours, and if he be arrested your reputation would suffer."

"You are right," said Morgan, brusquely. "I had better tell you all."

"I congratulate you on your decision, sir; and I assure you that you will have no cause to regret having followed my advice."

"Ah, well! the woman up there is mad, and has been mad for fifteen years."

"It is a woman, then," said M. de Mornac, who was perfectly well aware of the fact, but who had taken good care not to mention the sex of the prisoner.

"Yes, my wife. You see I am concealing nothing from you. I married her in America. She brought me no fortune, so I have no interest in getting her out of the way. Her mind became affected while we were living in Havre. I had ceased to follow the sea and was contemplating a change of residence. She had not lost her reason entirely at that time; but her malady seemed to be making such rapid progress that I thought strongly of placing the unfortunate woman in an insane asylum; but Marcaudier dissuaded me from doing so and offered to take charge of her himself. I made a great mistake in following his advice, and have often regretted it since."

"May I inquire if Madame de Malvoisine knows of this affair?"

"So you know—"

"Yes; I am perfectly aware of your former relations with her, and also that the fruit of your *liaison* was a daughter whom you have not acknowledged in order that you might be able to leave her your entire fortune."

"I do not deny it."

" Then you have had no legitimate children, I suppose?"

Morgan turned pale, but he had resolved to keep nothing back.

" Yes; my wife bore me a daughter," he replied, " but she was stolen from me."

" Who stole her from you?" inquired the colonel, hastily, greatly surprised by this confession.

" I have no idea. I was in America at the time. It was in consequence of this calamity that my wife became insane."

" But did you make no effort to find your child?"

" It would have been useless. Marcaudier ascertained for a certainty that she was dead. The persons who stole her embarked on a small vessel with the intention of taking her to England. The vessel was run down in the middle of the Channel by a large ship and every soul on board was lost."

" So it was Marcaudier who—"

" I loved the child very much, and grieved a great deal over her loss; but of course I got used to it after awhile. And it was all for the best that she died, perhaps, for my life has been a hell ever since my marriage. My wife found out about Madame de Malvoisine and was continually making scenes. I live in peace now; but I am not much happier."

" I should think that Mademoiselle Herminia—"

" Herminia has no heart; and her mother has brought her up very badly. She is about to be married, Marcaudier writes me, and I am glad of it. I shall give her a large dowry, and she will inherit my property. I am thinking strongly of going to sea again, and I shall die as I have lived—a sailor. I have told you all. Have you any more questions to ask?"

" But one. I shall be obliged to report to the prefect; and as I can not do that upon mere hearsay, I must see—"

" My wife. You can do so if you like. I haven't seen

her myself since she's been up there; but I have the key to the garret where Marcaudier keeps her. It is in my secretary; I'll go and get it."

He re-entered the house, but the colonel remained in the garden. He was satisfied now that Morgan's statements were true, and that he was not such a great criminal after all. That he had formerly been engaged in the slave-trade —that he had even been a pirate—was more than probable; that he made his wife's life very unhappy was certain; but there was nothing to prove that he told an untruth when he said that he had placed his wife in confinement because she was insane. And it was equally probable that he was sincere in asserting that his daughter had been stolen in his absence, and that he had deeply mourned her loss.

Besides, however this might be, he was certainly ignorant that the daughter he supposed dead was imprisoned with her mother in Marcaudier's garret; and the colonel, who had previously regarded him as the chief culprit and the prime cause of Violette's misfortunes, now saw in him an unscrupulous man and cruel husband, but not an unnatural father. The real culprit was Marcaudier, Mme. de Malvoisine's accomplice, and Morgan's treacherous counselor, the inhuman custodian of the poor insane woman, the cowardly wretch who had just condemned Violette to the same horrible fate as her mother, and that certainly without Morgan's knowledge or consent.

In a few moments Morgan reappeared with a key in his hand.

"I will satisfy you now, sir," he said, coldly; "and I trust to your honor to render a truthful and impartial version of the facts to those who sent you here. You have only to follow me. I know where the room is and the way to it though I have never entered it."

"What! never?" exclaimed Mornac.

"No; Marcaudier is the only person that visits the room. He goes there every evening—whether I am in Paris or not

—to take the unfortunate woman food; and I assure you that she has never wanted for anything so far as I know."

"It seems to me, however, that a man is hardly the person to wait upon a—a sick lady."

"Oh, Marcaudier is a sort of general utility man. I can trust him; and he has often assured me that my wife never complained of her surroundings or fate."

"But how about these cries that the neighbors hear?"

"Oh, she shrieks and raves when fits of frenzy seize her —which is generally at night, unfortunately. But at other times she is very quiet."

"One question more, sir. If she had died in her prison-house what would you have done?"

Morgan seemed a trifle disconcerted, but he replied, with much hesitation:

"I confess that I never thought what I should do in such a case."

"Would you have made her death public? Hardly, for it would have been necessary for you to admit at the same time how she had been living for fifteen years, and who she was."

"I could not have done it even if I had wanted to, for when I brought my wife here on my return from a voyage to America I told people that she had died in New York."

"So everybody supposed that you were a widower. Consequently you would have been obliged to bury her secretly in the garden, probably."

"I don't know. Marcaudier would have attended to that."

"I don't doubt it; but see the situation in which this would have placed you. You might even have been accused of murder. I tell you this to show you that you have acted very wisely in putting an end to a state of affairs which was certainly fraught with serious danger to you."

"Nothing would please me better, I am sure," said

Morgan, "but how? What are you going to do with my wife? I can not live with her any longer."

"You must place her in an asylum, where your fortune will enable you to give her every possible comfort. No explanation of the past will be required of you when you take her there; and this reappearance or resurrection of your lawful wife will make very little change in your life, for you have no idea of marrying Madame de Malvoisine, I suppose?"

"Oh, no. Marcaudier has urged me to do so several times, but I have never given him any encouragement. I've had enough of married life, and of the countess. I have made my will. Herminia will inherit all my property. She is my daughter, after all. If the other one had lived—"

"What other one?"

"The one who was stolen from me!"

"Well, what then?" inquired M. de Mornac, eagerly.

"If the other one had lived Herminia would not have had my fortune, and it would have been a good thing, for she isn't worthy of it. I should have left her plenty to live upon, however; and as her mother is very well off she might have succeeded in capturing a marquis after all, and that is the height of her ambition."

These remarks dispelled the colonel's last lingering doubts. The real culprit was certainly Marcaudier.

So there was nothing to prevent Violette from becoming a wealthy heiress! But at what a price! The father who stood ready to acknowledge her as his child was certainly not a parent to be proud of, and M. de Mornac found it difficult indeed to believe that she was the daughter of such a man, and even the half-sister of a girl who was so utterly unlike her.

"Come, sir," said Morgan; "come, I beg of you, and let us have it over with."

They walked toward the building at the other end of the

garden, and the colonel then followed his companion up a winding staircase that led to a massive door.

"This is the place," remarked his guide. "I will open the door for you, but I don't care to go in. You can make your investigation without my assistance."

"I would rather you accompanied me," replied the colonel, who had his reasons for not wishing to appear before the two prisoners alone.

"As you please."

Morgan looked for the lock, and as it was rather dark in the passage he had considerable difficulty in finding it. He succeeded at last. The key he inserted was so rusty that it did not enter the lock very easily, and when he tried to turn it it resisted his efforts—a fact which proved beyond a doubt that he had rarely or never made use of this key. Marcaudier had his own, and Marcaudier came every day.

The lock finally yielded to the pressure exerted upon it, and the door opened; but instead of entering Morgan hastily recoiled, for his wife, who had been attracted thither by the noise, suddenly appeared before him, changed almost beyond recognition by the frightful sufferings and privations through which she had passed. He recognized her, however, and she knew him, for she cried

"Wretch! you have come to kill me at last."

"No, no," faltered Morgan.

"Ah, well, then kill your daughter too," replied the unfortunate woman, pushing Violette forward.

"My daughter!" repeated Morgan in profound astonishment.

"Yes, my daughter Simone, whom you stole from me, but whom God has restored to me! Look at her! do you see the birth-mark on her shoulder? Do you dare to deny that it is she?"

The colonel had kept a little in the background, and the prisoners had not perceived his presence; but when he did step forward Violette threw herself in his arms, crying wildly:

"Save me! Save me!"

She might have added: "from my mother," for she had no idea that the man who had entered first was her father, and it was the insane woman that so terrified her.

Morgan devoured his daughter with his eyes, and undoubtedly recognized her, for he stepped toward her and offered her his hand. Seeing her draw back with a gesture of surprise and aversion, he said, curtly:

"Very well. I know what I have to do. Sir, I ask you to grant me a quarter of an hour—time to repair the wrong I have done."

And without waiting for a reply he rushed down-stairs, leaving the colonel alone with the mother and daughter.

The demented woman had regained just enough reason to realize the terrible wrong that had been done her, and she began to shower the fiercest imprecations upon her persecutors, while Violette briefly related her strange adventures to M. de Mornac.

The way was clear now, and there was nothing to prevent the colonel from taking the prisoners from the dungeon in which Marcaudier had confined them. He rather shrunk from the idea of taking them out into the street and putting them in the carriage. dressed as they were, but it would not do to leave them here, for Morgan might change his mind.

"Come," he said to them, motioning Violette to support her mother upon one side while he sustained her on the other.

The unfortunate woman offered no resistance, and they descended the stairs three abreast; but when they reached the garden the light dazzled her, and her strength seemed to fail her, so they were obliged to seat her upon a bench.

She was perfectly quiet now. The excitement caused by Morgan's unexpected visit had given place to a deep torpor.

"Where is Robert?" inquired Violette, as she seated herself beside her mother.

"He is waiting for me a few steps from here. Have you the courage to take your mother home with you in her present condition?"

"I will not leave her again. But that man—"

"That man is less culpable than you suppose. Besides —he is your father."

Violette burst into tears.

"Do you not think with me that it would be better to forget the wrong he has done your mother?"

"Alas, yes."

"Then you will consent to abandon all idea of avenging your mother. I approve your decision; but it is not necessary that he should see you again, and if you are not afraid to remain here by yourself for a few moments I will let him know your decision—and mine."

Violette nodded her assent, and M. de Mornac walked straight into the house.

He met no one in the hall, and seeing an open door he entered a room that seemed to be the private office of the master of the house; but that gentleman was not there.

He was about to call him, when a voice cried:

"One minute more and I will be at your service."

The sound came from an adjoining room, which was separated from the office by a rich curtain, purchased probably by Morgan on one of his voyages to the far East.

M. de Mornac thought he might surely grant a few moments to this repentant father, so he walked to a window that looked out upon the garden in which the mother and daughter were sitting side by side.

"Here I am, sir," said Morgan, entering the room, with a large envelope in his hand. "Will you be kind enough to give this envelope to the person to whom it is addressed? It contains the certificate of my daughter's birth, and a full description of her, authenticated by the testimony of witnesses, and recorded in the city clerk's office at Havre, shortly after her disappearance, and before I had received the false intelligence of her death. With these documents she will have no difficulty in establishing her rights; besides, they will not be contested, for I have just burned my will. I have also inclosed in the envelope the certificate of my marriage with her mother. Simone Morgan is my legitimate child, my only child, and consequently the sole heiress to all my property."

"You have certainly done the handsome thing, monsieur," said the colonel, surprised and touched. "Do you desire to see her again?"

"See her again! No, it would only pain her."

"She is in the garden."

"Then I can certainly take one more look at my child."

He gazed at her in silence for some time, and the colonel, who was watching him, saw two big tears roll down his swarthy cheeks.

His emotion transfigured the face of the old corsair, and the colonel saw now that he must really have been quite handsome in his youth.

"She would have loved me," muttered Morgan. "My life has been a failure, and it is too late to begin it over again. Farewell, sir," he continued, turning from the window. "I bear you no ill-will. You have really done me a service, and I rely upon you to prevent this affair from becoming noised about. I take no interest in Marcandier, and if you deliver him up to justice you will be doing perfectly right. I really think, however, that it would be better to let him go and get hung elsewhere."

"That is my opinion, and—"

"Tell my daughter that I implore her to forgive me, and pray for me."

With these concluding words Morgan disappeared behind the curtain, and the colonel dared not follow him, though he foresaw the possibility of a tragical *denouement*.

Putting the envelope in his pocket, he passed out into the hall, but he had not descended three stairs when he heard the report of a pistol.

"Ah!" he said to himself, with a *sang-froid* Robert de Becherel would certainly have envied, "I thought it would end in that way. He has killed himself, and it is a good thing I guess. He had the right sort of stuff in him, after all. You wouldn't catch that cur Marcaudier doing the same."

He saw nothing of the valet when he reached the hall below, so instead of going out into the garden he opened the door that led into the street.

Robert was awaiting him there.

"Violette is found," said the colonel, "and her mother, too. Don't ask me any questions now, but tell the coachman to drive up to the door. Send the officers away, and tell them I will be at the prefecture in an hour. Get up on the box beside the driver. I am going to take Violette home, and I don't want her to see you. I won't have any explanations and lover's transports in the street, nor would it be well for the crazy woman to see you. We should only have a scene."

Becherel obeyed without even a protest, and everything passed off as the colonel desired.

He had certainly done a good morning's work, this intrepid colonel! Thanks to his efforts, Violette was saved, and Robert was troubled with no further fears of losing her. There was nothing for them to do now but be happy.

———

EPILOGUE.

A YEAR has passed, and Paris has forgotten the story, though it must be admitted that it knew only a portion of the facts.

Violette's disappearance in the middle of a performance

at the Fantasies Lyriques created a great stir, and the papers talked of nothing else for a week; but nobody suspected the truth. Everybody attributed it to some love affair or a pretty woman's caprice.

Poor Cochard was the greatest sufferer, but Violette, on finding herself the possessor of immense wealth, indemnified him in the most liberal manner for the pecuniary loss the sudden closing of his theater had caused him.

Herminia and her mother heard of Morgan's death and his daughter's reappearance at the same time.

Their feelings on learning that Morgan had destroyed his will before he killed himself may be better imagined than described.

The investigation made by M. de Mornac, after Morgan's tragical death, told him all he cared to know about the infamous scoundrel whom Morgan had enriched, but who had been his evil genius.

Devoted to Josephine Lureau, who was not then a countess, Marcaudier had taken advantage of his benefactor's absence to kidnap Simone, with the assistance of Rembriche, whom he had afterward rewarded by taking into his service. It was Rembriche who had taken the child to Rennes, and left her on a public promenade in that city; and Marcaudier had taken advantage of the distress of mind into which this misfortune had plunged Morgan to induce him to deprive his poor, partially demented wife of her freedom. He had offered to take charge of her, and Heaven only knows the sufferings and privations he had imposed upon her!

This in itself would have more than sufficed to insure his arrest and subsequent imprisonment, but M. de Mornac, after a consultation with his friend at the prefecture, decided not to seek any legal redress on account of Violette, who would be obliged to testify before the court that tried her mother's persecutor; but the wretch, on finding that his guilt had been discovered and that he was likely to be arrested at any moment, fled from the country as rapidly as steam would take him, and is now carrying on his old business of usury in England. He may prosper on the other side of the Channel, but in France no one regrets him, not even Julia Pannetier, who has found consolation in the devotion of Florimond, the handsome tenor of the Fantasies Lyriques.

But though the gallant colonel had accomplished wonders, he had a far more difficult task to perform.

He was now of the opinion that his young friend should marry Violette, but how was Mme. de Becherel to be induced to consent to his son's marriage with the daughter of an insane woman and a former slave-trader?

Morgan had died without leaving any trace, so to speak. He was scarcely known in France, and the origin of his wealth was already forgotten. But the mother was living, and there was no hope of her recovery. Indeed, after a few days of comparative sanity, her condition became so much worse that it was necessary to place her in a private insane asylum.

But God, in His infinite mercy, granted this poor suffering soul rest at last, and about a month afterward she died peacefully and quietly in Simone's arms.

Violette's past remained a past irreproachable, so far as conduct was concerned, but marred by a single brief appearance on the boards of a Parisian theater. Immense importance is attached to such crimes as this, in the provinces, and a woman is regarded with suspicion merely from the fact that she has been an actress, if only for a single day. It is needless to say that Mme. de Becherel fully agreed with her most bigoted compatriots in this matter.

The colonel adopted a very sensible plan. He went to Rennes, and instead of making a direct appeal to Mme. de Becherel, went straight to the superior of the Convent of the Visitation. That venerable lady, who retained a very favorable recollection of her former protégé, admitted the justice of the colonel's arguments, and finally consented to serve as an intermediary between him and Robert's mother. It would be almost too much to say that Mlle. Morgan's millions did not influence Mme. de Becherel somewhat in her decision—for in Brittany the power of money is universally conceded—but if Violette had had fifty millions and a blemish on her past, she would never have married the last scion of one of the oldest families in Brittany with his mother's consent.

Violette and Robert were married in Paris the following autumn, and spent the winter in Rennes, where everybody petted and made much of the beautiful bride.

They are rebuilding the old château of the Becherels in the Prevalaye, and the newly married pair will reside there. Jean has been promoted to the dignity of *valet-de-chambre,* and tells all the country youths of his acquaintance that Paris girls are deceitful hussies.

Herminia, they say, is about to marry a gentleman who has just spent all the money he had left in purchasing a foreign title, so she seems likely to be a countess—like her mother.

The colonel has resumed his former habits. He rides every day, and dances attendance upon all the handsome widows of his acquaintance; but he has agreed to spend two months of every summer with his young friends, and whenever he meets Robert in Paris, where the newly married couple go quite often, he never fails to say to him:

" You still owe me satisfaction, recollect. You must be prepared to receive a visit from my seconds at any time."

THE END.